A Flight Delayed

BY

KC LEMMER

A FLIGHT DELAYED

ISBN 978-0-9555283-8-5

First published in Great Britain in 2010 by Rose & Crown Books
www.roseandcrownbooks.com (Sunpenny Publishing)

MORE BOOKS FROM ROSE & CROWN:
Embracing Change, by Debbie Roome
Blue Freedom, by Sandra Peut
Redemption on the Red River, by Cheryl R. Cain (coming soon)
Heart of the Hobo, by Shae O'Brien (coming soon)

MORE BOOKS FROM SUNPENNY PUBLISHING:
Dance of Eagles, by JS Holloway
Going Astray, by Christine Moore
My Sea is Wide, by Rowland Evans
The Mountains Between, by Julie McGowan
Just One More Summer, by Julie McGowan

Thanks

Thank you Gran, Mom and Bob for your encouragement and support, not only while I wrote this book but also in sharing life. And thank You Daddy-God for Your amazing and unwavering love that continually leaves me awed.

Chapter 1

She presided over the fireplace in death, just as she had presided over whatever room she had occupied in her life. The fact that she was incapable of speaking did little to lighten their despondent hearts. Even in the dim light, Amanda could see her sister's shoulders slumped forward wearily. Great Aunt Marie had always had that effect on those who'd been in her company for longer than an hour.

The sole light in the room came from a fine china lamp on the mantelpiece. It illuminated the green alabaster jar in an eerie way, especially as its shadow fell across the portrait behind it—Aunt Marie's portrait.

The whole effect was sinister.

Just like Aunt Marie!

Amanda shuddered, rubbing her upper arms briskly to rid herself of the sudden chill. She glanced over at Polly, so still and pale, with dark rings under her eyes. Polly wasn't handling this well—or was it the pregnancy? Aunt Marie and a pregnancy were a super-bad combination, Amanda thought, pitying her sister's misfortunes.

"So what are we going to do?" she asked, moving slowly over to the window. It was such a clear day that the Ochils looked like they were just minutes away, rather than all the way across the Firth of Forth. On a day like today, Amanda would have happily driven across the bridge and gone jogging up one of the mountain paths. Anything but this.

She turned back to the dim room. All she could see was a dark huddle in the chair, until her eyes re-adjusted to the lighting.

As Polly stood, she could make out the familiar pointy chin, fluffy pink slippers, and bulging stomach. It was

1

impossible to know what was going through her sister's mind as she crossed over to the mantelpiece and touched the alabaster jar gingerly.

The stomach turned to face her, exchanging the distorted shape for a slim one. From this aspect, one might never know Polly was almost eight months pregnant. It was amazing how shadows and angles could hide the truth.

Once again, Amanda gratefully rejoiced that it wasn't herself. She frowned as she watched her sister gently rub the round bulge, her focus once again on Aunt Marie's ashes.

Amanda flopped into the rocking chair that her sister had just vacated. It was still warm.

Polly tapped the jar. "What choice do we have?"

Was she checking to see that Aunt Marie really was dead?

"Great Aunt Marie was a tough nut, Pol, but I think she is well and truly gone," Amanda remarked dryly. "We no longer have to live under her wrath and dictatorship. We are finally free."

"Oh, Mandy!" Polly scolded with a shaky laugh, "she wasn't all that bad…"

"Says you!" Amanda exclaimed. "You didn't have her stalking you at every possible chance, waiting to pounce, or start an argument. She could never pass up an opportunity to begin some hullabaloo with me!"

Polly didn't argue. She smiled sweetly and tapped the jar with a little more confidence. "Well, it doesn't change the fact that we have to come to some decision about what to do with her. It's a pity Dad and Mum aren't here to sort this out."

Rolling her eyes, Amanda bit back her sharp retort. She wouldn't upset Polly further, not tonight.

"Well, they're not, and that's all there is to it." The words still came out in a snap, despite her resolve.

Sighing, Amanda pushed out of the chair and paced restlessly to the window again. The little china lamp made Aunt Marie too much of a focus. Growing more and more angry, Amanda crossed the room and with an open hand slapped the main switch on. The room was flooded with sweet light; the china lamp was just a dim glow now.

Glaring balefully at the jar, she shook a finger at Polly in warning: "This won't be the last request from Aunt Marie; there's *always* something more when it comes to her!"

Polly began to shake her head in defence of Aunt Marie, but stopped as she met Amanda's quelling gaze. The two sisters stared at each other, green eyes sharp as they bored down into the softer blue ones. They had the same curling black hair and big eyes, but beyond that the similarities ended.

Polly was slightly shorter than Amanda, and more rounded, thanks to the pregnancy. Amanda, at five foot seven, was her senior by two years. Some of the older church folks said Amanda took after her father and Polly after their mother...*But what would she know of that?* she thought bitterly, reflecting on their years of separation.

Polly was gentle and thought too well of people. Amanda considered that it was just as well she'd had a big sister who tended to become more cynical than anything else when in doubt. There were countless memories of times when she had stood up for Polly, defended Polly, protected Polly. She'd needed to be tough. So had they all, what with Dad and Mum never at home. And as far as Amanda was concerned, those two years between their ages had made all the difference in the shaping of their characters. Polly friendly and warm, Amanda reserved and suspicious. Polly positive and enthusiastic, Amanda driven and independent. And here they were, once again, the two of them trying to make decisions that should never have been their responsibility. And, once again, Polly was looking to her for leadership.

Heart heavy, Amanda rubbed her right cheekbone. If she had her way she would smash the jar out in the backyard, or toss it over some cliff. Maybe a holiday to the White Cliffs of Dover...? What a joy that experience would be! If nothing else, at least some of her own tension would be released.

Scrutinising the tired features before her, Amanda bitterly pushed aside thoughts of her parents. They hadn't been around physically in times of need, and she certainly wasn't going to let them occupy any space in her mind either. It was her time to make the call on what to do.

She tried to be gentle as she said, "Polly, there is no way we can get Aunt Marie's ashes back to Africa. It is an impossible request, and she knew it was too, the old crone. I can tell you this – I'm not going!"

Polly said nothing, her eyes on the red patterned carpet.

"It's true!" Amanda insisted, striding back to the window to glare out at the frosted grass. "The woman won't let us rest and get on with our lives. She planned this to rile us all up." An image of Polly's peaceful eyes sprang into mind. Giving a half-hearted laugh, Amanda corrected herself. "Or rather, to rile *me* up."

The bird tray under the spruce tree had one lone pigeon on it. There wasn't room for any others, judging by the size of the fat bird.

"Greedy thing."

A door banged just then, and the quick step in the hallway caused both women to turn as a slim man, just an inch taller than Amanda, pushed open the lounge door and grinned at them both.

"Hello hello, ladies!" His lively eyes were warm as he bent to give Polly a quick kiss. "You're both looking very subdued." He glanced over at Amanda, noting the fire in her eyes. "Or perhaps subdued isn't the best word to use?"

"We *are* a little put out," Polly admitted, leaning against her husband for support.

"Put out!" Amanda exploded. "I am *more* than put out." She turned on Sam. "Tell me you agree this is a ridiculous request. Great Aunt Marie wants her ashes taken back to Africa! For goodness sake, the woman was only there for the first three years of her life. And what's more, she had the nerve to go as far as to quote some Scripture about Joseph asking for his bones to be taken back to Israel when the Israelites returned there from Egypt."

Sam's face twitched, and then, unable to hold it in, he chuckled, and was promptly rewarded with a firm warning nudge in his ribs.

"I'm sorry—" his smile broadened, "—but look at it from my point of view. Aunt Marie up to her usual pranks of winding up Amanda—and she can always do it. Why, Amanda is fairly bursting..."

"Sam," Polly hissed, "hush up!" She glanced cautiously at the scorching eyes of her sister and tried to be diplomatic. "I'm sure we can work this out sensibly. I'll get in touch with the family and tell them about the will, and then we will calmly come to a decision, alright?"

Hands on her expanding waist, Polly dared Amanda to argue—and for once, she won.

Ramming the car keys into the ignition five minutes later, Amanda laughed bitterly. "The family! Poor little Polly. Beats me how you're going to find Cobs' address, never mind get hold of the parents! And if you get Ruth to co-operate, that *will* be a miracle."

She twisted the key and felt the car shudder and then splutter into life. Shaking her dark curls, Amanda reached for the black gloves on the passenger seat and absently pulled them on, her thoughts clouded with Great Aunt Marie's request.

She just knew what was going to happen. Ruth and Cobs, if Polly located him at all, would both have some *very* valid excuse as to why they were not the right choice for Aunt Marie's mission. And Polly couldn't go, what with her being so near to delivering her baby. No one wanted their smooth little lives to be disrupted by one difficult old woman's request.

Would Polly tell Ruth and Cobs the truth – that Great Aunt Marie had actually asked for Amanda to go?

"Maybe we can just post the ashes and pay someone to bury them somewhere," Amanda mused, smiling thinly. "That'd get you hopping, Aunt Marie. Tit for tat! Or even better, let's just wait for Polly's children to grow up and we'll pass your message on to them. After all, it was generations later when Joseph's bones were finally carried to his homeland!"

Her shoulders sagged as the fight slowly slid out of her. Clutching the steering wheel, Amanda laid her forehead against its cold leather and groaned. "Oh God, why did this have to happen? You know it'll be me who has to go. They'll all think: 'Single Amanda with the good-natured boss she can wrap around her finger—*she'll* be available.' But please, God, I *really* don't want to go trekking across Africa. I have my job to do, deadlines to meet, a career to think about. I'm happy!"

Sighing heavily, she released the handbrake and pulled

onto the road, guiding her car through the neat residential area. Her sister's neighbour looked up, from where she was pulling shopping bags out of the boot of her car, and waved. Flashing up a hand in response, Amanda glanced down at the Bible and the thick green folder on the passenger seat. It was five-fifteen. There was at least half an hour in which to run into the office before evening church.

And no Aunt Marie to whip me afterwards. Some of the heaviness lifted. *It's just a pity the office is right next door to the church.* Amanda felt faintly uncomfortable as she heard her thoughts. "Well, it *is* a little awkward if anyone sees me going into the office on a Sunday," she argued aloud, "even though this is crucial work that needs to be done."

When she reached Almond Avenue Amanda hesitated at the intersection, then steered the Fiesta into the back parking of the church. This would leave more parking spaces at the front for the elderly, she reasoned. It was much easier for them to go into the church from that entrance, wasn't it? Nothing furtive about it; she was being considerate.

A quick glance around showed the car park was deserted. Grabbing her office keys from the cubbyhole, Amanda picked up the green folder and slid cautiously out of her car, glad of the wintery darkness of the evening. The street lights gave a pretty orange glow that created a cosy effect, rather than an exposing light as in some more suspect districts.

Head held high, Amanda hopped the stairs up to the office block two at a time and punched in the door code to the office. Just half an hour in the office would relieve some of the pressure of work tomorrow.

"Amanda?" Her sister's voice was tinny across the telephone line.

Amanda silently groaned and shifted the phone to her other ear. Forcing a brightness into her voice she answered, "Polly, is that you? What's up?"

"I never saw you at church. I thought you were coming tonight?"

The disappointment in her sister's voice made Amanda feel like a convicted sinner. "Oh Pol..." Amanda wriggled in her seat uncomfortably. "I did mean to come, I just got caught up." Her gaze flicked over the neat piles of paper, the desk lamp focussed on the single sheet in front of her, and the black laptop pushed over to the right of the paper.

Trying to sound open and interested she asked, "How was church? What was the sermon about?" She regretted the questions the moment they were out of her mouth.

"I was a wee bit distracted," she heard Polly admit.

Amanda fidgeted while she waited for Polly to ask Sam about the sermon. She heard his deep rumbled answer: "Jonah". Just great!

Lord, this had better not be You talking to me. This is not the same as Jonah's situation. Great Aunt Marie's ashes have nothing to do with warning a city of Your anger and impending destruction.

"Amanda, are you still there?"

Clearing her throat, Amanda nodded, before realising Polly wouldn't see her response, "Yeah, I'm here."

"Look, I managed to speak to Ruth, but I couldn't track down Cobs."

"No surprise there," Amanda muttered under her breath.

"Ruth is committed to her school until July holidays, but she said she really wants to be involved so she's willing to pay for the flight."

Amanda rolled her eyes. Ruth couldn't care two pence about Aunt Marie and her ashes and who went, except to clear her conscience and feel she was doing something. And Polly was swallowing the story hook, line, and sinker.

"Good news, though—I also got through to Dad. He and Mum agree we need to honour Aunt Marie's request."

Amanda's heart sank at her sister's soft words. It was all very well for Dad to talk; he was too far away to have to worry about it. As usual.

Scooting the lap top over, Amanda opened up a Spider Solitaire game. There was no way she was going to disrupt the smooth flow of her research work for even a few days. There would be jet lag, lost time...

"—So I've tentatively booked the first available flight."

What! Amanda froze, her knuckles whitening around the phone. "Look Polly, that's out of the question, in your condi—" She stopped short as her sister's words sank in.

There was silence on the other end of the phone. Amanda

gulped nervously. She just *couldn't* go instead of Polly! Hand pressed over her mouth, Amanda closed her eyes—waiting.

"Sam's agreed." Polly's voice was small, small and scared. "I'm leaving the day after tomorrow—on Tuesday."

"Amanda McCree!" The triumphant bellow had Amanda clinging to a lamp post in fright. A diminutive figure emerged from the shadows of Amanda's car, her cane knocking against the sidewalk as she approached.

"Mrs May!" Amanda gasped, squinting through the darkness as she recognised the familiar shape.

"That's right, hen." The little woman reached up and caught Amanda's jaw firmly in her small wrinkled hand. "When I saw your car, and the light on up in your office, I just knew you were bunking church."

Flushing, Amanda tried not to shift under the scrutinising gaze of her former teacher. She opened her mouth with some excuse but was instantly shut down.

"Don't argue with me; we both know who always won the war in the end." Mrs May clucked her tongue, as though the memories were fond ones. Amanda could only remember nightmarish fights with this strong-willed teacher who refused to budge one way or another. She had dreaded Biology lessons, which was probably why she had been more difficult than usual in them. The fact that Mrs May and Great Aunt Marie had been great pals had not helped raise Amanda's regard for the woman.

Amanda backed out of the firm grip and circled cautiously around Mrs May, to her car. "What are you doing out so late?" she queried, unlocking the back door of her car to lay down the green folder, which was now joined by a matching blue one—her current research on children suffering from depression. The fact that Mrs May was stalking around in the dark near her car, waiting for her, was possibly worse than a carjacker hiding there, Amanda thought, slamming the door shut.

She turned back to the little eyes and sagging cheeks, wearily wondering what the persistent woman wanted this time. She had long since wondered if Aunt Marie and Mrs May were part of a conspiracy, with the sole goal of imbuing her with their opinions and concerns—usually on spiritual matters.

"I just wanted to give you this," Mrs May said, peering up at Amanda and leaning heavily on her cane as she held out a slim white envelope. "Open this when you have time."

Insides churning, Amanda suspiciously accepted the letter.

"God will get you, my lassie." Mrs May reached up in a loving gesture to touch Amanda's cheek.

Amanda jerked back before she realised what was happening. The hurt that filled Mrs May's eyes was awful to see.

"Mrs May!" Amanda was horrified at her own response. "I—I'm so sorry. I don't know..." She stared at the pile of grey curls below her, trying to find something to say—anything that might explain her appalling response.

"It's alright Amanda." Mrs May shook her head, and then glanced up. Her eyes were watery. "You are in my prayers, Amanda..." She hesitated, as though suddenly unsure what to say, and then catching Amanda's hand briefly she whispered, voice breaking: "I truly care about what happens to you."

Hugely disturbed, Amanda watched the little frame shuffle along the dark car park and head up the lane behind the church. She watched until Mrs May was out of sight, and then slid slowly into the driver's seat. Out of the corner of her eyes she could see her still-zipped up Bible lying where she had left it.

Chapter 2

"Hal–loo! Anyone home?" Amanda called, hanging up her coat in the coat cupboard under the stairs.

"In here, Mandy."

Amanda followed the sing-song call into the lounge. "Okay, what are you up to now, Kari?" she asked, smiling as she rounded the corner. "I know that tone!"

Her two flatmates were perched on the same seat in front of the flat screen computer. Both turned to grin guiltily at her.

"Come and check this out!" Dark-haired Kari grinned at Amanda as she stood up. Brown eyes dancing, she leaned in to say, "There are some *cute* characters here, and some real duffers too!"

Kari winked at Amanda before heading into the kitchen. A moment later the sound of a boiling kettle was heard. They must have been making coffee when she arrived.

Amanda perched on the vacant half of the seat. "What is it Sal?" she asked, studying the screen curiously. The web page was an unfamiliar one, and at present it only showed some random bloke's face. There was nothing particular striking or abnormal about him.

Sally shot Amanda a laughing glance. "Kari was searching for some info and spotted this web page. I heard her laughing like crazy and came to find out what was going on," she explained, clicking on the 'back arrow' at the top of the screen. A string of male faces slid down the display.

"Pick your hubby!" Kari burst back into the room, sloshing dark liquid out of the mug she was carrying, as she waved her hand in a flourish at the screen. She thrust a lime green mug at Amanda and pulled up another chair, tucking her knees up against her chest. "It's crazy!" Her eyes sparkled with excited laughter.

Amanda raised a curious brow, and lifted her mug to breathe in the beautiful aroma of the coffee. Just the smell of the steamy liquid soothed her fraying edges.

"It sounds like those mail order brides from the olden days that you read about," she observed, tentatively dipping a finger into the black depth of the cup, testing to see if it would scald her. Uttering a sharp whimper, she quickly popped her finger into her mouth to cool it down. Sally gave her a reproachful look.

"Some of these guys look do-*dgeee!*" Kari exclaimed, pushing back her chaotic rumple of curls. "There should be rules to this thing."

"But some look very sincere." Sally's gentle voice tried to bring in some fairness, as she rubbed her slightly turned up nose thoughtfully. She reminded Amanda of Polly in many ways. Sally never wanted anyone to get hurt. She'd rather be put out of her own way than cause anyone else to be.

Unperturbed, Kari rattled on, grabbing Amanda's arm dramatically: "And all of them want a *Christian* bride!" Her lively eyes sparkled at Amanda. "Our game is to work out which ones are genuine and which ones are just playing around."

Amanda grinned, warming up to the fun as she listened to her friends playfully debate the causes of the men who had put their profiles up for grabs. She took a quick sip of her coffee and leant forward. "Okay, which is our first candidate?"

Sally's rounded cheeks dimpled into an impish grin, "How about that one with the bushy sideburns?"

Kari nodded eagerly, her animated features lighting up, "Alright Amanda, we couldn't decide on this one. Sally says he's genuine, and I say he is stalker-potential. It's up to you to make the final call."

"Whoa!" Amanda clutched Kari's shoulder, "move *on!*"

Three hours and three coffees later, Amanda was fully into the swing of the new game. Laughing, Sally clicked on to the next profile.

"Well, look-ee *here*," Amanda grinned, studying the angular features of the next profile. "What's his claim to fame?"

Kari leant in. "He's quite a looker," she winked at Sally, who also moved in for a better look. Nodding, she nudged Amanda, who obediently studied the man's features.

She couldn't decide for sure what colour his eyes were, maybe hazel. But his thick brown hair, clear cut features and smiling mouth were certainly attractive. His profile read that he was six foot two, twenty-eight years old, and a doctor. Amanda silently read the single description of the man's character: *A man devoted to doing God's will.* She glanced back at his face, noting the clear eyes with approval. Kari was right; there was something very appealing about this one.

"Well?" Kari ribbed her.

"Not bad," Amanda admitted, leaning back against the chair, hands cupped around her cooling mug. "It doesn't say much about him though, does it? Not even a description of the kind of woman he is hoping to meet, or anything."

Sally nodded. "Yeah, not much here. It just says his name is Caleb. And his home is in Africa." She lifted a curious brow at Kari and then Amanda. "Now that is a *very* general description. It's almost as though he doesn't want to be found."

"So you're saying he's shy?" Kari accused, turning back to the man's profile. "I don't know about that. He looks very confident; I wouldn't have said shyness was an issue with him."

Suddenly feeling uncomfortable, Amanda gazed into her mug. For some reason she did not feel right about verbally dissecting this man. "Anyone want another cup?" she offered, afraid she'd be asked for her opinion if she didn't say something quickly.

Kari glanced up at the clock on the wall and grimaced. "I'd love another, but it's—*yikes!* Three o'clock in the morning! If I don't get some sleep I'll be dysfunctional tomorrow."

"You already are dysfunctional," Amanda remarked dryly.

"A ha-ha!" Kari playfully punched Amanda's arm. They both waited while Sally logged off the computer.

"You must have got home about twelve," Kari said casually, studying the clock again. "What took you so long?"

Amanda gathered up the empty mugs, depositing their

apple cores all into one mug. "I got nabbed by Mrs May." She wrinkled her nose at Kari. "She was skulking around my car when I came out of work."

"Mrs May!" Kari sighed dramatically. "When I left school I thought the days of Mrs May were over."

"It sounds to me like the days of Mrs May are never over." Sally turned to smile at the two of them. "I'm just sorry I haven't yet met this infamous Mrs May."

"She has already cast a spell over you," Kari growled deeply. "She must have, for you to have uttered such a wish."

For once Amanda was unable to join in the usual mockery of Mrs May. Her response to the elderly woman had unnerved her, embarrassed her. It was a topic that was too sensitive tonight. But at least Kari felt the same way; she'd had almost as many head-on encounters with Mrs May as Amanda had.

When the last dripping mug was placed on the drying rack, the three friends gathered up scattered belongings and trekked up the stairs, Sally bringing up the rear and switching off the lights as she went. Lying in bed, Amanda ran through the events of the day, before deciding that any further contemplation of either Mrs May or Aunt Marie would have far from healthy consequences.

The last thought she had as she drifted off to sleep was of Mrs May handing her the white envelope.

"Rise and shine, Amanda!" The door was flung open; Kari erupted into the room and plonked something down on the bedside table.

"Hmm..." Amanda stretched and covered a yawn, reluctantly peeking one eye open to squint at the dark shape looming over her. She heard Kari groping for the lamp switch.

"No, not the desk lamp!" Amanda squawked, trying to block Kari's hand. Too late, the focussed light splashed right down into her eyes. "Too bright! Too bright!"

"It's already seven-thirty, lazy bones! We both know how your boss will respond if you arrive late," Kari warned severely.

Amanda giggled softly, her eyes still closed, "You're just

jealous that he couldn't care less if I was there at seven or eleven." She peeked open an eye. "Is that coffee I smell?"

The lime green mug with the daffodil was sitting beside her bed, steam rising out of it. "'Mmm—thanks. You're a pal," Amanda whispered, licking her dry lips as she leant on an elbow and sipped at the drink.

"Sure thing." Kari made no move to go, but instead sat down on the edge of the bed.

Amanda hid a smile in her mug as she watched her friend try and tuck a wayward curl back into the main body of hair, which was pulled back into a pretty pile.

"There are some clips in my top drawer," Amanda offered. She waited while Kari fixed her hair, knowing she had something on her mind. Sure enough, the moment the clip was firmly in place Kari turned knowing eyes on her.

"Now, we've known each other since the day you beat me up in the school gym." Kari folded her lean hands onto her lap.

Amanda felt her chest squeeze up in concern as she saw the veins in her friend's hands so clearly today. Was it her imagination, or were Kari's cheekbones more pronounced than before? And were eyes looking larger against her narrowing face?

"And I know something's up," Kari said, shaking a finger at Amanda.

Smiling, Amanda cut in smoothly, knowing Kari's familiar pep talk off by heart: "And you don't need to be Mrs May to work out I'm a sinner."

"Quite right, I couldn't agree with you more. You took the words right out of my mouth," Kari smiled. She arched a shaped brow. "Well?"

"You're right," Amanda nodded, trying to observe her friend discreetly. She could see the dark marks under Kari's eyes, and the usual spark in the dancing brown eyes had definitely grown dimmer in the recent months. If only Kari would talk to her about this thing! It was destroying her. Couldn't two bear the load better than one?

As though reading her thoughts, Kari turned away to stare at a poster on the wall; a map of Scotland. There was a red drawing pin on South Queensferry to mark their flat.

Unwilling to start a rumpus right now, Amanda quaffed

her fears about Kari. Clutching her mug close, she tried to arrange her thoughts. The bed creaked as Kari shifted her position. Downstairs Amanda could hear the sound of a broom knocking against cupboard doors. The dirty kitchen floor must have finally got to Sally.

"It's Aunt Marie."

Judging by the enlightened look on Kari's face, Amanda guessed she would not have had to say much more for Kari to have understood what she was feeling. But she explained anyway: "Polly and I read through Aunt Marie's will yesterday. Aunt Marie had asked that her ashes be taken back to Africa when she dies. She specifically requested that *I* would take them!" Amanda wrinkled her nose at Kari, not offended by the grin that briefly touched her friend's face.

"Oh Mandy!" Kari reached out a sympathetic hand, which Amanda gratefully took. "She always did have it in for you."

"I don't want to go Kari," Amanda pleaded, tears so suddenly filling her eyes that Kari was taken aback by the depth of her conviction. "Aunt Marie *did* always have something in for me, but not so much for the others. She was always ordering me to do something or other. And now another task—from beyond the grave!" She squeezed Kari's hand. "How many more letters and instructions, from her, will we find stashed away somewhere?" The tears flowed in earnest now.

"Oh Mandy," Kari said again, scooting over to wrap a comforting arm around her friend.

"I'm just so tired," Amanda whispered, "and this is just one more thing added to everything else. There's the family disunity, the busyness of work—the Mrs Mays of this world," she tacked on, and laughed brokenly through her tears, silently adding, *And I'm worried about you Kari.*

"And you're also afraid to go to Africa," Kari said perceptively.

Amanda felt a jolt inside of her at Kari's remark. It took her a moment to respond, but she nodded, marvelling at how well her friend knew her.

"Yeah, I am scared to go. Africa seems such a—a wild place. I've heard statistics of the crime rate in South Africa. It's horrific. I feel like I've been handed a suicidal mission..."

Her voice faded away.

Kari waited a moment before saying, "And Africa stole your parents, huh?"

The hardening inside of Amanda was answer enough. She didn't deny Kari's pointed question. "Aunt Marie was born in Cape Town." Amanda skirted Kari's question. She traced over the Winnie-the-Pooh picture on her duvet cover miserably. "It's apparently a pretty city," she added, unconvinced, "so it *could* be okay?"

Amanda paused, then admitted to Kari: "Polly says she'll go."

Silence again, broken only by the sound of the shower running. Sally must be running late today.

At last Kari asked, "So what are you going to do then?"

Heart trembling, Amanda's eyes met her friend's, tears trickling miserably down her cheeks, "I guess I go."

After the other two had left for work, Amanda pulled on her green caterpillar slippers and padded down the stairs to the kitchen. It sparkled with cleanliness. Slipping her mug into the soapy water in the sink, Amanda dug out a cereal box and some yogurt and then went in search of her cell phone.

"Please help," she breathed, wondering just who she was talking to as she punched in her boss's number.

"Hi Doug, this is Amanda here..." She nodded, listening. "Yes, I stopped in yesterday evening, it seemed a good time to do some catching up. No that's alright; I definitely will be in today because I want to carry on with my research on child depression in girls under twelve."

Kari would be bristling mad to know Doug had offered her a day off. He thought she worked too hard. "Doug, I'm—uh, I'm phoning because my Aunt Marie...Yes, the dead one. She asked for her ashes to be taken to South Africa." She gave an embarrassed laugh. "Yeah, Cape Town. It's crazy, but I had to ask—"

Amanda's eyes widened with horror as she listened to her boss's response. Pushing the cell phone away from her ear, she stared at it a moment. Cautiously, she raised it back to her ear and her eyes fluttered closed as Doug gurgled on.

This was absolutely crazy! She knew her boss was

relaxed, but this was *outrageous*!

He finally stopped talking, and she thought fast. "Do you really think such an idea is valid? I mean, there will be cultural differences that could hide the symptoms we are used to. Perhaps they don't even get the same psychotic disorders there." Shaking her head, Amanda gritted her teeth: "This is a bad idea. I need to be in the office..."

She hesitated, searching for an escape route. Why didn't Doug just tell her she had a project to finish and a trip away was out of the question?

"Yes, I have a paper and pen," she heard her dull response as she picked up the black ball point pen from beside the kettle. *Psychotic disorders, stresses, symptoms, treatments,* she scribbled. Drawing an arrow off the words, she added a note: *Research social and cultural factors, environmental influences, any other relevant factors that contribute.* She fiddled with the pen, wondering how to stop the excited flow of ideas that was pouring down the phone.

"When do I leave?" she repeated stupidly after him. She had to get control of this! "Now wait a moment. Hold on there. I understand that this could be an interesting research line but I just don't think this is a good idea, Doug...Well yes, but..."

Gulping, Amanda tried to get some grasp on this fast unravelling situation, "No, you don't need to sponsor the trip...Why not?" She stared at her distorted face in the silver of the kettle, black tresses spilling over her shoulders, green eyes wide with worry, her slender jaw taut. Her usually pert nose looked bulbous in the reflection. "Well, because my sister Ruth has the ticket covered. But..."

Despite all her efforts to get a word in that would clear up this awful misunderstanding, Amanda found herself listening to dial tone two minutes later, and in the possession of pocket money and research funding. The smooth calm voice of Doug was still ringing in her ears.

This was not meant to go this way! Amanda glared at her reflection, and then up at the clock. Groaning, she cupped her head in her hands. "God, this is not working out right! What have I done to deserve this punishment?"

There was no booming answer in reply, although she hadn't really expected any.

Sighing, Amanda looked back up at the brown teapot clock again. Eight-thirty.

"Eight-thirty Monday morning and I'm getting shipped off to Africa in less than forty-eight hours. What a nightmare! This is when I'd trade Doug for Kari's boss any day." She'd always had a habit of speaking her thoughts out loud to herself; it had got her into trouble more than once, growing up.

Shuffling into the lounge, Amanda fumbled for her work bag. "Add an extra dimension to my research," she muttered, mimicking her employer. "Yeah, right Doug!" For a brief moment the thought that Doug was trying to get rid of her flashed through her mind, but just as quickly flicked back out. She knew she was a valued employee and did more than her share of her work.

Perhaps this really *was* a great opportunity?

Amanda stuffed the green and blue folders into her bag. "Research child depression in Africa," she breathed, and her hands stilled. "Research it? That means *weeks* of sitting out there, not just days...No, no, no," she wailed, "*no!* God, what is going on?"

Flopping down in front of the television, Amanda absently picked up the remote and flicked through the channels, hoping to find some distraction from the turmoil inside. She paused on the news to check the weather. The frosted UK map switched onto news headlines, displaying the latest upheaval in... Kenya? Amanda shuddered. How far away was Kenya from South Africa?

"I'll book a fixed return flight for one month—" Amanda leapt to her feet "—and no one will convince me otherwise!"

Chapter 3

E xcuse me lady, you're blocking the way."
"Oh—sorry," Amanda gasped. She hoisted up her
bag and staggered over to the right of the exit to let a
barrel-chested man past. He glared over his bristly moustache at her as he strode by, his brown coat swaying behind
him.

The airport was hectic. The security check she had just
come through had long strings of people crammed into
roped rows. As Amanda was fumbling for her passport in
her jacket pocket, a couple of coins were knocked out and
rolled across the white floor. She scampered after them,
but just as she was bending to pick them up a passer-by
elbowed her in the head. She heard a vague apology but the
perpetrator was already scuttling away by the time she had
retrieved the coins and turned to confront him.

A group of five rumbled past, all talking at once, their
voices turned to top volume. They all but obliterated the
announcement on the Tannoy system for the next flight. A
couple of ski bags swung dangerously at Amanda's temple
as one of the young men in the group readjusted his grip.

Distinctly shaky, Amanda gathered up her kitbag and
slung it over her shoulder, pulling free her body warmer
that had got caught up in the bag's strap. Hopefully her
main luggage would arrive safely with her on the other side.
She'd heard stories of how suitcases were sometimes never
found again after that initial check-in.

She wandered along past different departure lounges
until she came to the Costa Coffee. It was a small comfort
to see the familiar maroon sign; she was still in Edinburgh,
even if she felt as though she'd already been shipped off to
Africa.

"A cappuccino please," she croaked through the tear clog

in her throat, digging in her bag for change. She carefully placed the two pounds and ten pence on the counter, taking her time while she tried to control her emotions.

"There you go; your cappuccino."

Amanda nodded her thanks and scanned the tables for an ideal spot to hide in. The corner table, away from the smiling man who was watching her hopefully, looked like the best option. It had families shielding it from any unwanted attention.

Sliding into the seat, Amanda slowly stirred the sugar in as she checked her phone. She tapped out a quick message to Kari and then tried to absorb herself in her coffee. Fear bubbled up again the moment her thoughts began to settle. She immediately began to dig restlessly through her kitbag and lighted upon her tickets once again. She must have checked them at least ten times already. She studied them mournfully, rubbing a finger over the seat numbers to memorise them. All of the flights were window seats.

"I wonder why Sam looked so concerned about the second flight?" Amanda mused, scrutinising the ticket in fascination. *20:30 hours from London Heathrow, arriving at Joshua Nkomo Airport at 13:05 hours,* Amanda read, hesitating over the foreign airport name, silently mouthing it to herself again. She flicked over to the third ticket with Zimbabwe Airways printed across the top. The Zimbabwe flag was spread across the top of the ticket, an array of bright colours. This flight took her from Joshua Nkomo airport in Bulawayo, to Johannesburg Airport, leaving at 14:30 hours and arriving in Johannesburg forty-five minutes later.

And then from there to Cape Town, a two hour flight. Amanda flipped over to the last out-going ticket, her eyes glazing over. *I wonder if Dad or Mum will come to meet me?*

The thought of seeing her parents again made her stomach churn. Was it really only seven years since she had last seen them? It felt so much longer.

I doubt they will remember.

Amanda tucked the tickets back into her bag and scowled across at the openly gazing man who had a clear view of her table now that one family had moved on.

She downed some of her cappuccino, scalding her throat as she did so. Polly said she had got this flight on a good deal, and that it had also been the only flight plan that was available so soon.

Had it really only been three days ago that Polly had found Aunt Marie's letter?

"Well Aunt Marie, I hope you're enjoying your free ride," Amanda chuntered. She smiled smugly at the thought of her Great Aunt tucked amongst her clothes in her hold baggage. She refused to share her flight space with her aunt. If the bag made it to Cape Town, then great, so did Aunt Marie. If the bag didn't make it, then tough, that was just the way it was. Some other poor blighter could decide what to do with Aunt Marie's ashes.

"This is the second boarding call for Flight 1201 to Heathrow, London," the announcer's voice blared out through the loudspeakers just as a blur of people scurried past with bags bouncing behind them, wobbling recklessly on tiny wheels. They overtook an elderly man who stopped in his tracks to let them past. He caught her gaze and gave her a friendly wink, one bushy brow lowering, before moseying on his way.

"Well, here we go God," Amanda breathed. "Between Aunt Marie and Doug I'm getting shipped off to fight in the trenches. If You're up to it, I wouldn't mind some help."

"Go *on!*" Amanda ordered in sharp disbelief.

Judging by the make-shift arrival area—it certainly could not be called an arrival *lounge*—the Bulawayo Airport must be under renovation.

"Really, madam," the dark-skinned man supplied, leaning forward in earnest, all former traces of ease gone as he nodded at the unoccupied chairs and bare concrete floors: "There are only a few departing flights, and *all* are fully booked."

Amanda glanced up at the sign over the man's head. It definitely read "Information Desk", though it was very faded. She turned and followed his gaze around the fairly vacant makeshift airport.

There was an elderly white couple sipping tea out of dainty cups at one of the eight little round tables tucked into one corner. They looked very content. Two restless youths stood near the exit of the building. Amanda recognised them from her flight; both looked as lost and misplaced as she felt. Dressed in the latest torn-style jeans and tight rock shirts, with shaggy dyed hair, they clashed with their neat (if shabby) surroundings.

A harassed young mother with three small children was spread over four or five chairs in the row of seats just beside the Information Desk. One child was asleep, but the other two were revving on full power.

The only other person in the building was an elderly African man with a broom. He swept the floor in smooth, methodical strokes and whistled a swinging tune in time with his sweeping. He looked up just then and grinned at her, showing off a couple of missing teeth. There was no stress in his aging eyes as he cheerfully called out, "There will be flights in a week or two. Don't worry, you will get on one."

Amanda stared at him in disbelief, astonished that a sweep had the cheek to interfere. Yet at the same time his words reverberated through her mind.

"It's *okay?*" she echoed in disbelief, turning from the sweep to the young man behind the desk—who was nodding in agreement with the sweep.

"He's right," the young man smiled, pleased that the situation was getting under control. He picked up a pen and tapped it on the lone notepad in front of him. The continuous tap-tap-tap only increased Amanda's anger and fright.

"What do you mean, *it's okay?*" she snapped, pounding a fist on the desk. "I refuse to be stranded out here in—in the middle of nowhere. Get me on a plane *now*."

The smiling eyes clouded over in concern. "But there are none," the young man insisted, his name badge sagging on his slack shirt.

Amanda blew out her breath silently. This was unreal. What had happened to order, to organisation? With forced patience she said slowly and clearly: "You don't understand. I have my ticket here to fly to Johannesburg. My flight is all paid for." She waved the not-so-crispy ticket at him again. "See, I have paid for the flight."

"But there is no flight." The man patiently folded his hands together and stared at Amanda in bemusement.

It's as though he thinks I'm the slow one, Amanda fumed.

Aloud she said, her voice strained, "I am holding a ticket, Mister. A ticket means a flight. I've had enough of your fun and games; I demand to get on my flight."

A soft chuckle behind her caused Amanda to swing around sharply, only to find the wizened face of the sweep smiling up at her.

"No fuel," he explained, leaning on his broom. "We must wait for more fuel to come before you can go."

"No *fuel?*" Amanda couldn't help responding. Despite the apparent lack of protocol in this place, the sweep seemed more knowledgeable than the chap behind the desk. "So just like that my flight is cancelled, without warning and without any plans being made? I could sue for this!"

They both looked intrigued, and a little confused, by this suggestion—which only frustrated Amanda further.

Realising that there was no way around this, Amanda glanced at the placid face of the young man behind the counter and then, against her better judgement, addressed the weathered face of the sweep. "Does the airport offer accommodation for passengers that are dropped with such inconsideration and lack of concern?"

The sweep shook his greying head sadly.

"Well, is there compensation?" Amanda queried, trying to control her frantic heart. "If I received compensation I could perhaps find another flight out?" She shrugged, seeing the weary patience on both faces. "Alright, not a flight—but maybe there's another way, such as a car or a train?"

Sighing at the negative response, Amanda swung on the young man behind the desk. "I demand to see someone in authority."

The floor sweeper leant against his broom thoughtfully, considering her questions. At last he looked up, confident in his response.

"No. There is nothing we can do but wait. You will go when a flight comes in," he assured her. There was peace in his eyes as he simply accepted the situation.

"Are none of you people at all worried that you have—" Amanda hunted for an appropriate word, but none seemed to fit; "—well, that you have disgruntled passengers that are stranded in a foreign land? Trapped!" Amanda stammered, hiding her fear with anger. "Does my predicament mean nothing to you?"

An idea struck her. "Is there a lawyer I can speak to? He can straighten this out." Her gaze swung between the peaceful face of the old sweep, and the youth tapping his pen on the desk, tears pricking her eyes as first the sweep and then the young man broke into boisterous laughter. They slapped their palms together as they laughed at her plight.

The whole situation was preposterous. This was an outrage! Was there no decorum? No obligation? No legal contracts that should be met?

"Eh—Miss." It was the young man who finally spoke, his teeth very white against his dark skin. "You just don't understand. No matter how much we want to help you, no matter if you find the best lawyer—there is nothing that can be done. No fuel means no flights. You must just wait. You will get to Johannesburg, I promise you that. But for now you must just wait." He touched his chest where his name tag hung on the faded blue shirt. "I, Samuel Chiwedza, will personally make sure you get onto a flight to Johannesburg as soon as possible."

Amanda stared at his name tag, attempting to memorise the foreign surname. She would certainly hold him accountable to his word.

"All right," she said wearily, giving in. "What do I do now?"

Samuel Chiwedza tapped his notepad again, very formally this time: "Go to Bulawayo and find accommodation there. Then phone us with your number so we can contact you."

"Phone you with my number," Amanda repeated numbly, accepting the piece of paper from the young man which now had a number scribbled across it. She stared at it, trying to grasp this foreign way of thinking. What had happened to customer service and support in a crisis? If this was Edinburgh the reporters would be all over the show. Where were the reporters?

She glanced around the airport. None of the people remaining in the airport looked like reporters.

"I told you so, Polly," Amanda berated her sister in hushed tones, "I told you people could disappear in Africa. I could be stranded here the rest of my life, for all the help

I'm getting!"

She backed numbly away from the desk, kitbag still slung over her shoulder. She'd just have to get a taxi into town and find a B&B, or a hotel, and stay there until there was a flight out. With that decision settled, Amanda shoved the airport phone number into her pocket, determined not to lose it.

Gathering herself together, relieved that she had a plan to work with, she strode confidently across to the exit, dragging her suitcase behind her. She barely glanced at the garage doors that were swung outward. She was immediately embraced by a hot breeze that drifted in through the exit; apparently there was no air conditioning here either. She rounded the corner, coins already in hand as she prepared to hop into a waiting taxi and ask to be taken to the nearest guest house.

The scene before her left her winded.

Instead of a black taxi and airport traffic there was an expanse of long brown grass rippling in the breeze. Trees were dotted here and there, peering up over the grass; up ahead a long line of neatly planted oaks headed off to the right. There were a couple of buildings on the left, and only two cars in the car park.

No city, no people, and definitely no taxies. Only blazing heat, and bird sounds.

Stepping cautiously back into the dark airport, Amanda closed her eyes.

"It's okay Amanda," she reassured herself, "this will all work out somehow." She took a deep breath and held it, counting to five before she let it out. And then she did it again, and then once more. It was a trick a child psychologist had taught her once when she was crying uncontrollably during one of their sessions; it always calmed her down and helped her get a grip on herself.

Taking a moment to absorb the situation, Amanda turned, deciding against looking back outside just yet. She waited while her eyes adjusted to the darker interior. It took her a moment to see the sweep was just where she had left him, leaning against the counter, caught up in some humorous conversation with Samuel, the Information man. Amanda glared at them suspiciously. "They'd better not be laughing at me," she muttered, glancing over at the elderly couple, who were pouring themselves another cup of tea.

They really were a picture of contentment. The woman was dressed in a soft brown skirt and apricot blouse, her white hair piled up on top of her head in some elegant but out-dated fashion. The man was dressed in a worn green shirt and dark green shorts, long grey socks pulled up to his knees. Neither spoke as they stirred their tea.

Amanda looked around for the two youths, but they were gone. How that was possible she didn't know. She could see the entire airport, all but the departure lounge—which obviously was unoccupied—or at least, it had better be! And there was nowhere to go outside, just grass and trees and blazing heat.

Shifting her bag for a better grip, Amanda approached the two men at the desk with trepidation. She knew she was out of her depth now. All her manipulative skills were lost on these two. This place, Bulawayo—it just didn't function the same way as home did.

"Excuse me..." She cleared her throat nervously.

The two men turned, their expressions open and welcoming.

"Are there any taxies?" She wondered why she almost felt stupid to ask the question.

A pensive frown covered both faces and they broke into a sudden babble of waving arms and words. Amanda could not understand a word of it, but judging by the intensity of their expressions they were debating what to do about her.

To her surprise, the sweep drifted away from the table and towards the exit, his broom swinging along beside him as he continued his animated conversation with Samuel Chiwedza—distance was not a problem, apparently.

When he reached the garage doors he suddenly broke off into a piercing whistle. No one else in the airport turned to see what the din was.

Amanda stared at Samuel Chiwedza, dazed. He didn't look at her; his focus was on the wizened old man at the door. She waited, wondering if she somehow had been forgotten or ignored.

"Oh please God, help!" Amanda whispered, anxiously tugging on a loose strand of black hair. She plucked nervously at a brown thread hanging off her shirt. If only Kari were here. Kari would somehow bring some sense to this whole situation, or at least lighten it up with her sense of humour.

"He's arranging a lift for you into town with some of the workers this evening," Samuel informed her, smiling triumphantly.

Amanda listened to all the laughing and loud chatter outside. So that's what the old man was doing...

"Huh," she grunted, regarding Samuel suspiciously. "In Scotland we would go over and ask someone in nice quiet tones if we could have a lift, and it would take one second."

Samuel nodded pleasantly. "Scotland is very cold, isn't it?"

Now what was that supposed to mean? Amanda glared at Samuel dubiously, and then sighed heavily wondering if anything would ruffle this peaceful man. She shifted her kitbag over to the other shoulder and observed dryly, "But then we would never be in a predicament like this so we wouldn't have to even worry about how to ask someone for a lift."

"Eh, five o'clock!" the old man shouted from the door, waving at them, before continuing his noisy conversing with the unseen friend.

"See?" Samuel's face split into a pleased grin. "He has arranged a lift for you at five o'clock."

"Five o'clock!" Amanda gaped looking down at her watch, horrified, "that's hours away!"

She looked up pleadingly at Samuel, almost panicking.

He gazed back peacefully.

"Ugh!" Amanda threw up her free hand in exasperation. Reasoning was impossible. Resigned to her fate, Amanda wearily thanked Samuel and moved slowly away from the counter.

Everyone else was in exactly the same position as last time she had looked.

Uncertain what to do with herself, Amanda made her way over to the one little shop tucked into a space opposite the exit.

"Hi," Amanda nodded at the buxom attendant, "can I

have a Diet Coke please?"

The woman turned her ample figure to gesture at the display fridge behind her. The clean white racks were empty.

"No Coke, we hope to get some more next Friday." She smiled pleasantly at Amanda.

"Why am I not surprised?" Amanda groaned, staring at the shelves intently, wishing for Cokes to appear there. Any Cokes, Diet or not.

"Would you like something else?" The woman lifted up the hinged counter and ducked through before lowering the board again. "We have some wonderful crocheted blouses. There are also table clothes, tea cosies..."

Amanda absently followed the woman's movements as she waved at various items that had been tastefully arranged in a display down the wall, and on adjacent tables.

What was Polly thinking when she booked a flight via Zimbabwe? Amanda silently ranted, an image of Sam's concerned face popping into mind. Sam must have known things were bad here. He must have!

Amanda racked her memory, trying to remember if she had heard anything on the news about Zimbabwe. She came up empty. If there had been, she obviously wasn't paying attention.

Amanda scowled at an elephant print table cloth. *So here I am, stranded in Africa...*

Sighing, she dug in her back jeans pocket and pulled out the pound that she kept there to put in the slot of the gym locker; she wouldn't need to worry about that for a while.

"Which one would you like?"

Amanda looked up and was taken aback by the warmth of the brown eyes before her. "Uh—" She tried to focus on the two table cloths the saleswoman was showing her. "That one." She pointed at a beautiful leopard-spotted cloth with four matching serviettes.

"Three pounds," the woman smiled, folding the cloth up neatly, "but I will give it to you for two pounds because we have no Coke today."

Fumbling in her other back pocket, Amanda pulled out the change from Costas. She could feel another pound and fifty pence in her pocket, but it would be a scandal to pay more than the price that was offered her. "Two pounds," she said, dropping the coins into the woman's worn palm and silently accepting the table cloth. Goodness knows what she would do with it. It wouldn't fit her colour scheme at the flat. Maybe Kari would like it...

Unwilling to stay inside any longer, Amanda made her way to the exit. The moment she stepped out of the shade of the building she was hit by the intense heat of the sun. Glancing around, her eyes fell on a rickety chair propped up beside the exit to hold the garage doors back. She doubted anyone would object to her sitting on it. Gingerly, she lowered herself down, not letting her full weight rest until she was sure the feeble legs would support her weight. Her feet were still in the sun, but the rest of her just made it into the cooler shade if she pressed right up against the metal doors.

For a moment Amanda just sat there, absorbing the scene before her, trying to take in the reality of her situation. A high pitched ringing noise filled the air. Some sort of bird perhaps, Amanda guessed, already beginning to feel restless.

She dug in her bag, grateful that Aunt Marie's ashes were in her big suitcase and not packed amongst her research papers and laptop. She dug a little deeper and felt an unfamiliar bulge. Fumbling for a better grip, Amanda pulled out the stowaway and smiled to see one of Kari's romance novels. "She must have tucked it in at the airport," Amanda whispered, tears starting up as she flipped open the front cover. She had to wait for her eyes to clear before she could read what Kari had written on the blank front page:

> *Happy travelling, my friend. Enjoy your adventures and bring back tons of photos. Perhaps you'll even meet the man from Africa. Wouldn't that be just crazy! Love you lots, Kari.*

Amanda's laugh turned to a cry as she traced her finger over the familiar handwriting. If only Kari were here, then things wouldn't seem half so bad! She giggled through her tears at the thought of finding the man called Caleb. Trust Kari to think of that one.

The spidery scrawl was not very enlightening, but it was a decent attempt to look busy and in control of her situation. A glance at her watch told Amanda she'd been here two hours, and only one man had driven up through the oak trees and parked his car against the far building, trying to get as much shade as possible to cover the metallic Jaguar. The only other even partly exciting thing to happen was when two spotty ground birds, the size of chickens, had raced past Amanda's feet and into the grass beyond. One little black feather spotted with white had floated softly to the ground on the other side of the exit.

This was exactly the kind of place where Cobs would have fitted in. Growing up, he had always loved being the cowboy character; he should have been the chosen victim for this little excursion—not her.

"This is absolutely *great,* Lord," Amanda growled sarcastically. "I've always dreamed of such an exciting day as this!" She scowled. "And to think tourists do this for fun."

"It's a scorcher today, isn't it?"

Amanda jumped, swinging round to see the grey-bristled chin of the elderly white man coming through the exit. She had forgotten the couple were still here. What on earth had they been doing in there for two hours? It just wasn't natural.

"The suicide month gets hotter every year," the old man continued, blue eyes looking down at her, assuring Amanda that he was talking to her. He stepped to the side and reached out a hand to guide his wife out. Amanda assumed it was his wife as they each wore a gold band on their wrinkled ring fingers. The woman had no engagement ring, only the wedding one. It was all very simple and down to earth.

Amanda watched the cautious steps of the old girl. She moved with little shuffles; the white trainers barely seemed to shift. Thoughts of difficult Aunt Marie rose up in her mind. Amanda tried not to glare at the couple, silently reminding herself that transference of feelings was not appropriate, although it did sound very appealing right now; Aunt Marie *was* the one who had orchestrated this little excursion to Africa. If it wasn't for her Amanda would have been sitting at her desk in her office, sipping coffee and engrossed in her work.

"Quite a change to the airport, isn't it?" The snow white head of the woman lifted to give Amanda a shy smile, but her faded blue eyes looked tired.

Amanda nodded mutely.

"An aeroplane hangar—not quite the same as the old smart airport with the balcony where we could watch the planes land."

Amanda nodded again, trying to think of something to say. Their strong accent made their words difficult to decipher, she understood the woman better than the man. "What was wrong with the old airport?" she asked lamely.

She was startled by the excited boom that erupted from the old man.

"Oh, you're Scottish!" He grinned benevolently at her, turning to his wife. "Did you hear that Margie, the little lass is Scottish?" The old woman was clutching his arm excitedly, her eyes alight with pleasure as she re-evaluated Amanda.

Amanda shifted nervously, fingers wrapped around the strap of her bag as she wondered what would happen next.

"My wife is originally from the Scottish borders," the old codger explained, his white moustache twitching. "Where are you from?"

"Uh...Edinburgh," Amanda shrugged, "but before that Inverness." The ringing call of the bird—or perhaps it was a beetle—grew louder; it was enough to drive anyone crazy.

"A Highland lass!" The shrivelled old woman's eyes shone, her voice faint as she asked. "What brought you to Zimbabwe?"

Apparently they were oblivious to the noise. The smell of musk perfume filled the air; Amanda tried not to breath. At least Aunt Marie had never worn musk perfume.

She groped for a response. "Well, I'm actually stranded," she admitted, shooting a quick glance between the two of them. "My connecting flight to South Africa was cancelled, apparently."

"Oh, dear!" The soft sigh of the old woman sounded genuine enough, as she nudged her husband.

He clearly didn't need any nudging, for he was already leaning close; his twinkly blue eyes were now intense. "Do you know anyone here?" He shook his head in concern at Amanda's response. "Well you must come home with us until you can get a flight out." Another firm shake of his head said he wasn't going to argue with Amanda or accept her refusal. Already he was grabbing her kitbag.

"Please come." His wife touched Amanda's elbow gently: "I would so enjoy having someone with a Scottish brogue around again."

Overwhelmed, Amanda found herself climbing into the back seat of a run-down Ford, her big suitcase stowed in the boot. She hadn't managed to tell Samuel Chiwedza that she was off, and the old man hadn't been anywhere about. She would have to phone them later. She fumbled with the seat belt, trying to get it to click into place, pausing to carefully place her hand luggage over the big rent in the faded cloth seat while she listened to the engine splutter, cough, and die.

Perhaps she wouldn't need to worry about getting the seat belt in—by the sounds of it, the car wasn't go to work either.

Chapter 4

He must have hit every single pothole in the dirt track.

Amanda clung to the door handle with both hands as she craned her neck around the broad-rim hat, trying to spot the next pothole so that she could prepare for it. Without a working seat belt (which lay limply in a useless heap beside her), she was tossed around the backseat like a rider on a rodeo horse.

The road up ahead bent to the right, disappearing behind a shield of metre-long grass. Grimacing, Amanda clenched the door handle with her right hand and pressed the palm of her left hand against the back of the old man's seat, which slid back against Amanda's knees, pinning her down, every time he careered around a corner. Bracing herself, Amanda held her breath as Jack—as he'd introduced himself to be—swung sharply to the right, whistling happily under his breath. Amanda bounced against her door while trying to kick his seat forward again, her kitbag squashing against her knee.

"She's actually quite useful, Margie!" Jack yelled above the rattle of the car, one hairy arm dangling out his open window. He grinned up at Amanda in the rear view mirror. "You just keep pushing my chair forward, lass—I'm reaching the accelerator all the time now, and it's great."

His cheerful grin did nothing to stop the embarrassed heat that rose up Amanda's neck. "I'm sorry," she stammered, "it's just that it keeps coming back at me."

Jack had some comment in response but his words were lost in the hot wind and dust that poured through his window, right into Amanda's face. The taste of dirt in her mouth was foul, clumping up every bit of saliva she had left. And every now and then, when Jack took a corner too sharply, the long grass would slap against the car door and splay across her window.

If Kari could see this she would be cracking up with laughter. At the thought of her friend, Amanda smiled half-heartedly. She missed Kari. Was she taking care of herself? Was she eating properly? *Please take care of her until I get back God!* Amanda pressed her forehead against the cool of the glass window, worried. When had things gotten so out of control for Kari and how had she—Kari's best friend—not noticed what she was going through, until the clinging tentacles of the sickness had already wrapped themselves tightly around those bony wrists?

Gazing out of the window, Amanda watched the long grass flip past. There was nothing she could do for Kari right now except try and get home as soon as possible. *I must get out of this place within the next few days,* Amanda determined, pulling away from the window.

The car was too low; all she could see stretching across the tops of the tall tasselled grass was pale blue sky, with not a cloud in sight. Swivelling around, Amanda watched the dust billow up behind them, obliterating any view of where they had come from. It was rather like being in a tunnel. The grass rose up high on both sides of the car, channelling them, and behind was all the dust, so the only way to go, really, was forward.

Yesterday at this time she had been safe in her flat, surrounded by friends, work, and familiar places. Twenty-four hours later here she was, bouncing about in the back seat of a stranger's car in the middle of the bush, sweating like the proverbial pig in the stifling heat, and absolutely clueless as to where she was going.

The fear she had so firmly pushed down now reared up again, threatening to consume her. "Oh Polly, I was so right," Amanda whispered, her vision blurry. "Anything *can* happen to you in Africa."

"Well, here we are lassie," Jack called, "Shamwari Ranch. That's a Shona name, but this area of Zimbabwe has a lot of Ndebele folk. My family moved down from the north east, so we know more Shona than Sindebele."

Amanda ducked her head to see a huge grey sign

approaching. It was in the shape of a rhinoceros, and just as it flashed by the car Amanda caught a glimpse of black ribbon-type letters spelling out "Shamwari Ranch". She twisted around and peered out the back window. The sign knocked against the metal pole in the wind. The back was blank.

"We have three rhinos on our reserve," Jack informed Amanda proudly. "One of them is our own little baby that was born here. We waited four years for Tsakupiti to be born."

"Tsa-koo-peetee..." Amanda tentatively tested the foreign name; it felt strange on her tongue.

"It means Little Stout Girl," Jack grinned, "and she fits her name for sure. Perhaps you'll get to see her while you are here."

The road straightened out and the grass fell back so that they came into a clearing. Up ahead was a large sprawling house. White curtains flapped out of the attic windows against the red tiled roof and the front door was flung open. Behind the house Amanda could see a woman, dressed in red and white checks, hanging washing on the rope that was strung up between three trees on the grass.

"That's Rosie—she's been with Jeff and Sophie for at least twenty years," Jack said, driving through the open gate and up to the front side of the house so that Rosie was blocked from view.

"Oh, longer than that Jack," his quiet little wife interjected. "I remember her being here when Andy was born."

Amanda studied the hooked nose and sagging cheeks of the old woman. What was her name again? Margie—that was it. She wasn't that bad. She didn't have a lot to say—unlike Aunt Marie or Mrs May!

"So this is your home?" Amanda asked, looking up into the rear view mirror.

Margie shook her head but Jack answered: "No, this is my daughter's home. We live a couple of miles down the road. Jeff and Sophie will be delighted to have you stay with them."

Amanda gasped, horrified, as she realised Jack and his wife had never intended to host her. They were pawning her off on their relatives! She might have known it would be like this. Old people were so unpredictable, and they had a way of putting you in a difficult spot.

"Come on in, one of the boys can get your bag out the boot," Jack ordered, yanking her sticky door open. "Are you coming in Margie?" he called through his window.

"Not today Jack, I'm a little worn out." Margie turned and smiled tiredly at Amanda. "Do come and visit us when you have time, Amanda; I'd love to have tea with you."

Amanda managed a shaky smile, "Thank you—" she couldn't bring herself to commit to a tea date; "Thank you for the lift...and everything." *Including putting her in a tight spot!*

Clutching her kitbag, Amanda scooted out the car and after her second attempt at pushing the door, it managed to crank closed. Jack was already almost at the front door. He had long strides for an old man.

"Here we go," Amanda breathed. Her jaw tightened as she trotted after Jack up to the house, muttering: "Sorry folks, but your parents have just landed you with a stranger to put up with, unless you can work a plan, fast!"

"Hello!" Jack bellowed through the front door. "Is anyone home?"

"Grandpa, that you?" a young male voice answered from somewhere deep within the house.

Jack turned and winked at Amanda. "That's Mickey, he's home on study break."

Amanda gave a quick nod; her stomach was churning over like crazy. She glanced back at the rusty blue car where Margie was waiting. Margie waved, so Amanda waved too. She turned back just as a lanky youth appeared in the door way. With ruffled brown hair, an easy grin, and bare feet, he was definitely having a home day.

"Hey Grandpa!" He gripped Jack in a firm one armed hug, blue eyes sparkling curiously at her over Jack's shoulder. "Were you out at the airport?"

"Sure were," Jack grinned. "They always have sugar there for my tea."

Amanda watched both of them laugh, not quite sure what was so funny.

"This is Amanda, Mickey, her flight was cancelled so Gran and I brought her home with us. Is your Mom in?"

One broad hand swung out at Amanda. "Hello, I'm Mickey," he grinned.

Amanda found herself smiling nervously back, liking the warmth in his eyes.

"Amanda McCree," she responded, taking his hand. It was firm, but unusually rough for someone of his age. He looked liked he could only be eighteen. She glanced at Jack and then back at Mickey; pride and self-esteem demanded she try and explain herself.

"Look, I'm sorry for the intrusion. I didn't realise your Grandfather—" Amanda hesitated, wondering how to tactfully put this while Jack was standing there, "—well, I misunderstood Jack's offer."

"You mean Grandpa is landing you with strangers?" Mickey cut in, rubbing his square jaw in amusement. "Yip, we're used to it. Funny how often it's young women, too," he teased his grandfather.

"Now don't you start that," Jack warned good-naturedly. "Last time I brought a single girl home to the family it was your Grandmother, and I married her. That was way before your time, so no tall stories. Our guest might get the wrong impression of you."

"Well, come in." Mickey stepped back to let them enter. "Mom's gone to fetch Penny, but she'll be home in about an hour. Dad's in, though." Mickey winked at Amanda as she passed him.

Amanda was assaulted by the strong smell of fresh polish as she followed Jack into the house. The wooden tiles were shiny and wet; the woman Amanda had seen hanging up clothes was mopping it with a dirty-looking mop.

"Right in there." Mickey pointed to a doorway on her left. Amanda found herself smiling in response. She rarely was taken with a person straight away but she knew she would like Mickey. There was something appealing about him.

"I'll call Dad and then I'm just going to say hi to Gran quick," Mickey called as he passed the lounge door, a tall athletic frame that moved with smooth grace.

He reminded Amanda of someone but she could not put her finger on whom. It would come back to her later, hopefully.

Jack was flicking through the magazine rack. "Nothing

new here," he complained, digging behind a newspaper. "A-ha, the October *National Geographic!*" He turned and waved it at Amanda: "I knew there would be something worthwhile here if I persisted." He glanced around the room. "Pick a chair, they're all pretty comfy." He settled down in a soft brown rocking chair near the stone fireplace.

Amanda looked around the room, debating what to do. She was too nervous to sit down. What if this family was completely put out by Jack dumping her on them? And when would the next flight out be available? She eventually settled for the seat opposite Jack's that faced the lounge door, and watched Jack flip through his magazine, completely engrossed. At the sound of heavy footsteps approaching, Amanda anxiously moved to the front of the chair, watching the doorway with wide eyes.

The man who walked in was definitely Mickey's father. His face was weathered and sun-burnt, and he was more filled out, but he had the same tall height and friendly blue eyes.

"Jeff Jacobs," he said as he shook her hand firmly. "Mickey says your flight was cancelled?"

Amanda nodded, mouth open but no words coming. She stood. Out of the corner of her eye she could see that Jack was still buried in his magazine, completely oblivious to her discomfort.

"Air travel is all mixed up at the moment," Jeff sympathised, "but we'll do as much as we can to make your stay in Zimbabwe enjoyable."

Amanda's straying eyes looked uncertainly into the concerned blue ones. Was he agreeing to her staying here?

"Is there anyone you need to contact to let them know what's happened? Our phone is just in the passage."

"Oh!" Amanda pushed back the dark curls from her face: "Uh, yes there is, but I feel just terrible throwing myself on you and your family like this..." She tried to contain her stretched emotions. "This is not at *all* how I planned it to go."

"Ah, don't worry about us." Mickey's father shoved his hands into his pocket and leaned back on his heels to survey her properly. "If you feel like this is putting us out of our way, it's no bother at all. We actually run a tourist resort so this is our line. I'm not sure if Jack told you that or not?"

Amanda shook her head, glancing across at Jack again. The old man was muttering as he flicked the page over. He looked quite upset.

"Sounds like Dad's style," Jeff grinned, and rocked forward onto his toes.

The silence that followed was extremely uncomfortable for Amanda, but a quick glance at her host-to-be showed that he was unperturbed. If anything his mind seemed somewhere else as he regarded her happily.

"So you're sure I won't mess up your plans in anyway?" Amanda double-checked. "Oh, and shall I pay you now for my stay? I'd feel much better sorting that out right away."

Jeff's brow wrinkled up as he rocked back to his heels, "Oh, I don't deal with the money, that's Sophie's business. I'm the guy who gets to run around in the bush and pretend I have things to do."

Amanda nodded at his roughened hands that clearly demonstrated he did indeed have things to do. She glanced up at her host's hair. It was coppery-brown, slightly flattened, and moist, as though he had just taken his hat off. His straight nose and square jaw were just as familiar as Mickey's were. Who were they reminding her of?

"Well, I must get back to work, but I'll ring up Sophie and she'll make things nice for you; that sound okay?" Jeff checked.

Amanda nodded bleakly, "Yes, that sounds wonderful. Thank you so much, you have no idea how grateful I am for a place to stay. I really thought I was going to be getting to know that airport intimately."

Grinning, Jeff waved a hand past her shoulder. "Bye Dad, we'll see you on Friday."

Jack grunted but never looked up.

"Just make yourself at home, phone up whoever you need to phone as well," Jeff told her, backing into the passageway to point at a little telephone table in the corner. "If you need anything ask Mickey." He strode over to the front door and lifted a black broad-brimmed hat off the hook. "See you this evening."

Amanda nodded mutely and watched him jam the hat down over his brown hair and stride out to the jeep, his long grey-black socks pulled up to his knees in the same style that Jack wore. It was obviously the fashion around here.

Feeling lost, Amanda went to the front door and peered out. A cloud of dust all the way up the road marked Jeff's departure. She glanced across at the old car where Margie was still sitting. Mickey was now stretched out in the driver's seat beside her, his door open to let air in. His low rumble carried across the heavy afternoon air. It was all so still, as though everything was too tired out by the heat to move or even make a squeak. Everything but Mickey, that is.

Studying the teenager, Amanda could not imagine that he would easily be subdued by a little bit of heat. She watched him with interest, intrigued that he genuinely looked pleased to be talking with the old woman. Amanda could recall no time in her life when she had ever been pleased to talk with an old woman! She had Aunt Marie to thank for that.

"If you had Aunt Marie as your Great Aunt you would be just the same as I am," Amanda muttered blackly at the sprawled out teenager in the driver's seat.

As though he heard her, Mickey turned just then and, seeing her in the doorway, waved at her before turning back to his grandmother.

Amanda waved back. Now she felt emboldened to step just outside the front door for a better look.

To the left was the automatic gate that they had driven through, a high wire gate that gave the feeling that she was in a fortress. The equally high electric fence it linked to only confirmed her impressions. The fence ran off to the left and behind the house. Beyond it stretched an open area of grass at a slight downward slope. To the right, thick clumps of bushes and grass were tangled in the fence for part of the section, but further to the right Amanda could see that the bush thinned out, because she caught glimpses of local people moving along the road.

Two children came into view, pushing a wheel barrow. Frowning, Amanda squatted down to try and get a better look at them through the bushes. Wasn't this a game park with wild animals? What were children doing wandering around in such an unsafe environment? Where were their parents?

Suddenly a pair of solid hairy legs were planted in front

of her face. Frayed socks pulled up under big knees filled her view. Gasping, Amanda wobbled and fell back onto her hands.

She looked up from the bulging calves that filled out the socks, up the thunder thighs, past the well-fed stomach, to a weathered red face at the top. A fair moustache, a bulbous nose, and caterpillar eyebrows completed the foreboding character before her.

A meaty hand was thrust in her face. Amanda stared at it dumbly before realising he was offering to help her up. She reached out and felt the chunky fingers wrap over her hand, completely covering it. She winced in anticipation of a crushing hold, but to her surprise found herself being effortlessly raised off the floor without so much as the hold going beyond a firm grip.

A pair of bright eyes scrutinised her closely as Amanda dusted off the seat of her jeans and tried to compose herself.

A voice blared out from somewhere behind, startling Amanda once again: "Hey Georgie, did you bring Jeff's axe back?"

The man in front of her remained unmoved as he continued to watch her, but Amanda guessed he was the one being addressed.

"Well hello!" From behind Georgie came his splitting image.

Amanda's eyes flicked between the two men as she realised they must be twins. Georgie's brother glowed with enthusiasm and energy—the complete opposite of Georgie, that was for sure.

"I'm Fabio," the cheerful red face announced, and stuck out a hand.

Amanda smiled cautiously, her glance flicking back over to Georgie. "Hi."

"And you are...?" Fabio asked, dusting off his hat on his thigh.

"Just a guest of the family," Amanda shrugged. "My name's Amanda."

Fabio nodded, "Good to meet you. Is Jeff in?" He looked past her into the house.

Shaking her head, Amanda said, "No, only Jack."

"The old boy's here?" Fabio looked pleased. "In the lounge, is he?"

Amanda nodded, stepping to one side to let him past. She watched in fascination as he approached the front door, wondering just how he would get through. These men had to be about six foot four and were as solid as elephants.

Fabio dipped his right shoulder down and ducked his head. Georgie nodded at her before following suit. Amanda noticed he did not carry a hat. She heard Jack grunt at Fabio's enthusiastic greeting before launching into a fully-fledged complaint about the *National Geographic*.

"You'd think they would put something in about us," Jack complained. "We're falling apart at the seams!"

Amanda leant against the door frame, listening to Jack elaborate on the poor quality of the magazine. He seemed quite devastated to find that once again Zimbabwe had not made it into its pages. Fabio couldn't get a word in, although he tried quite persistently. Amanda could hear him try to cut in frequently, only to be completely drowned out by Jack's tirade.

Smiling to herself, Amanda turned to watch the two children. The elder could not be more than ten years old. They were calling to each other in high happy voices, their bare feet kicking up red dust. Seeing them pass the entrance gate made Amanda wonder how Fabio and Georgie had got in. There must be another entrance, because they definitely had not come through that one!

Two minutes later a teenage boy appeared, letting out a shrill whistle to keep together the dozen or so cows he was herding. He slapped the rump of a straying heifer with a thin bendy stick; Amanda craned her neck to see where they went, but the herd and the boy simply disappeared into the bush. Feeling somewhat concerned, Amanda hoped that they would be okay. Hopefully if a wild animal attacked it would go for a cow before a skinny boy.

"Although the cows don't look all that fat, either," Amanda muttered. She wondered whether she would go for small skinny boy or big skinny cow, and immediately tried to shake off the dismal direction of her thoughts. Obviously the children here could take care of themselves. If no one else was worrying, why should she? She was just a visitor, a tourist. It wasn't her business to worry about the local children wandering alone through a game park.

"You'll find Jeff out on the north fence, I think." Jack's voice roused Amanda out of her worries and she turned to watch the three men coming out of the lounge. It struck her that none of these men actually belonged in the house, yet all looked very comfortable and at home there.

"Well Amanda, we're off," Jack grinned at her, back to his sociable self now that he had let off steam. "Do come and visit us sometime. Margie's biscuits are humdingers."

"You should try Anna's!" Fabio slapped Jack on the back and, turning to Amanda, said: "Georgie's wife is a terrific baker and cook."

Amanda noticed, only because she was watching him very closely, that Georgie's eyes crinkled at the corners in pleasure.

To Jack Amanda said, smiling: "Thank you for rescuing me—" But Jack was already strolling out into the sunshine, his white hair silvered by the light.

"Just as well, too!" he called back. Pulling out a mass of jangling keys, he sifted through them for the car key. "Would have been a long night if we hadn't." He grinned warmly at Amanda. "You've got God to thank for that. We were aiming to drive into Bulawayo today but didn't have enough petrol to do the whole trip."

Smiling stiffly, Amanda linked her fingers together behind her back and watched Jack chase Mickey out of the front seat. The two big visitors planted themselves beside the car. Silent Georgie watched, massive arms folded across his chest, while his grinning brother teased Mickey unmercifully about his skinny frame.

Amanda listened, growing more indignant as the teasing went on. Mickey wasn't that thin, it was just because he was almost as tall as Fabio that he looked so lean next to him.

"Besides, Mickey is just a youth, you overgrown buffoon," Amanda muttered severely, stepping closer. Her movement caused Georgie to look her way. Their eyes connected and Amanda felt the anger snuffle out of her when she saw Georgie's eyes flicker with understanding.

"They're playing," he said simply, unmoved.

Amanda turned back to the pair, Georgie's deep voice still rumbling in her ears. For the first time she noticed that Mickey's eyes were alight with pleasure as he gave back as good as he got. There was no animosity there. She glanced back at Georgie, reluctantly prepared to admit he was right. Fortunately, he was looking back at the car, perhaps at Margie. Amanda watched him, wondering if anything missed those observant eyes.

Amanda stepped back a safe distance while Jack jerked the car backwards and forwards until he finally got it facing the way it had come in. No one looked impatient as they waited for him to leave. Everyone waved as the electric gate rolled smoothly back and let them through.

Amanda felt uncomfortable as she stood with the three men, who all towered over her. Because Georgie was watching her, she tried to look in control and relaxed, but everything in her was strained from exhaustion and stress.

"Mickey, where can we find your dad?" asked Fabio. "We said we'd go with him to the other farm to help with the dipping."

"Dad's on the north fence. Part of it's been damaged." Mickey looked concerned: "Could be poachers."

"No surprise there," Fabio nodded. "People are hungry."

Amanda tried to follow their conversation, but she was watching a woman who had just walked up to the electric gate. She stood there expectantly, dressed in a blue and white checked uniform with a cloth tied around her head. *The Jacobs must have two maids,* Amanda mused.

"There's Mary; I'll just let her in." Mickey dashed inside, leaving Amanda alone with the two giants. She stared intently at the gate, as though absorbed in her own thoughts. Out of the corner of her eye she could see that both Georgie and Fabio were watching her curiously.

"So—you were stranded at the airport?" Fabio's curiosity could be heard in every syllable.

"Something like that," Amanda nodded coolly, watching the gate slide back, its wheels sliding along its rut.

"Yip, that's the way things are around here—" Fabio stretched his hands above his head and groaned as audible creaks were released in his back "—always some new challenge to work with. The Jacobs are convinced that God is at work in this place," Fabio smiled benevolently. "But they're good people."

Amanda cocked her head, forgetting her discomfort. "So they are Christians?"

Fabio nodded, "The whole pack of them. They pray about everything, even getting a stuck bull out of the water hole."

Amanda thought of Jeff, and mentally compared him in size to Fabio and Georgie. She suddenly giggled; all Fabio would need to do was pull and the bull would probably come flying out of the water hole!

Georgie leant forward and, in his bass rumble, said very seriously: "Bulls are expensive."

"I know that," Fabio argued. "My point is, they pray about everything. They're *practising* Christians, is what I am saying."

Georgie nodded.

"So I take it you're not?" Amanda queried.

Fabio shrugged, "Nah, I just get on with life and handle it as it comes—but sometimes I wonder if Georgie..."

Both turned to study Georgie, who stared back at them complacently.

Realising that Fabio was likely to ask about her own faith, Amanda quickly changed the topic. "How did you get in? You didn't come through the gate."

"We have a farm on the north side, so we came through the gate on that side of the house. Don't worry; this isn't a break and entry." He grinned widely at her.

Squirming, Amanda was relieved to see Mickey hopping across to them just as the gate knocked gently closed once more.

"The ground is scorching," Mickey answered Amanda's questioning look, jumping from one foot to the other. "Uncle Fabio, why don't you head straight to the other farm? I think Dad will go there as soon as he's checked on the fence. Have you already sent your cattle over to the dip?"

Fabio nodded. "A couple of the workers took them over this morning. Hopefully most of your cattle will already be dipped." Fabio turned to Amanda: "Enjoy your stay. We'll probably be seeing each other again."

Georgie lifted a hand in parting. "Study hard Mickey— nothing but A's."

"That's what Dad says," Mickey grinned; "nothing but A's for a Jacobs."

"Maybe you'll beat your brother's results," Georgie suggested.

"Not likely," Mickey scoffed. "He wrote four A-Levels and got A's for all of them."

"You're doing four, aren't you?" Georgie persisted.

"Yeah, but..."

Georgie shook his head firmly. "Get A-pluses. Your brother and I have a bet on you. Don't let the team down, boy." The big man's pat sent Mickey jerking forward.

Amanda suddenly found those dark blue eyes turned on like lamps. She had the distinct feeling that Georgie was smiling inside, although his features remained serious. He nodded at her before striding away—his brother was already out of sight. If Fabio's story was true—and it appeared it was—their car must be parked on the other side of the house.

"Georgie likes you," Mickey stated, sounding intrigued.

Amanda laughed disbelievingly: "Go on!"

Mickey shook his head earnestly, "I'm telling you. And Georgie doesn't usually like people straight away. He takes ages to warm up to someone new. The only other person I've ever seen him like straight away was Mom's Auntie Joan—but she was pretty cool. She used to sneak food out the fridge and blame my eldest brother."

"Great," Amanda responded unenthusiastically, "me and Great Aunt Joan."

She followed Mickey into the house, pausing in the hallway mirror to check her mascara hadn't smudged, making her green eyes look over-large for her face. It hadn't, and her black curls were all still looking fairly tidy, fortunately.

"You hungry?" Mickey led the way into the kitchen. "Rosie, is there any food?"

The buxom maid grinned, her teeth very white against her dark skin. "Today I will make rolls, just for you."

Mickey grinned back, pulling his stomach in so that his ribs appeared to press against his shirt. "I've missed you Rosie; do you see how they have been feeding me lately?"

The rich chuckle from the maid made Amanda smile.

"This boy—" Rosie shook her dripping finger "—you watch him closely. He's trouble!"

"Rosie!" Mickey exclaimed, sounding hurt. "You've cut me deep. Amanda, I've known Rosie since the day I came home from the hospital and this is what she says about me."

"Then she must know," Amanda responded, smiling at the maid who was leaning against the sink watching Mickey with a motherly look on her face.

"Shocking!" Mickey clasped a hand over his chest. "Even our guest has turned against me and she's only been here less than an hour."

Amanda flushed, wondering if she was being reprimanded.

"So now you can believe me!" Rosie shook her finger again at Mickey. "Now *hamba*. Go away."

"But the food!" Mickey protested. "Our guest is hungry, Rosie. She has travelled far."

The maid's rounded features pursed together as she summed up the situation, "I can give her something nice."

"She can't eat alone," Mickey shook his head seriously, "that wouldn't be right."

Amanda found herself and Mickey leaving the kitchen with two thick hunks of vanilla sponge cake and two mugs of tea. The tea had been sugared without anyone asking whether she took sugar. Kari wouldn't have touched either if her life had depended on it.

Amanda cringed at the thought. Kari's life did depend on it.

"Mom and Penny will be home in an hour or so, so you're stuck with me until then," Mickey said, settling down into an armchair in the sitting room. "Dad and Andy are working on the farm and Mom is doing some stuff in town before picking up Penny from school."

"Your grandfather said you're studying?" Amanda asked, wincing at the sweetness of the tea. How many sugars had they put in here?

"Yip, my A-levels. I've got my first exams next week." Mickey shrugged. "Not the most exciting thing to look forward to, but I'm determined to beat both my brother and Rob's results."

"Who's Rob?" Amanda asked, breaking a tiny piece off the rich butter-iced cake. How many calories were in this thing?

"Rob's my friend at school. It's either him or me who comes first in class. I can't let him take the lead now." Mickey shook his head, his eyes intense: "But most of all I want to beat my brother's results. He did all three sciences and Maths and got A's for them all." Mickey sounded slightly overwhelmed. "I know I can do it if I just keep studying."

"Stiff competition," Amanda observed, popping a chunk of cake into her mouth and feeling it melt on her tongue. Absolutely delicious!

"You're telling me," Mickey agreed. "What did you get for your A-levels?"

Amanda stopped chewing and stared at Mickey. "You're asking me?"

Mickey grinned, looking pointedly around the room.

Sighing, Amanda smiled in resignation, "Well, I wish there was someone else to ask. I didn't work very hard in high school, not as hard as I should have. I did English, Biology and History. I got one A and two B's."

"Not bad..." Mickey shrugged, looking at her empty cake plate. "I'd offer you another piece but I don't think Rosie would oblige. No use pushing her too far—otherwise next time she won't budge an inch."

"Oh, this was plenty," Amanda answered honestly. "Delicious, actually." She picked at the last few crumbs on her plate guiltily; she had just wolfed that down. She glanced up at her host. He must think she was an absolute pig. However, she was met with a friendly grin. If anything, Mickey looked pleased with himself. Unable to detect any ulterior motives, Amanda found her lips turning up in an answering smile. She quite liked this young man.

"I'm going to have to abandon you now," Mickey said, making no attempt to move. "I've got some more studying to do before the day is up."

"How much more?" Amanda was curious.

"Three hours; my goal is eight hours a day." He pushed on the arm rests and, straightening his arms, hovered over the seat for a moment while keeping his body in a sitting position, before he collapsed back into the seat. He glanced up at Amanda, a wicked flicker in his eye, "I bet you can't do that."

Amanda stared at the dancing eyes and lopsided smile. He really *was* actually suggesting she attempt to prove she had some arm muscles, and hover over her seat like a...like a teenager! This was ridiculous. Here she was, stuck in the middle of nowhere in a third-world African country, being entertained by a teenager, and he had the nerve to ask her to play the clown!

"I certainly can," Amanda retorted, spreading her palms over the top of each arm rest. She ignored Mickey's smile as she concentrated on pushing off the chair and straightening her arms, feeling the seat disappear from underneath her. For a moment she hovered above the seat, her arms shaking, and then they gave way and she collapsed down with a soft thump. "Ha!" Triumphant, she crowed: "You thought I couldn't do it."

Mickey just grinned as he pushed off the seat and gathered up the plates and mugs.

Once he had left, Amanda slid off the seat and crossed over to the bookshelf, an image of Mickey's face lingering in her mind. What was that look on his face? Had he looked pleased, maybe impressed? She shrugged, her eyes scanning along the book shelf. A glance at her watch told her it was three o'clock, but it couldn't be. It must be heading towards late afternoon now. How many hours was Zimbabwe ahead of the UK?

Amanda glanced out at the sunshine and then at the bookshelf. Her options seemed limited. How did she make herself at home when she wasn't sure where she was and what she was allowed to do?

"And soon the mother is going to arrive home and find her parents have cast a visitor on her," Amanda groaned, anticipating the awkwardness of the meeting ahead. "This whole thing is a mess."

In the end, she pulled out a book called *Jock of the Bushveld* and headed out of the front door. Perhaps there was a shady tree she could read under until everyone came home and she had to explain her presence. She cringed at the thought, wondering what she would have done if Polly had dropped some stranger off and given them the freedom of her flat until she came home from work...

Stepping out into the bright light, it took a moment for her eyes to adjust. The sky was so wide, and such a pale blue, as though the sun had bleached it. And high up, only a black speck, she could see what she thought must be an eagle. It almost didn't seem to be moving. She watched for a while until it looped just above the distant tree line and headed back the way it had come, on that lazy, almost unnoticeable, glide.

Turning right, Amanda walked along the shadow of the house. She didn't doubt Fabio when he said there was another gate, but she did want to see it for herself. No one seemed to be around, although she could hear hammering in the distance.

"Big house," she muttered, finally rounding the corner. She saw only more fence, and outcrops of bushes neatly trimmed back from the wire. Beyond were some rambling buildings.

Must be for farm use, Amanda thought. *They're not houses, anyway.*

She scanned the fence, looking for the gate. "None," she muttered grimly, striding along the west wall of the house until she came around the back.

Her breath caught at the landscape before her and she clung to the edge of the wall, mouth hanging open. Just beyond the fence stretched land as far as the eye could see. Long brown grass swayed gently in the breeze. In the far distance were purplish hills, a transmitter tower on the peak of the highest one. She could only just make out its thin shape.

Right below the house, nestled in a dip of land, was a natural collection of water. Judging from the large stretches of baked mud it must have once been bigger, but now it had receded.

But it wasn't the waterhole itself that caught Amanda's attention; it was the huge animal standing with its back to her that had her gawking. Its legs were stretched wide apart and its long neck was lowered to drink from the remaining pool.

A giraffe, right here!

Amanda was stunned as she watched the graceful neck

rise and the beautiful large brown eyes of the giraffe turn in her direction. She was close enough even to make out the whiskers on its face. "Absolutely incredible," Amanda breathed, the breeze causing her curls to wrap around her neck. For a moment she allowed herself the luxury of just watching the animal, the gate forgotten. The wind was blowing in her direction from the giraffe, and she got a strong whiff of animal smell and dried mud. It wasn't unpleasant, but neither was it a pretty smell.

The sound of hammering started up again, rousing Amanda back into action. With her eyes she followed the fence along until it dipped out of sight behind the rise on the left. But to the right there was definitely no gate.

Not to be beaten, Amanda went left, strode up the rise and stared down. She was almost disappointed to see the spoken-of gate just about where Fabio had said it would be. There were hardly any trees, and because she was standing on higher ground Amanda's gaze could follow the strip tar road for quite a distance. For a moment she was captured with the absurd desire to know where it went. There was something very appealing about the skinny double track with long grass rising up either side of it.

"Pull yourself together," Amanda told herself in business-like tones. "What you have to do is tell Kari and Polly what has happened and then sort out getting on a flight as soon as possible."

She lingered there a moment longer, enjoying the sun and the scene. It was the sight of the giraffe again that undid the immediacy of her resolution. She didn't see a giraffe every day, nor was the sun this glorious and warm very often...

Besides, Samuel Chiwedza assured me there were no flights today, Amanda remembered bitterly. With that in mind, she checked the dry grass patch she was standing on before sitting down.

"Ow!" Amanda bounced back onto her feet, slapping the seat of her jeans and gazing at the floor. "That's *hot!*" She stared at the spot in wonder, still feeling the burning ground through the denim.

A little scurry of movement caught her eye. Crouching down, she realised that the apparently lifeless patch of ground was actually buzzing with activity. Tiny black ants trailed through the dust, all heading in the same direction. She shifted over, following their trail until she saw their destination. The little black ants had cornered a long black insect and were swarming over it. The creature was writhing and squirming under the attack.

"Hey!" Amanda exclaimed, swinging around in search of a stick. "You mean little things." She pushed the stick under the squirming creature's body and flicked, sending the black carapace sailing through the air to land a good five metres away. She followed it up and saw that it was able to crawl away now, even though a few ants still clung desperately to it.

She stood, her gaze swinging over the dry trees with their long white thorns, across the scraggly grass and over the drying-up waterhole, the heat blazing down on them all. The harsh aridity was a far cry from the lush green of her Scottish hills.

She crossed over to the scattered shade beneath a nearby tree, scrutinising the ground before sitting cautiously down and opening the hard-cover book. Maybe she would at least learn something about Zimbabwe while she was here; then her delay would not be completely wasted.

"Never know," she murmured, trying to get comfortable on the prickly grass tips as she flipped to page one. "This might add an interesting twist to my research...somehow."

Chapter 5

The afternoon sun was setting on the horizon when Amanda was jerked out of her reading by the honk of a car hooter. The shade had long since moved on. For a moment she was dazed. Images of a tough Staffie dog called Jock merged with the spectacular array of colour on the horizon; then the horn sounded again, fully bringing her back into the present. Sucking in a slow deep breath, Amanda closed the book before exhaling gently. There were two grey pig-like animals at the water now—warthog or bush pig, she guessed—but otherwise the scene before her was deserted.

Deserted, but very beautiful in the orange glow of the setting sun that seeped right across the land and touched her, so that her arms too seemed to glow a soft orange shade. The sound of crickets and frogs filled the evening air and every now and then a dove called.

Rising with dignity, Amanda touched her face. It felt dry and stretched.

"Well, here we go," she breathed, tucking the book against her hip. "Mrs Jacobs and co, meet your unexpected and no doubt unwelcome guest."

She hesitated at the corner of the building, debating the best time to show herself. She could hear voices, so whoever it was must still be at the car. Perhaps it would be better for Mickey to reach them first.

"Mickey!" A girl's voice rang out through the evening air. "Mom says to come help with the shopping."

Amanda leant against the wall smiling to herself. She remembered how often Ruth had tried to convince the rest of them, especially Cobs, to come and help with the shopping.

"Yo yo!" The young masculine voice bounced through the

air, causing Amanda's brow to lift with pleasant surprise as she listened.

"*Ndeipi* Ma. What's up, kid?"

"*Ndeipi* yourself," the girl's voice retorted.

"Hi Mickey, had a good day? Will you grab that packet there please?" an older feminine voice asked. It had a pleasant ring to it.

"Which one? This one?" There was soft shuffling and crinkling of shopping bags and then Mickey said, "Yeah, I've clocked in about seven hours I'd guess; one more to go."

"Good job."

Amanda waited, thinking: "Now is a good time to mention me, Mickey." But Mickey said nothing as their steps faded into the house.

Sighing, Amanda rubbed the bumpy brick wall, crumbling pieces off it while she debated what to do. This was totally absurd. Time to get it over with.

"Hello?" Amanda cut through the happy bustle in the kitchen. She watched as mother and daughter gasped in unison, swinging around to see who had broken into their home.

"Amanda!" Mickey's easy grin lit up the room. "Ma, this is Amanda. She got stranded at the airport because there are no flights out to Jo'burg, so Gramps and Gran brought her home with them."

The woman's shock immediately turned into concern. "I'm so sorry! You must be exhausted and overwhelmed. Thank the Lord that Dad and Mom found you!"

Amanda waited, wondering what would happen next. She could see out of the side of her eye that the little girl was goggling at her with an open mouth, while Mickey continue to rummage through grocery bags to see what had come home.

"No mealie-meal?" he burst out.

"There was none Mickey, we searched everywhere," the child answered, moving over to stare into the packets with him.

Suddenly it was taking all Amanda's self-control to hold herself together. She could feel her legs trembling and hoped it wasn't visible.

"You poor girl!" Mickey's mother came over and, to Amanda's horror, gave her a warm embrace. When the woman stepped back, she was smiling in a motherly sort of way and apparently was not aware of Amanda's discomfort. "I do hope you'll stay with us for as long as your waiting takes?"

Amanda gripped the door frame, heart beat starting up again, "I wouldn't want to get in the way," she said stiffly.

"Nonsense!" The woman clapped her hands briskly. "We love having visitors, so this is wonderful. Has Mickey helped you settle in?"

Amanda glanced over at the teenager, engrossed in friendly banter with his sister. She gave a reluctant smile, "He did wheedle a decent cake from your maid."

The woman laughed merrily, "Well, it's up to me then to show you your room. Where are your bags?"

Amanda shrugged. "Mickey and his dad brought them in, but I'm not actually sure where they went."

The woman shook her head in mock dismay, "Such hospitality, and you probably exhausted as it is..."

Amanda followed her down the passage and into a daffodil-coloured room.

"Here you are—oh, and I am Sophie," she laughed as she stuck out a small hand and then clasped Amanda's in both of hers. "I do hope you'll love staying with us Amanda. Consider this your home while you are here." She shrugged, gently releasing Amanda's hand to go and check that the cupboards were empty. "You don't know how long you'll have to stay, what with the situation being as it is in the country, so you might as well make yourself comfortable and enjoy it," she grinned. "In my biased opinion you couldn't have picked a better place to have your holiday, either."

Amanda smiled, keeping her impressions of the harsh conditions to herself.

"We run a game park so we'll take you on game drives and show you our favourite haunts. And if you're here long enough we can take you over to look at our cattle farm. We rent land about half an hour away and graze some beef cattle on it." Sophie crossed briskly to the bed and pulled back the duvet slightly. "Yes, it's all clean and fresh," she confirmed, smiling up at Amanda. "Oh, I'm so glad God sent you to stay with us. This will be so much fun!" And then she was out of the room and down the passage, calling that she would hunt down Amanda's luggage. Amanda followed the sound of her short quick steps until they abruptly died. She must have stepped onto the sitting room carpet.

Mickey looks nothing like his mother, Amanda decided, comparing the lanky Mickey with his chocolate brown hair and blue eyes to his petite mother with her soft shoulder-length hair and gentle brown eyes *—except perhaps for the smile.* She stared around at the very bright room before crossing over to the window. It was dusk, shadows blending mysteriously into shadows. Every now and then Amanda could see movement beyond the fence.

Sophie had given her a room facing north; facing the dying water hole.

"Here it is!" Sophie hauled in Amanda's huge suitcase before letting the kitbag slide off her shoulder. "There you go."

"Thank you—" Amanda took the kitbag "—and thanks for being willing to let me stay. Just tell me how much the bill is."

She thought she saw surprise flare up in the brown eyes but all Sophie said was, "Let's not worry about that now. We'll sort it out later. Now, the bathroom is down the hall. Supper will be in about an hour so there's no rush if you want to have a bath first, or just settle in. A nap, maybe? You must be so tired!"

Amanda slowly unzipped her suitcase once Sophie had gone, discovering that the lock had been broken off her bag somewhere along the journey.

Well, I'll just keep a record of what I eat and how long I stay for, she decided. *I certainly won't take advantage of their kindness, and goodness knows that Doug certainly deserves to be paying out for my accommodation, considering he practically forced me into coming here.*

She thought of her boss and for the first time wondered when he had last left Scotland, let alone the UK. It paid to be rich and have a lot of money so you could tell everyone else what to do while you did exactly as you pleased. What was everyone from home doing tonight? Were Sally and Kari cooking the evening meal? And was Polly waiting eagerly for Sam to come home?

The street lights must be on by now. Amanda peered out

of the window at the purplish orange sky. There would be no street lights for her tonight, but she wouldn't complain—not with a sky like that.

Perhaps she would just have a brief lie-down. Just for a few moments...

The dinner call came sooner than Amanda would have liked. She procrastinated, tidying herself up and washing in the small basin, until she knew she was bordering on being rude, then nervously made her way down the passage, following the voices. The family was already gathering around the dining room table when she entered.

"Have a seat, Amanda," Jeff said, gesturing at the place setting opposite Mickey's. He waited until she was seated before beginning the family introductions.

"This is Penny, my sunshine." He leant over and ruffled the already untidy hair of the pre-teen Amanda had seen earlier in the kitchen with her mother. "And this is Andy. Andy and I run the game farm together, especially now that we're also raising beef cattle."

Amanda nodded politely at the young man, whom she judged to be about her own age—twenty-five or so. He was more the colouring of Sophie, and slightly shorter than Mickey and his dad, which made him about six foot. She noticed that his smile never reached his eyes. Or if it did, it was a sad sort of smile. She was glad when Jeff moved on to Mickey.

"And then you've met our Mick," Jeff smiled at Amanda as Mickey stretched lazily. "This boy is no fool, no matter what impression he tries to give. He's razor sharp under all that gangliness."

Amanda gave her first genuine smile of the night as she met Mickey's bright eyes, "I believe you."

"Oh-ho!" Mickey pretended surprise. "Well *that's* a change of tone from this afternoon. You should have seen how she and Rosie were ganging up on me, when I had no moral support or protection."

Amanda flushed as smiles lit up the table.

"Here it is, be careful—it's hot." Sophie came out of the kitchen with a steaming pot held in gloved hands. "Jeff, will you dish it out?" She bounced energetically back into the kitchen and returned with a big dish of vegetables.

"'Mmm-hmm...'" Penny sniffed deeply. "Beef stew, my favourite!"

Amanda had to agree with the young girl that it looked good; the aroma of the stew was wonderful.

"Now the only one you haven't met is our eldest son," Jeff said as he ladled stew onto Amanda's plate.

"And you're not likely to either," Sophie's soft voice interjected. "We don't see him for weeks, if not months, on end. He's a recently graduated doctor and works at a Mission."

"Oh?" Amanda feigned interest as she stared at the mountain of food on her plate.

"Along with one other doctor, he usually gets spread out between three different Missions. None of them are too far away from us, but it keeps him busy," Sophie explained. She suddenly clapped her hands together and announced: "Alright, enough chitter-chatter. Let's pray."

Amanda felt a small hand slip into her own. She turned to stare at Penny, wondering what on earth the little girl was playing at. Penny smiled sweetly back at her. Amanda glanced around the table and saw that everyone was holding hands, and waiting for her to take the hand that Andy was holding out to her.

Jeff smiled at her before bowing his head and praying: "Thank You for this delicious food Lord Jesus, please bless us as we eat it and bless the food to us. And thank You that Amanda has come to stay with us. I pray that You will do wonderful things in her life and ours in the time she is with us. Amen."

Amanda was still sorting her thoughts out when she heard the clatter of forks on plates and realised everyone had begun eating. What did Jeff mean by 'that You will do wonderful things in her life'? She was unsure of that prayer; it seemed to echo some of the things Mrs May had said to her that night in the church car park.

"You're looking sunburnt, Amanda, compared to when I saw you earlier," Jeff observed. "Did you spend the afternoon in the sun?"

Amanda looked up. Across the table from her, Mickey stabbed a piece of tomato with his fork and held up the red skin pointedly at her.

"Oh!" Amanda swallowed her half chewed food, "yeah, I guess so."

"You'll need a hat—I have a spare one," Sophie said. "Better use it while you are here."

"And I'll warn you now—" Jeff leant forward earnestly "—my wife is a hard task master. We are continuously being whipped into action. You might have it easy tonight; it's just the lull before the storm. Tomorrow..." He shook his head sadly. "Tomorrow your holiday is over. You'll be reined in for duty." Jeff looked around the table at his family before coming back to Amanda and saying piteously: "There is no rest for the wicked."

"Jeff!" Sophie gave a squeal of laughter as she flicked her serviette at him. "Don't you listen to him Amanda, or he'll have you re-packing your bags."

Amanda smiled. She hadn't *un*packed her bags yet. She didn't mean to stay very long.

"We can take it easy tonight, Jeff," Sophie added as she flicked back the straight fair hair that slid into her face, "but the five guests for Black Rhino arrive tomorrow, and the other three on Tuesday."

"We have guests arriving tomorrow?" Jeff looked up in surprise, his mouth full.

Sophie nodded, "Yes, they phoned today." She turned to Amanda, "Black Rhino is our biggest lodge for tourists, and Black Eagle is another."

Amanda nodded, wishing she hadn't changed into a polo neck. She was absolutely steaming. So much for hoping the heat would subside as night came on. It was Great Aunt Marie's fault she was here; Great Aunt Marie, Doug, and Mrs May. Somehow she was sure Mrs May had something to do with this. Remembering her old teacher's prayers and all the things she had said in the car park, Amanda just knew the little old woman had a part in all this. And from the little she knew of Him, it would be just like God to mess up her well ordered plans.

"I am cooking!" Mickey exclaimed, holding out his empty plate for seconds. "This heat is incredible."

"Don't talk with your mouth full Mick," Sophie chided, spooning stew onto the rice, "and well done for finally moving your muddy shoes off the veranda."

Mickey grinned, "That was Spooks, Ma."

Sophie rolled her eyes in exasperation and laughed in defeat, "Just as well you have a dog, because I was going to put you to work on the veggie garden if they weren't moved by tomorrow. Spooks is Mick's puppy, Amanda, he's a little menace."

Amanda didn't bother to respond this time. She was so uncomfortable and unhappy inside, so hot on the outside, and her eyes were burning with tiredness. She'd been without sleep now for about thirty-six hours, she realised!

"So you're driving Penny to school tomorrow, Mick," Jeff confirmed, "and coming back mid-afternoon? Andy and I will be at the fence, so I'll need you to supervise the cattle going to the market."

Mickey nodded, "I'll drive straight there, then."

Amanda looked between Jeff and Mickey incredulously. Was Jeff really putting Mickey in charge of something as big as getting cattle to market? She didn't doubt that Mickey was capable of handling it, but it seemed such a big responsibility for an eighteen year old.

"Would you like to come and check it out?" Mickey suddenly offered; blue eyes keen.

Amanda looked up and realised he was talking to her. "Oh—no thanks." She shook her head emphatically. "I might get a flight out tomorrow, and I wouldn't want to miss it."

The table suddenly grew quiet and everyone turned to stare at her. Then Sophie said very gently, "Amanda, I don't think you'll be getting a flight out for a good two weeks at least. Jeff stopped by at the airport this afternoon. There is one more flight coming in tomorrow, and then our planes are grounded until there is enough fuel and until the flight situation gets straightened out."

"So you mean..." Amanda stared wide-eyed at Sophie; "so you mean I'm stuck here?" She felt the last spiral of hope and control inside of her sink slowly into the pit of her stomach and become a dead weight. "But...what can I do, then? I have work to do, people to see, things to do...I—I have a schedule...to keep..." She trailed off miserably.

Sophie looked so sad and sympathetic as Jeff said, "You're just going to have to enjoy our good company. We're not that bad. It's only every other day we eat our visitors."

The family chuckled dutifully, but no one seemed to know what to say after that.

Amanda stared at her half-emptied plate and slowly placed her fork down on it. So that was that, she was stuck here indefinitely. What would she do?

"What is *wrong* with this country?" Amanda heard herself ask brusquely. She stared around at the faces and suddenly felt guilty that she was so ungrateful, after all their kindness towards her. But she was exhausted, disappointed, frustrated, and just plain...ugh! And now this lovely family was putting up with her horrible rudeness, even smiling at her in understanding...

Jeff responded gently: "We're going through a tough time at the moment. We have a drought, a severe financial crisis, food and fuel shortages all over the place...We're pretty much making do with what we've got. Everyone is. God has been very gracious to our family, we're doing fairly well. We still have tourists, still have some fuel, still have sugar..."

"Although our phone wasn't working today..." Penny wrinkled her nose at her dad. "I tried to phone Sarah this morning and it was dead."

"It's been like that two days, Smartie," Mickey said, wrinkling his nose back at her.

Sophie ignored her children, concentrating on Amanda. "Please know we are *so* glad you're staying with us," she pleaded, "and I really hope you can just rest and enjoy your visit. You are no imposition *at all*. Truly."

The woman sounded genuine. Amanda glanced at Jeff and he nodded in firm agreement with his wife. Both Mickey and Penny were openly watching, interested to see how she would respond. Only Andy carried on eating as though he couldn't hear any of what was going on around him.

Amanda gulped, hands clenched together under the table. What choice did she have? She literally had absolutely no control over the situation. For once she was completely dependent on other people, something she had always worked so hard at avoiding.

"Well then, I *must* pay you," Amanda said firmly. "You've all been so kind—and I must do what I can. I have foreign currency, so that will be a help, I think?"

To her surprise both Jeff and Sophie shook their heads

in unison.

"I won't take no for an answer." Amanda gritted her teeth in determination. She would not be a charity case again. She had spent too many childhood holidays pawned off on relatives and distant family friends, preying on their stretched hospitality.

"Well...I actually had another idea in mind," Sophie admitted. "I'm really needing some support around the ranch, and would gladly make a trade of your time for our accommodation. How does that sound?"

Amanda frowned, "I don't think that's fair to you. I can still help out, but I do think I must give you *some* money."

Sophie shrugged. "If you insist...but in all honesty, your help would be more valuable than your money. It's been crazy trying to keep up with all the things we have to do around here lately."

"You'll be part of the family," Jeff said. "Muck in and do what you can where you can, and receive the praise or the pain along with the rest of us."

Hands clenched tightly, Amanda stared at Jeff, wondering if he realised what a fearsome proposal he was offering her. She had barely ever been part of a family, and when she was it hadn't been all that fun.

"Well..." She moistened her bottom lip nervously, trying to think of something reasonable to say. Two weeks, they'd said—she could do 'family' for two weeks, couldn't she?

"It's a deal," she whispered, and regretted the words the moment they were out. "As long as you tell me what needs doing and what I do wrong, so I know how to correct it."

"Sounds good," Jeff nodded, looking pleased. Sophie smiled radiantly at her.

"So?" Mickey knocked his fork loudly against his plate: "You wanna come and check out the cattle?"

Amanda shrugged, giving Mickey a half-hearted smile. She couldn't resist his youthful zest for living, or that smile. "Okay."

In her room that night, as she lay under the thin sheet and stared out of the open curtains at a fantastic sprinkle of stars, Amanda couldn't hold back a miserable trickle of tears.

"What on earth are You doing, God?" she whispered. "I'm stranded in the middle of nowhere. Sure, these people are amazing. I know I would never have picked up a stranger and brought them home, or welcomed them so warmly and eagerly into my home." She brushed a finger along her hot cheek, beginning to notice the pain of the sunburn. "But God, I don't want to be here and I'd like you to get me out. Can't I *plee-ease* get a flight out tomorrow?"

Heart heavy, Amanda's even heavier eyes finally closed and her breath grew slow and even. Once, she woke and thought she heard the back door open and footsteps pass under her window, but after listening a moment she heard nothing more. She was asleep again within moments.

Chapter 6

"Hmm-mm, too warm!" Amanda groaned, stretching out a hand on the pillow. Kari must have left the heating on.

Even with her eyes closed, she could tell it was day already. Opening them up a crack, Amanda was embraced by a stream of sunlight. And not Scottish sunlight, either...

Rubbing blurry eyes, Amanda tried to focus, and as her fingers brushed against her sunburnt cheeks she yelped in pain and leapt up—only to find herself in a strange room. The trauma of her trip came rushing back in full force, sucking the life out of her legs so that she collapsed wearily back down onto the bed.

"So I'm still here," she breathed, gazing around at the unfamiliar furniture, at the yellow walls and at her suitcase lying open beneath the window. There would be no research on depression today. No Kari and Sally to come home to. No Polly to call on the way home from work and find out how she was doing. No Forth of Firth estuary to look at from her window on the drive home. No Ochil mountains...

"I don't even know where I'd find myself in the atlas right now," Amanda moaned, somewhat awed as the reality of her situation sank in. She was utterly at the mercy of these strangers, for not even her cell phone had signal on it.

Pulling on yesterday's jeans and a black and white T-shirt, Amanda grabbed her pair of sneakers, tugged them on and softly cracked her bedroom door open. She could hear Sophie's voice coming from the kitchen area but she wasn't speaking English. It sounded the same as Samuel Chiwedza and the sweeper at the airport had been speaking.

She made her way up the passage, her treads squeaking on the tiled floor, and up to the kitchen. Hovering in the doorway, Amanda debated what to do. She had just about decided to go back to her room when Sophie swung around and spotted her.

"Amanda, good morning!" The bright welcoming smile soothed some of Amanda's fears. Apparently Sophie had not had a change of heart overnight. "You're up early." Sophie lifted up the teapot questioningly.

Amanda nodded, accepting the tea offer as she slid onto a kitchen stool, "Up early? I am?"

She glanced around the kitchen walls until she found the kitchen clock, "Five o'clock! Wow, is that right?" she checked.

Sophie grinned, "Yip, you're welcome to take your tea and go back to bed?"

Amanda shook her head, not even considering the option. "No, I'm up now," Amanda said, accepting the mug of tea. "Is there anything I can do to help?"

"Not right away," Sophie answered easily, "but as soon as Mickey and Penny leave for school we'll drive up to Black Rhino Lodge and get it ready for the guests. Now I've got to go and meet Jeff at the compound, that's where the workers live. Help yourself to porridge. It's in the pot on the stove."

Amanda obediently scooped two ladles of creamy white porridge into a bowl and sprinkled some very dark sugar onto it.

"Do the workers also live in the game reserve? Do they have a fence protecting them from the wild animals as well?"

Sophie shook her head. "No, they live just outside the game reserve but sometimes they pass through it." She shrugged, "It's not at all advisable but they still do it."

One of the maids came in just then, closely followed by the other. Taking her steaming porridge, Amanda left Sophie chatting with them and wandered out the back door onto the veranda.

The air was pleasantly cool. She stood for a moment staring out at the waterhole. There were no animals visible. Picking the woven basket chair with the red cushion, Amanda tucked her legs up and balanced her porridge bowl on the arm of the chair. She slowly stirred the sugar in, watching streams of brown whirl through the white as the sugar melted.

From the corner of her eye she saw a small form glide silently out the kitchen door and settle in a chair nearby. It was Penny. Amanda surreptitiously studied the girl. She was dressed in a blue and white uniform and her brown hair was pulled back into a neat pony tail, two clips holding her fringe back.

Unhappy that her space had been invaded, Amanda nevertheless croaked: "Morning." She watched Penny's young face light up. Gaining a little bit of confidence, Amanda relaxed slightly and attempted to make light conversation. What did pre-teen girls like to talk about?

"What time does your school start?"

"Just after seven." Penny's voice was very soft. Was she suddenly shy this morning?

Amanda stirred her porridge some more. If the girl was so shy why had she come to sit with her? They sat in silence, Amanda uncomfortable as Penny watched her adoringly.

"Have you had breakfast?" Amanda asked.

Penny nodded.

Sighing inwardly, Amanda hoped that the girl would go soon. She didn't know how to relate to children. She tentatively tested her porridge and was pleased to find it tasted just right. Not too salty and not too tasteless.

"Penny, let's go!"

Amanda sagged in relief on hearing Mickey's roar from somewhere in the house. She gave Penny a bright smile, "Off to school."

Penny nodded, looking disappointed, "I wish I could come with you and Mickey to the cattle ranch."

Amanda shrugged, trying to look sympathetic.

Mickey appeared in the door way just then, all spruced up in a crisp white shirt and black trousers.

Seeing Amanda he flashed his grin: "*Ndeipe* Amanda?"

Amanda smiled back, responding to the contagious enthusiasm and energy Mickey brought. "*Ndeipe*. Is that a greeting?"

"Shona slang. It means 'what's up?'," Mickey answered. He grabbed the back of Penny's chair and rocked it. "Stop dawdling Penny and get moving. Amanda will still be here when you get back."

Amanda watched Penny's face flush with embarrassment as the girl scrambled to her feet. Taking pity on her, Amanda called out as she was leaving, "Bye Penny, have a good day."

Penny flashed a quick smile and ducked into the kitchen after Mickey.

"Well!" Amanda let out her breath. "I'm not sure what I did to deserve her attention."

Relieved to be alone, Amanda listened as an engine coughed deeply into life and minutes later an old Bedford truck rattled past the veranda. Amanda caught sight of two scowling faces in the front seats. She giggled a little, especially when both Mickey and Penny turned to wave brightly at her before returning back to whatever argument they were having.

"Sibling warfare."

Amanda turned to see Sophie flop down into the seat that was still cooling from its last occupant.

"They have me clawing at the wall, quite often," Sophie admitted. "Some days I'm quite relieved to wave them goodbye and pack them off to school. But they're good kids." She flashed Amanda a smile. "You know something Amanda, Penny's taken to you fast."

Amanda sighed, "I'm not sure why she has." She hesitated and then said frankly, "I'm much better with books than people. My sister Polly is the people person."

Sophie's eyes smiled, "What is it you do, Amanda?"

"Research." Amanda stared out towards the horizon. The sky was so blue.

"So were you flying to Jo'burg for business or pleasure?" Sophie asked.

"Work and family." Amanda tucked her empty porridge bowl under her chair and picked up the tea. It was still hot. It didn't cool quickly like it did in Scotland, the air was too warm. Sighing softly, Amanda cautiously expanded her answer: "At the moment I'm working on a research project that investigates depression in children. We're comparing depression between males and females, as well as differences in symptoms of depression. Along with this, we hope to also see how depression in children differs from depression in adults."

Amanda glowed as she mentally processed her work. "It's quite a mammoth task," she admitted, "but I love it. When my boss found out I had to go to Cape Town he jumped at the chance to expand our research." Amanda smiled wryly. "So our already huge project has just stretched to include a quick look at cultural factors that influence the causes and effects of depression in children."

She must remember to ask Doug if she could have an extension to work on the differing symptoms of depression between boys and girls; she had not covered that area properly. Perhaps there were also age differences, stages when boys were more vulnerable to depression than girls, and vice versa.

"Madame, it's the man for the cows. By the back door." Rosie appeared in the doorway, waving a hand into the house.

"Thanks, Rosie." Sophie pushed off her seat, but paused at the door to break into Amanda's reverie. "Amanda, I'm glad you're here. I know this is a God-thing." She slipped into the house, leaving Amanda staring at the empty doorway.

"A God-thing," Amanda echoed, her worst fears confirmed.

What did God want with her now?

Chapter 7

Amanda pulled herself up onto the passenger seat of the Land Rover while Sophie ran back into the house for extra towels to take up to the lodge. It was a beautiful day. The sun was already high in the sky, and incredibly hot. Just as well she had packed a sleeveless shirt, and with the sun-cream Sophie had lent her she should be set for the day.

In the tree on her left, perched on a long white thorn, was a bird with an enormous curved yellow beak. It had one eye fixed sternly on Amanda.

"What's that?" Amanda whispered, poking a finger at the bird, as soon as Sophie returned.

"Yellow-billed Hornbill," Sophie answered starting the engine. The bird fluttered but did not fly away. "And that's an Acacia tree it's sitting in."

"Huge thorns," Amanda murmured.

Sophie shifted into gear. "Our home has a double name. It's called *Shalom*, meaning 'peace' in Hebrew, and also *Shamwari Ranch*. Shamwari means 'friend' in Shona. Sindebele is one of the main languages in this area, but both Jeff and I came from Mashonaland so we know more Shona than Ndebele. We pretty much speak Chilapalapa with our workers if we're not speaking English."

"Chilapalapa?"

"Chilapalapa is a hybrid language, a mix of this and that."

Amanda nodded. Sophie's story was matching with what Jack had told her yesterday.

She sat up a little straighter in delight as Sophie drove around the house and down to the back gate that Fabio and Georgie had come through. Sophie slapped the centre of the steering wheel twice, letting out a loud double hoot.

"Rosie will open it for us," Sophie explained. "Now this morning we'll go to Black Rhino Lodge first and then on to Black Eagle. Both of them are pretty places, but my own favourite is Duiker Cottage. It's just a one-roomed cottage that overlooks the dam, but Jeff and I have many happy memories of times spent there."

"Oh?" Amanda clutched at her seat as the left wheel ramped over an anthill.

"Yip, we built it together. I thought I'd never get rid of the calluses I got from that." Sophie casually swerved to dodge an animal that darted across the road.

"Whoa!" Amanda gasped. "A deer!"

"It's a kudu," Sophie grinned, looking very much like Mickey just then. "An antelope, as opposed to a deer. They do spice up the drive, don't they?"

She guided the four-by-four up a steep hill and paused at the top to give Amanda a chance to take in the breath-taking view. A plain of honey-coloured grass spread out before them, almost treeless, and far ahead Amanda could see a stretch of water. It must be the dam Sophie had spoken of.

Amanda suddenly spotted a grey lump in the water.

"Look at that!" Amanda cried, excitedly clutching Sophie's arm. "Is it an elephant?"

"A bull elephant I think." Sophie jerked the vehicle forward, looking just as pleased as her guest.

Amanda couldn't contain her excitement as they threaded their way through the bumps in the road to get a closer look at the huge pachyderm. "I really didn't expect to see this."

The depression and anxiety of her turbulent trip began to lift as they approached the elephant, and by the time they had watched the animal, chatted in soft whispers, and then continued on towards Black Rhino Lodge, Amanda's spirits had risen enormously.

"So this is all your own game park?" she asked.

"Yes, a private game reserve," Sophie nodded. "Tourists come and stay with us, and Andy or Jeff take them on game walks, or sometimes hunting if we need to cull—to control the population. I mostly do the guided game viewing and keep the accommodation up to scratch."

Amanda felt a measure of relief as she listened. If she

was to be stranded here for two weeks as a paying guest, she might as well enjoy her holiday.

"Here we are—Black Rhino Lodge," Sophie announced, pulling up next to a neatly thatched stone-walled building.

The cabin was exquisite. Following her through the khaki door, Amanda could see Sophie's tasteful touch in the design and arrangement. Thick wooden gum poles stretched across the roof to support the thatch, and the inside of the lodge smelt woody. Big fireplaces were already set for a fire.

"We thought of putting televisions in, but the electricity is from generators—the cottages are too isolated out here to have power lines—so we decided against it." Sophie staggered into the kitchen with the basket of supplies she had brought with her. "Besides, you can watch TV anywhere, but you can't enjoy a game reserve just anywhere. Do you mind unpacking this while I go and make the beds?"

Sophie did not wait for an answer. Lifting the cloth off the basket, Amanda happily rummaged through it, pulling out packets of fresh meat, eggs, milk, and a couple of assorted tins. In another container she found home baked biscuits, and then there were tea bags and fruit left lying at the bottom of the basket. Hunting through the cupboards, Amanda found a collection of tins and added the new supplies to them, then stacked the meat into the freezer. Humming softly under her breath, she discovered that Sophie had written out a 'To Do' list.

"Check dustbins have new liner," Amanda read, pushing back loose curls from her face. Obediently she wandered through the lodge, slipping into bedrooms to check that each straw bin had a liner in it and then, spotting a big grey bin through the bedroom window, made her way back to the kitchen.

Stepping out the back door, Amanda gave a grunt of dismay. A grey monkey was rummaging through the bin using one hand, its head jerking up frequently to scan the area. Amanda watched it for a moment, debating what to do. After much deliberation and soft "shooing" noises, she grabbed a broom and warily approached the creature. It leaned back and wiggled dark eyebrows at her, making its eyes go wide and threatening.

"I don't like your attitude," Amanda informed the vervet forbiddingly, clutching the broom in both hands. "We both want the bin and I'm going to win. It's up to you how you leave..."

She thrust the broom out in front of her. The monkey gave a mock lunge forward, sending a rush of adrenaline through Amanda.

"Ha!" She swiped the air and charged forward. The monkey leapt from the concrete bin and scampered a safe distance away. "Better," Amanda muttered, keeping one hand firmly on the broom while she gathered the black plastic bag up. She cautiously leaned the broom against the bin while she tied up the black bag.

"Now, I don't have a personal problem with you," she informed the monkey, "but this is just the way it is. I'll put a fresh clean bag in, like this, and when I've gone you're free to play in it as much as you like. You'll be someone else's bother next time."

It was with a flourish of triumph that she carted her prize back into the house, waving cheerily at the watching black eyes as she passed the tree into which the monkey had withdrawn.

Amanda picked up the 'To Do' list and read the next point softly.

"Remember God's grace extends to me as well." She stared at it. "Funny."

Shrugging, she skipped on to the next one: "Boil three eggs for lunch. Now *that* I can do." And once she had figured out how to work the gas stove there were no further problems.

"Bedrooms done!" Sophie breezed back into the room and nodded in approval. "Great job! Now, how about tea before we move on to the next lodge?"

"'Mmm," Amanda nodded, settling on to a stool while Sophie retrieved the silver flask with ready-made tea in it.

"You ever thought of coming to Zimbabwe before this?" Sophie queried.

Laughing sheepishly, Amanda admitted, "I'm still not sure I want to be here now. I don't even precisely know where Zimbabwe is."

"That can be easily solved with a map, I'll show you when

we get home," Sophie said, just as her cell phone started ringing. "Where is that thing?" Rummaging through her pockets, Sophie tried to find the phone.

"In the basket!" Amanda dove for it and handed it over.

"It's my eldest son," Sophie whispered, pressing the answer button, "Hello darling."

Her nose wrinkled up. "I can't hear you very well at all, only every fourth word or so. If you can hear me I am at Black Rhino Lodge. We'll be heading up to Black Eagle just now, so try again then, the signal may be better. I love you, Sunshine."

Pocketing the phone, Sophie dug in the cupboard under the sink. "We don't hear from him often. He's quite absorbed in his work, and due to petrol shortages and poor network we have little contact with him. I really miss him, but he seems very content in what he believes is God's call on his life—Aha!" She rose, brandishing a pocket of candles. "I knew they were here somewhere. The generators can be so unpredictable, it's important to know where the candles are kept."

"It sounds like living in Zimbabwe is like living back in the hunters-and-gatherers times," Amanda observed.

"Close," Sophie grinned, smiling slyly at Amanda. "Some people are scared to even come into the country because of the situation, so whatever guests we have are God-sent."

Groaning, Amanda rolled her eyes: "You can thank my sister Polly for that. I told her I wanted a return ticket for a month and between her and my eldest sister they booked my ticket so that it would change flights here on the way to South Africa."

"Uh-huh..." Sophie nodded, but Amanda could see she disagreed.

Half an hour later they were on the rise up to Black Eagle when the phone rang again.

"Would you answer that?"

Amanda took the phone, "Hello, Sophie's phone—can I help you?" She smiled, thinking how Kari would have called that a call centre answer of sorts.

A clear masculine voice answered. He sounded quite similar to Mickey.

"You can't hear me?" Amanda repeated, frowning at

the dashboard. "The line sounds pretty clear to me." She listened, "Yes I know, I heard you the first time. I can hear you very well." She frowned, pressing the phone closer to her ear. "You can't *understand* me?" she said, scratching a bit of mud off the dark plastic cubby hole in front of her. Lowering the phone and pressing it to her knee to block out sound she whispered to Sophie, "He can't hear me. I think its your son again."

"Keep talking, he will," Sophie encouraged, her lips turned up in a smile.

Amanda repeated her first line into the phone, and tapped the dashboard softly in frustration. "I *am* speaking English," she growled, struggling to rein in her annoyance. If this wasn't her hostess' son she might have insisted he phone back later to talk to Sophie, whether or not there was network later. "Sophie is driving at the moment but we are almost at the lodge. If you would hold on you can talk to her in a moment."

Amanda handed Sophie the phone as they pulled up at the lodge, "I'm sorry but he just couldn't understand my accent," she apologized, staring at the attractive rustic sign that read 'Black Eagle'.

Sophie accepted the phone with a soft thanks. "Hiya... Yes, you were speaking to Amanda. She arrived yesterday... No, she's staying with us. Gramps and Gran invited her and we are delighted to have her. How are you doing, and where are you?"

As she listened, Amanda had a growing suspicion that he had been able to understand every word she had said. She could just see Mickey pulling a stunt like that, so why not his brother?

Fuming inside, Amanda listened with growing intrigue, trying not to look too obviously interested.

"Well, take care of yourself darling. We'll see you when we see you. Alright. Love you. Bye." Sophie tucked the phone in the cubby-hole. "He was just touching base. He's at his home Mission station and doing well, just getting over a bit of a cold but otherwise as busy as ever."

"He's a doctor, you said?" Amanda confirmed.

"Yip, it's quite a struggle to get enough medicines, but then again—" Sophie's brown eyes shone with trust "—God provides time and again for that too."

"If you say so," Amanda murmured, hopping off the Land Rover to follow Sophie into the lodge. Sophie seemed very determined to believe that God was behind an awful lot more things than the average person would allow.

Each to her own. Amanda yanked the bin liner out of the concrete bin before following Sophie into the house. She found some of Sophie's comments quite unsettling. What would Kari think of these beliefs? They must have covered every topic under the sun except religion. Neither had much use for it—at least, she didn't, in spite of going to church to please Polly. But Kari?

She couldn't even begin to guess how Kari would respond to Sophie.

On arriving back at Shalom they were greeted by a gaggle of excitement. One of the farm workers had fallen into the river and broken his leg. He was also the driver who was supposed to be going into Bulawayo to do the shopping and bring Penny home.

"Oh, man!" Sophie let out a heavy sigh. "What now?" She followed the workers onto the veranda. They were all talking together at the tops of their voices, arms waving as they shouted.

"Patrick," she said as she crouched beside the injured man, "are you in much pain?"

He shook his head, lips tight, but glazed eyes said otherwise.

"We must get you into Bulawayo, to the hospital," Sophie decided.

"But the guests!" Patrick protested.

"There's the *Sekuru*," Sophie pointed out, and then groaned, even as Patrick shook his head. "You're right. Dad would have already gone into town. And Jeff and Andy are away on the other side of the ranch."

"I can fetch them—the guests, I mean," Amanda volunteered.

"Of course!" Sophie spun around. "You can drive, right?"

Nodding mutely, Amanda was already regretting her impulsive offer. Anything could happen to her. She could take a wrong turn and end up in another remote place where there was no Jack to rescue her. Or she could be attacked by...by an elephant, or gored by a—what was that thing that had jumped across the road?—a kudu.

"Great. I'll draw you a quick map, in case you don't remember how you got here, and then Patrick, Jason and I will head into town. Hopefully we'll be home by supper time."

A set of keys were shoved into her hand, accompanied by a rough map on a piece of toilet paper, and then Amanda found herself sitting in Sophie's Land Rover heading along the winding road she had travelled just yesterday, dust whipping up from the wheels.

Please get me back to Scotland alive, Amanda prayed, joggling over a grid on the road before having to stop to open a gate that was linked to the high electric fences that separated the game park from the communal land. Thoughts of Scotland diminished as Amanda negotiated a cart pulled by two enormous oxen, which weaved across the road ahead of her. The three small children in the cart waved excitedly, pulling the cart to a stop to watch her go by.

"Probably wondering what a stranger with wild black curls and a red face is doing with this vehicle. Maybe I'll get reported for stealing!" Amanda muttered, exaggerating her plight while absently scanning the road ahead for speed cameras. In truth, she was actually beginning to enjoy her adventure.

The rest of the drive was fairly quiet. The bush road blended into double-strip tarred tracks which later blended into a full tarred road. There was no yellow line, and the grass rose up like a hedge alongside the road so that it sometimes scratched against the side of the Land Rover. If she had been in a lower car, as yesterday with Jack, she would never have been able to see the cattle grazing in the grass beyond, or the tiny herders who could not have been much older than seven years. At one point she came across scatterings of children who had to move off the road to let her past. They were dressed in school uniforms and had bags slung over their backs. Most were not wearing shoes. A few waved and Amanda waved back, intrigued that none looked at all depressed with their poor living conditions.

Something to look into for my research paper.

She glanced down at the toilet paper map, held down on the seat by her shoe which she had taken off for that very purpose. The map showed that she must zigzag until she reached the long line of trees that marked the entrance road to the airport.

A plane was just landing when Amanda pulled up into the airport car park. She watched it wistfully, wondering what her chances were of getting a flight out today.

Glancing around, she nodded in approval: *No parking meters.* She strode business-like into the airport. Samuel Chiwedza was still manning his post.

"Eh—hello!" he called, greeting her like an old friend.

Unable to keep the smile in, Amanda went over to him.

"No flights to Jo'burg today," he informed her cheerfully before she could ask him.

"Worth a try." Amanda leant an elbow on the counter, keeping an eye on the narrow doorway from which the guests would arrive. "Today I'm picking up people."

She watched Samuel's face cloud with confusion.

"Here's my phone number. I'm staying with people called Jeff and Sophie Jacobs."

"Oh!" Samuel grinned in understanding. "Where is Madam Sophie today?"

"Madam Sophie?" a voice cut through the air.

Both turned to see the sweeper strut through the entrance of the airport and look around expectantly. His eyes lit upon Amanda and he trotted over.

"Ah..." Samuel's eyes shone. He pointed at Amanda. "She is the one who has come from Shamwari Ranch in Madam Sophie's car." He turned to his old friend, his voice growing loud in delight. "Yesterday she was lost, today she has a job."

"That Madam Sophie," the old man chuckled, slapping his hand against Samuel's. "Ehhh, I would not work for her; I would never sit down." The two burst into laughter.

"So—you are at Shamwari Ranch?" Samuel was still smiling at their joke when he turned back to Amanda. "Good," he nodded in approval; "I know where to find you when your plane comes."

"And you had better run all the way to the ranch if the phone is not working!" Amanda was only half-joking.

"Here are your guests." The old sweep pointed at the first person to emerge through the doors.

Something sparked in her at the sight of the cowboy hat jammed down on the man's head. It reminded her so much of the way Cobs had worn his hat.

"How do you know this is them?" Amanda queried, gazing at the man doubtfully.

That brought another laugh.

"They have 'tourist' written all over them," the sweep grinned. "Come, I'll help you put their bags into the car."

Amanda paused a moment, trying to see what the old man meant, but seeing nothing unusual about the passengers, she followed the man over to the door.

"Sophie Jacobs?" The passenger who'd been indicated by the sweep approached her, cowboy hat in hand and dressed in khaki clothes. He looked at Amanda expectantly.

Amanda shook his hand nervously, "Amanda McCree. I'm here on behalf of Sophie Jacobs." She tried to smile with the same warmth that Sophie would have given, but knew she was failing. "Welcome to Zimbabwe."

She and the old man led the five-person troop to the Land Rover. Amanda gratefully let the old man organize the bags while the bearded leader of the group climbed into the passenger seat, and the four remaining guests squeezed themselves onto the bench seat behind.

"It's all in—just check behind you whenever you hit a bump hard, in case a bag jumps out!" The old man waved, stepping back from the car. "We will see you."

Amanda stared at the packing dubiously. "Thanks, I think," she said, and after pulling a worried face gave him a grin. "Yes, I definitely will be seeing you again. Soon, I hope!"

"So this is Zimbabwe." The tall guest, with his cowboy hat jammed on once more, began talking before Amanda had even slid into the driver's seat. "It's not how I thought it would be. It's actually quite dry and derelict. Not much of an airport either. Looks like an old aeroplane hangar."

Amanda hid her annoyance at his open appraisal by concentrating on the road determinedly, though she also studied him out of the corner of her eye when he wasn't watching. A thick beard and moustache covered the thin face. There was a distinct kink in his nose and a scar beneath one eye: a rough customer.

"Where is the game?" one of the women whined from the back seat. "The brochure said there would be game!"

"Oh hush up Velda, we're not at the game ranch yet," the front passenger ordered.

"Ross, surely you are not going to let him speak to me like this!" Velda turned on the second man. "He may be your friend, but he is not *my* friend. We are married—remember?" She waved a bejewelled hand. "You're supposed to protect me from verbal abuse like this!"

Completely dominating the conversation, the man in the front seat continued as though Velda had never spoken. He said very knowledgeably, "So—you must be struggling with the situation as it is. What with the huge inflation, and all the food and petrol shortages. In fact, it's quite something you could fetch us in a vehicle at all. I imagined a donkey cart would be waiting for us."

Amanda's brow rose. "Oh?" Inside she was thinking, *Food shortages as well!* Sophie had mentioned nothing about food shortages, had she?

Amanda gritted her teeth as she hit an unavoidable gully in the road. She hid a dark smile when she heard the women in the back seat squeal as they were bounced off their seats.

"And what about the political unrest?" the man went on. "Is there open fighting, or is it all hush-hush?"

Political unrest? Amanda felt something deep inside of her tremble.

"Gosh, but is this hot or what!" the same whining woman complained, fanning herself with a flimsy paper that Amanda guessed to be the brochure. "I'm parched!"

In her rear view mirror, Amanda could see Velda's pouting red lips and heavy make-up as her dissatisfied, hard eyes scanned the scenery.

"And it's so dry," the red lips said, turned down at the corners, "one spark could set this whole place into a blaze."

"It hasn't rained lately," Amanda heard herself say defensively, not knowing whether she spoke the truth or not.

What was wrong with these people? They were horribly

critical.

Yet, why were they getting under her skin so much? What did it really matter how they viewed it all? Hadn't she thought the same way just yesterday? Maybe even now? Only, she had expected taxies and a city, while these people were an assorted mixture of expectations that seemed to range from donkey carts to well-watered green fields. They probably also expected a five star hotel with on-hand servants to attend to every whim.

"I heard that people were starving in some of the rural parts," the second man leaned forward to shout in Amanda's ear.

She cringed.

"It's shocking!" The third man—Ross?—shook his head gravely and looked intensely at Amanda. "If there is *anything* I can do while I am here please do not hesitate to ask."

It was with great relief that Amanda roared up to Black Rhino Lodge. She must have beaten Jack's speed record of yesterday and taken the corners with twice as much vigour as he had in her eagerness to get there.

Grabbing the lodge key from the cubby-hole, Amanda jerked the first bag she could get her hands on out of the Land Rover and marched up to the lodge. The five guests followed behind at different paces. The eager know-it-all was close on Amanda's heels, his wife hurrying behind, while the other man and the brochure woman—Ross and Velda— followed more slowly, hanging back to argue over whose bag was whose. The leader simply stood quietly, taking in his surrounds, before following them inside at a leisurely pace.

"This is it, Black Rhino Lodge." Amanda squeezed out a false smile, priding herself in being able to hide her true feelings of annoyance. "There are three bedrooms; one to the right, and two to the left. The kitchen is straight ahead, and then obviously this is the lounge." She looked around with pride at the attractive lodge, seeing touches of her own handiwork here and there.

"There's no TV." The brochure woman put on her dark sunglasses in horror before taking them off again. She stared at Amanda. "This is outrageous."

The carefully controlled anger bubble inside of her wobbled dangerously, "Well, the reason for that is—"

"Stop complaining, Velda." The tall bearded man turned his back on the woman scornfully. "Did you really expect anything different?"

Amanda's mouth dropped open. She could hold herself in no longer. "Well—of all the low-down attitudes to have!" she exclaimed. "Why did you bother coming, if you all have such foul opinions? I can take you back to the airport right now; *you* might be enough to convince them that they desperately want to organise a flight out of here!"

Adrenaline coursing through her, Amanda dared any of the visitors to speak. But they were all too overwhelmed to even move. They stared at her in shock.

"Well hello!" A friendly masculine voice rang through the room.

Amanda reluctantly turned from the battle scene to see who was intruding into her moment.

A man in his late twenties was standing in the doorway, dressed in knee-length shorts, an amused smile on his face. He gave Amanda a wink as he turned towards the guests.

"Welcome to Shamwari Ranch," he said warmly, holding out his hand to greet the leader of the group.

The guests all began to talk at once, but all Amanda could think was that, by some ridiculous coincidence, she had stumbled across *the* attractive-looking man from the Christian singles web site who was based somewhere in Africa; the man she and the girls had debated about less than a week ago! The chances of such a meeting must be one in a million. It was next to impossible—wasn't it?

"I'm Caleb Jacobs." Blue eyes swept around the faces and came to rest on Amanda: "Welcome to my world."

Chapter 8

Amanda coolly waited for Caleb Jacobs to finish his smooth flow of conversation. With his dark hair curling onto his forehead and his warm easy smile, he made a charming conversationalist. The brochure woman had actually managed to stop whining and was now pressed up against Caleb, revealing all thirty or so teeth. *Eugh!* And this Jacobs chap had the audacity to play her along. Sickening! Now she could see why he had put his profile up on the Christian singles web site. He knew he was handsome, he was used to charming the women, and now he hoped to sucker some poor naive Christian girl in, too. Why? To please his parents?

Jaw set, Amanda flicked her eyes crossly over the five tourists. The second woman smiled tentatively at her, but under Amanda's furious look the woman faltered and she averted her gaze. Amanda silently harrumphed, fuming inside at this whole situation.

It was all God's fault! He had messed everything up. Not only was she stranded out in the middle of the bush in a derelict country, but she was now playing servant to some family who in turn were playing servant to strangers. What a mess!

She noticed everyone was smiling, and wondered what honeyed words Jacobs had uttered to get them that way.

"Well, that's it then." He turned and included her in the smile. "Someone will come and check on you all tomorrow and see how you've settled in and whether you need anything. Have a good evening—and stay inside at night, there'll be animals around your lodge and they will be hungry."

Caleb's friendly smile belied the seriousness of his words. Looking at the five tourists, Amanda decided that at least two of them were not really listening to what Caleb was saying. The tall man was, of course, an old hand at safari and could cope fine with five lions at once, and the fluttery-lashed Velda was all eyes and no ears. She was probably only hearing a deep voice rumbling by as she fairly swooned into Caleb.

But something of what he'd said must have been taken in, for she clutched at Caleb's arm fearfully: "Oh my, will we be safe here?"

"Most of our guests come out with all their limbs," Amanda swiftly cut in before Caleb could answer, giving Caleb a sweet smile as she added, "except for that one woman who stepped outside to light a cigarette, do you remember that, Honey?"

Caleb's eyes reflected shock, and then began to sparkle as he eased himself loose from the woman's clutching grip. "No need to bring up such ugly memories, Sunshine," he answered, nodding politely at the now-pouting guest as he put a hand on Amanda's back and gently guided her towards the door. "Until tomorrow then, everyone!"

Amanda waved, her eye catching the second woman's wide eyed gaze just before she stepped into the sunlight. The poor woman was overwhelmed!

Amanda felt a spark of remorse for her bad behaviour, but that was quickly forgotten as she found herself being propelled towards Sophie's Land Rover.

"Hey, easy!" she snapped, digging in her heels to try and slow down their pace.

"Easy, nothing!" Caleb retorted, yanking open the driver's door. "What were you playing at?"

Amanda glared at Caleb, lips firmly closed.

"Ha, you won't even answer me because you know that you were as rude as they were," Caleb scoffed. "You obviously have no self-control, woman."

"How dare you accuse me of that!" Amanda exclaimed, "You know nothing about me."

"I know enough to know you don't want to be here, that you *are* here, and that you have no self-control and a stupid temper when things don't go your way," Caleb shot back, all his words even and firm. "Now get in," he ordered. "Drive behind me and I'll make sure you get safely to my parent's house, before you do any more damage."

"Ha! Now if you—"

"Excuse me," a timid voice interjected.

Amanda and Caleb both swung around to find the second woman standing warily behind them. Her gaze flitted nervously between them, and then she thrust a note at Amanda, before scampering back into the lodge like a frightened rabbit.

"I suspect no wild animal will get *her*," Caleb remarked dryly, "thanks to your helpful input."

Amanda shoved the note into her jeans pocket and pulled herself up into the driver's seat, glaring at Caleb mutinously. "Let's just go."

She waited for him to pull his vehicle—an open Jeep, old style—ahead of hers, and then joggle up the road at an easy pace. She purposely chose a different route to the one he did when trying to avoid the potholes and corrosions in the road. She was her own woman, even when it came to which way to go around a pothole!

About twenty minutes later they pulled up to the homestead and Caleb hooted for someone to open the gate. After one of the gardeners had pulled it wide and then shut it behind them, Amanda parked the Land Rover under the big shady tree just inside the property, dubiously eying the dove perched on the branches over the bonnet. There was no way it wasn't going to leave its mark.

"Is there anything I can help you with?" Caleb came over and asked, leaning against the 4x4.

Amanda eyed him suspiciously, wondering what he was up to now. Was he questioning her intellectual abilities? Or perhaps her character? He was a doctor, not a shrink!

"Uh...you did go to the airport, didn't you?" Caleb confirmed, the sternness still in his eyes. "So did you see any sugar or flour, or anything like that to buy?"

Amanda shook her head, letting out her breath slowly in an attempt to answer civilly, "Was I supposed to buy something?"

"No, not unless there *is* something to buy; we always just grab what we can, when we can. That's the law of the land now." He pushed off the car and waited long enough for Amanda to follow him into the house.

Once indoors he headed straight for the kitchen. "Hi Rosie," he called.

"Eh, you have come home at last!" The maid laughed teasingly. "The village life is too hard for you, eh?"

Caleb grinned, the former sternness leaving his face. Amanda sighed, somewhat relieved, just as a truck hooted. That must be Mickey, about to leave to attend to the cattle. She peeked out the door and waved. The beckoning arm from the window of the Bedford made her gleefully step back into the house long enough to say, "I'll just open the gate, maybe one of you could shut it once we're gone?" Without waiting for a reply she pressed the button that was tucked behind the rain jackets near the front door and scuttled back out into the sun, jogging quickly across the grass.

"Hi Mickey," she grinned, gratefully scrambling up into the seat next to him.

"You look like you've just escaped a prison sentence," Mickey observed, reversing before going slightly off the road to turn around.

Amanda grinned sheepishly. "I guess I feel like I have."

They bounced along the road for a while before Mickey turned suddenly off to the left, onto the faintest of tracks. "We'll just cut across here; this joins up to the road that'll take us to the other ranch."

Amanda nodded, tilting her hat slightly back so she could feel the full impact of the wind and the sun at the same time. "Wow, I'm so glad you came," she admitted, letting out her breath and feeling her tense muscles relax. "I left your brother *blethering* with Rosie."

"Blethering?"

"Talking, chatting, you know?"

"Hmm," Mickey mused. "I wonder what Andy's doing home?"

"Andy?" Amanda stared at him: "Not Andy—Caleb."

"Caleb?" Mickey was surprised. "Caleb's home? I can understand you running away from Andy, but not Caleb! What happened?"

Amanda sighed. Why had she brought this up? "I just got frustrated with the tourists. They're such a lousy bunch. The one woman was whining until she took up flirting with your brother. The other one was sure he knew more than the local people, and the rest just looked dazed or frightened."

"So you blew your top," Mickey guessed, smiling. "Now that must have been interesting to see."

"Your brother didn't think so," Amanda growled. "He arrived just in time to be a wonderful mediator and then escort me safely home, leaving them relatively unharmed. I think he would have spanked me if he could have."

"Probably," Mickey agreed amiably, "but Caleb also has a great sense of humour, he'll see the funny side when he's gotten over the shock. What did you say to them?" Mickey was curious.

Amanda rolled her eyes, and gave a sudden giggle. "Well, I offered to take them back to the airport, amongst other things."

Grinning, Mickey grunted something about understanding why Caleb was in shock.

"That reminds me, one of the women gave me a note..." Amanda dug in her pocket and pulled out the crumpled paper. She carefully unfolded it. "Huh, an old receipt. Thanks, lady!"

When Mickey looked back up at the road she flipped it over. In blue ink, lightly scrawled, were the words: "I need to talk to you alone."

Amanda thoughtfully shoved the note back in her pocket and shot Mickey a quick glance to see if he was paying attention. He wasn't; he was too busy fiddling with the rear view mirror to notice what she was up to. Well, she wouldn't be hunting the woman down to talk to her – not after today.

"Got a problem with it?" Amanda queried.

"There seems to be someone following us," Mickey said, adjusting the mirror again.

Amanda swivelled around and her heart jerked at sight of the familiar open Jeep that was rapidly approaching.

She sank slowly back into the seat, her heart hammering nervously against her rib cage.

"It's Caleb." Mickey lifted his foot off the accelerator.

"Maybe he's just driving the same route as us," Amanda suggested without conviction.

"No such luck," Mickey grinned. "We all have to face up to the consequences of our actions. Sorry for you, but Caleb takes that Scripture one step further and solves a problem straight away rather than waiting before night falls."

"Which Scripture?" Amanda asked fearfully.

"Slice down your enemy before she dare contaminate your home with her heathen ways one day longer!" Mickey slashed the air dramatically, and then laughed, flashing Amanda a quick grin. "Just teasing."

"Ooohh!" Amanda exclaimed, having been completely taken in. "Well which Scripture then?"

"It's not a bad one, all it says is that we must not let the sun set on our anger, but to solve a problem before it's dark. Caleb solves a problem as soon as possible—" Mickey rubbed his jaw "—and I'd hazard a guess that he's here to sort out his differences with you, which means I will no longer be needed at the cattle ranch."

"What?" Amanda hissed, clutching at Mickey's arm. "Oh no! Don't you dare leave me with your brother. Mickey!" She shot a worried glance over her shoulder when she realised they had come to a complete stop. They both turned to look up at Caleb who ducked his head in the window just then, his intense blue eyes lighting on Amanda before he said, "Howzit bru?"

"Caleb!" Mickey scrambled out the car and pounded on his back cheerfully. "'Bout time you showed your face again."

"How's the studying going?" Caleb queried.

Amanda stared at the two torsos through the window and listened with bated breath while they caught up on the latest cricket news.

"Mickey, Rosie told me about the cattle business. I'll sort it out, you've got studying to do and A-levels only happen once—or *should* only happen once."

Amanda quaked. Mickey had better stand by her!

"Thanks Caleb, I have three biggies next week."

"Good, well, see you at home then."

Amanda watched the unmoving torsos. Heart in her throat, she waited.

"I think I should take the truck. It looks like it might rain later," Caleb said, his hand reaching for the door handle.

Amanda immediately reached for her own and as the driver's door opened she scrambled out, scurrying after

Mickey to Caleb's Jeep. She didn't care that Mickey was laughing at her as she hopped up beside him in the seat, and looked straight ahead when Caleb climbed back out of the Bedford she had just abandoned and turned to stare at her, his brow furrowed.

"You've got him all wound up," Mickey chided softly, starting the engine. "Let's see how he sorts this one out." They both watched as Caleb retraced his steps to his Jeep and stared first at Amanda and then at Mickey.

"Look, I thought Amanda wanted to see the cattle?"

"Not true!" Amanda shook her head vigorously. "Mickey insisted he wanted to show me, so I came along to keep him company."

Caleb's brow rose sceptically.

"It's true, it took some convincing to get Amanda to come along with me," Mickey inserted.

The three of them waited, Amanda clutching the seat nervously.

"Well, I think it would be good for Amanda to come and have a look at it all anyway," Caleb said firmly, addressing Mickey.

Mickey shrugged, abdicating from decision-making.

Caleb swung on her. "Amanda," he said firmly, "come with me."

Amanda shook her head.

"Look woman, don't be difficult. Just get out and let's go."

Amanda tried to appease him with some sort of apology, "Look Caleb, I know I wasn't too friendly to your guests and I did lose my temper. I admit that. I'm sorry. Can't we just let it go?"

Jaw set, Caleb stalked around the bonnet and opened the door for her pointedly. "I'm not angry with you but I do want to resolve this situation. We got off to a bad start and I don't want to leave it there."

"Mickey?" Amanda quavered as she felt herself gently being tugged from the car.

"Go on Amanda." Mickey gave her a sympathetic smile. "I've survived all these years, you'll survive an afternoon."

Seeing no way around this, Amanda reluctantly followed Caleb back to the closed truck and cautiously took up her seat again. "You're a bully," she told him in no uncertain terms, making sure the car was clear of all possible weapons first.

Caleb said nothing as he started the engine. He continued on down the bush road for about five minutes in silence—the longest five minutes of Amanda's life.

"What do you want?" Amanda broke the silence, unable to bear it any longer.

She watched as he seemed to be finding his words before he said, "I just wanted to sort this out. We got off to a bad start and I am sorry I was so abrupt with you. I just didn't want to leave any space for the devil to get a foot in the door."

"The devil?" Amanda nervously moistened her sunburnt lips. "What's the devil got to do with this?"

"Nothing, yet—if we sort this out," Caleb answered relentlessly. He swerved to the right and onto a more formal dirt track. "I'm sorry, Amanda, for being impatient. Will you forgive me?"

Amanda stared at the straight nose and stern jaw in his disbelief. Seeing that he was serious she shrugged, "Sure, I guess I was as much at fault as you were."

"So it's a closed case," Caleb confirmed, glancing at her. "Well that was nice and simple." He smiled: "Are you ready for a fun afternoon?"

"Huh?"

"The cattle ranch is fascinating and if you've never seen one before I think you'll like it."

"But what about the tourists and...all that?" Amanda asked. "We haven't finished discussing it."

"What more is there to discuss?" Caleb asked, his face relaxed now that the issue was closed in his mind.

Amanda took a deep breath as she tried to grasp the whole situation. Shaking her head, she breathed out slowly and said, "Fine, we'll do it your way. Yeah, I'm ready for a cattle ranch afternoon."

They crossed what looked like a main highway and then bounced back into the bush and across a grid made of rolling bars that was set into the road between two fence posts.

"That grid keeps cattle from leaving the farm, and we don't need a gate to open and close, then." Caleb explained. "They're afraid to cross in case their hooves get caught in the rollers. Too unstable for them."

Intrigued, Amanda said, "When we go over another one will you slow down so I can have a look at it?"

"Sure, there's one more just before we cross into our farm."

Trees raced past and the grass slapped against the side of the truck as Caleb swerved sharply to the right at the last minute to avoid a massive gully in the road.

"So!" Amanda clapped her hands together: "This *is* a great country."

Caleb steered slightly to the left, just in time for the wheel to hit an anthill and send Amanda careering against the door. "I agree," he said cheerfully.

"Hey! You did that on purpose!" Amanda exclaimed in disbelief. "You could have easily avoided that bump. That was malicious intent to injure."

The sun-tanned features beside her were alight with glee as Caleb shook his head innocently. "Sometimes these things are unavoidable."

Sighing, Amanda pushed down her unspeakable thoughts and tried to breathe slowly and calmly. One lone bush boy would not get the glory of making her lose her temper, especially after he had so wrongly accused her of *having* a temper.

The road stretched out before them, long and flat, and the heat seemed to be trapped inside the truck so that the sweat streamed down Amanda's face from her temples. She must look a wreck, and her mascara was probably smudged across her face by now like she had been playing in soot.

Flipping down the sun visor, Amanda was disgusted to see that there was only an indentation where the mirror had once been.

"Your make-up is still perfect, and every hair is still in place."

The amused voice beside her made Amanda flush with embarrassment.

"I was merely blocking the sun out of my eyes," she answered stiffly, glaring at Caleb.

"I just thought I'd try and help, what with the mirror being gone and all," he said, still looking at her as he rode over a branch that had been abandoned in the road.

"So thoughtful."

Amanda did not dare touch her face now, even though she could feel that the hair at her temples was damp. Instead she rolled down the window and stuck her palm into the wind. Rather dust than sweat if it came down to the two options.

"So...I thought you were at the Mission where you work?" Amanda asked casually. "You were when you phoned this morning and could not *understand* me. I notice you have no problem now."

"It must have been poor phone signal." Caleb patted the steering wheel. "Signal's not good around Black Rhino lodge." He abruptly changed the subject. "We usually take our guests on a game viewing walk early in the morning. The Old Well is our starting point."

"Huh!" Amanda patted her bottom lip thoughtfully. "And all your guests go? What time does the walk start?" Was this an opportunity to talk to the woman? She frowned, wondering what the woman could say that could possibly have any connection to her.

"About five-thirty. Why? Do you want to go on it?"

"Why not?" Amanda turned and smiled at Caleb: "I've never been on a game viewing walk before, so it could be interesting."

Caleb nodded, his face thoughtful.

Half an hour later Caleb broke the long silence. "The grid's coming up, if you're still interested in having a look."

"Uh-huh..." Amanda was already scrambling out the cab before Caleb had turned the engine off. What a relief to be in the little bit of breeze that there was! She was half-sorry to see that Caleb was coming over to the cattle grid. She didn't understand the way his mind worked; an odd combination of thoughtful and sarcastic.

"The fence keeps the cattle in on both sides, and then the grid keeps them from crossing the boundary. Plus it saves us from having to open a gate," Caleb grinned at her. "We avoid opening gates wherever possible." He stepped onto the grid, balancing himself easily before squatting down over it.

Amanda cautiously followed suit, gingerly easing herself across the grid. Clutching the fence pole, she cautiously squatted down as well, and peered into the furrow below the rollers.

"Hey, there's a big beetle in here." Amanda poked a finger at the little black insect, which immediately scuttled to the darkest corner.

"A tic-toc beetle." Caleb slid his hand into the gap and tried to corner the beetle but it scurried Amanda's way, its long legs and round body covering the distance quickly. "You put your hand over there and push it towards me and I'll grab it when it comes," Caleb instructed, changing his position slightly to get a better angle.

"I don't know about this," Amanda said, reluctantly wiggling her fingers at the beetle.

"Good..." Caleb's hand hovered in the gap ready to grab the beetle as it came by. "Put your hand a bit lower, it'll be more convincing."

Rolling her eyes, Amanda obeyed and watched the tic-toc beetle charge in Caleb's direction. Caleb swiped at it and sent it scuttling Amanda's way.

Squealing, Amanda flung her hand out of the hole. "It's got yellow legs!"

Grinning, Caleb shuffled over, taunting. "And so its yellow legs gave you a fright, huh?"

"No—that's not what I meant!" Amanda dipped her hand back into the grid. "There, now get it." She watched Caleb's hand chase the beetle into her corner and then close over the insect.

"Gotcha!" Caleb rose triumphantly. "You want to hold him? His legs are ticklish."

"No!" Amanda clambered off the grid and watched as Caleb released the beetle into the grass beside the road. The black-shelled body scuttled into the grass almost in pleasure, Amanda thought, feeling like she'd conquered the world in rescuing the beetle from its dark grave.

"Can you hear that buzzing noise?" Caleb asked from where he was still crouched, his face turned towards the grass. "That's what we call a Christmas beetle, it makes that monotonous ringing sound."

"Not very pleasant," Amanda agreed, studying the athletic profile of her companion. He wasn't wearing long socks and shoes like the other men she had seen so far. Instead he had a pair of rubber sandals. What was it that Penny had called them last night? *Slops*—that was it. A strange name. Maybe it was derived from the word 'sloppy' because they were such casual shoes. And in his golf shirt and baggy shorts Caleb looked like he was dressed for the beach. All he needed was a towel slung over his shoulder. Perhaps she would have to find some *slops* while she was here, because this heat was killing her.

"This is a beautiful land, Amanda." Caleb turned to her and his eyes were shining with conviction. "The people here are friendly and warm, the land is good—" he dug his hand into the ground and let the sandy earth trickle through his fingers "—although very dry at the moment," he admitted. "But there is so much good and beauty in this place..."

He stood and stretched to his full height. "The heat, the birds, the smell that promises rain, the feel of hot dirt beneath your feet. This is when I know that God is a God of favour and blessing. But we are hurting at the moment. People are starving, trees are being cut down for firewood, family members are dying of starvation, the economy is *frot*..." He turned and his eyes were ablaze. "We need God's help big time, because this place has been seriously messed up."

Amanda hung onto the fence pole and marvelled at his passion as he openly poured out his thoughts.

"The corruption in Zimbabwe is sickening, and there are so many in authority who are lining their pockets with wealth while those they should be caring for are living on one meal a day—or less! And you should see the cities! They are filled with waiting people; people can wait for days for mealie-meal and bread, never mind all the other things like fuel, milk, oil and so on."

"But...why does no one speak out against all this?" she said, feeling his outrage and her own helplessness.

"People have—and they now are gracing the darkness of a gaol. There are political prisoners who are being tortured in secret. A group of youths called the Green Berets run through the high density suburbs in the cities beating people up, putting fear into the hearts of our people. We are a nation living in *fear,*" Caleb scowled. "Sometimes the intensity is so strong I can smell it, I can see it in the hollow eyes of those around me, in the unspoken words that pass between people as they silently communicate with one another. Last year I went down south to South Africa and I met a young Zimbabwean woman who was also there on holiday. I tried to find out how she was coping in Zimbabwe and what she thought of the whole situation. Do you know that all she would say to me was, 'It's hard.' The woman was too frightened to speak about it, even though she was in another country! She kept looking over her shoulder the whole time I spoke with her."

"This is crazy!" Amanda exclaimed. "So no one *can* do anything unless they are willing to end up beaten up, or something?"

"That's pretty much the way it is. Farmers are being chased off their farms I know a family who was given five hours to get out of their home, just like that."

"But all their stuff? Their furniture, their clothes...and what about their photos, their memories—well, *everything?*" Amanda was horrified.

"The neighbours came in and piled up trucks and helped evacuate the area. Unfortunately they weren't able to get the expensive farm equipment off, though. And what's worse is that the government says the farms are for those whose ancestors owned it, but in truth it's certain high officials who are taking the land—not those people they claim it is for. Some officials have taken over two or three farms."

"That's just...ridiculous!" Her own passions were rising to meet his.

"And—" Caleb waved a hand angrily "—on top of all that they've displaced hundreds of farm workers who are now jobless and desperate for food. Some of them have been beaten up, even killed...It's a mess!"

"Well, *someone* should do *something!* I've vaguely heard about Zimbabwe on the news in the UK, but never really paid much attention, so I admit I'm a bit ignorant—and anyway, it just doesn't sink in until you become part of it—but it seems crazy that the people haven't yet united and come up with some force against the corruption and greed, and just..." Amanda pounded a fist into her left hand, "and just *crushed* this horrible government and taken control themselves! Take back freedom for the people!"

Caleb regarded her in surprise. "Sounds like an uprising to me." He crossed over the cattle grid and sat down on the bonnet pensively.

"It's more than an uprising that's needed," Amanda said forcefully, "we need to eradicate the leaders who are torturing the people! From what you're saying and I've seen for myself, the conditions here are inhuman! We need to shake up the British government somehow, make them *act*...I could write to my MP in Scotland, for a start, and then— then..." She finally ran out of steam, beating the air with frustrated hands.

Her brief tantrum had surprised even herself, but conversely it seemed to have soothed Caleb. He was shaking his head, calmer now. "God knows what we're going through Amanda. This is the time for us to pray for His mercy, and for the hearts of the people to turn to Him."

"God?" Amanda spat. "Like *praying* counts as an action! Now *that* is just a weak excuse to escape doing anything yourself."

"A weak excuse?" Caleb cocked his head thoughtfully, and then he smiled thinly, "I think not. I think it is harder to wait on God's timing than it is to go ahead and act in my own strength."

The two locked eyes, silently clashing in their opinions.

"God *is* at work in Zimbabwe, Amanda. What I haven't mentioned in my zeal to air my thoughts is that the way God provides is incredible. And if you could see how people are working together, caring for one another, watching out for those around them—" Caleb squinted at her: "There is such unity in the midst of this trouble. Crisis brings out the best in people, bonds them...God *is* in it, Amanda."

Sighing dubiously, Amanda went over to sit beside him on the car bonnet. "Well, I haven't been here long enough to say whether I agree with you or not, but I do think the people need to do *something* to help themselves—otherwise nothing will change!"

She frowned at him: "Why are you smiling like that?"

Ruffling his hair, Caleb answered, "I was just thinking

how much change there would be if people would pray." He looked at her pensively. "I bet someone is praying for *you*."

An image of Mrs May flashed to mind. Amanda scowled, "Perhaps, but if that's supposed to prove prayer works, I wish they'd stop! Life just seems to get more and more complicated."

An image of Kari flashed into her mind. If Caleb spoke the truth then she was guilty of wasting time in helping Kari fight the sickness that ravished her mind and body, instead of simply praying for her. The thought sickened her. Her own helplessness sickened her! Caleb was wrong! She *would* help Kari—she just needed to get home to do that!

Grinning, Caleb decided it was time to change the subject. He pointed to the left of the road. "About ten minutes that way we'll come to the paddocks where we keep our horses for the cattle, and then just past there we'll get to the fields where our cattle will be. You ready to go?"

"Sure. I just wish I had brought your mother's sun-cream with me. I thought I couldn't possibly get more burnt than I already am, but I think I'm about to be proven wrong."

"Sure are. It could easily be about thirty-two degrees out there, probably more."

Amanda followed his lead and climbed into the truck. She suddenly thought of the match-making internet page and felt squeamish inside. How many women had he got sitting at the end of a computer waiting for him to contact them? And perhaps that was just the beginning. There obviously were women around his home and his job, even though it all seemed to be extremely isolated. Or maybe it was the tourists he preyed upon—people like her! He had pitched up at the house very suddenly. What had they decided about Caleb—stalker, or genuine? She just couldn't remember their final verdict.

"You've gone very quiet," Caleb observed. "Is the heat getting to you?"

"A bit..." Amanda stared out at the vast expanse of open land, all the things Caleb had told her churning through her mind. The condition of the land seemed to reflect the condition of the people. It was so arid, so brown; some areas were even bare of a stick of dry grass—just dirt and dust. She missed the greenness of home. "But I was just thinking about the cattle ranch," she lied, smiling at Caleb. "What are we going to do there?"

With only one hand on the steering wheel, Caleb followed the bend of the road. His right hand disappeared through the open car window and Amanda could hear it tapping absently against the door.

"Well, we have to make sure all the right cows are chosen for market, check that they are healthy, and then get them onto the trucks and off to the market."

"Sounds easy," Amanda nodded.

Caleb pulled the car up beside a long fence. In the field beyond it were big rangy cows milling together and bawling in each other's faces, bumping together while workers in blue overalls pushed through them, letting off shrill whistles through their teeth.

"It does *sound* easy," Caleb agreed, smiling to himself.

Chapter 9

That one, there!" Caleb shouted, pushing through the huge bony cows' bodies and pointing excitedly at a fawn-coloured one that was charging away in the opposite direction. Two workers followed his direction and immediately joined in the chase.

Amanda covered her eyes with her hands, afraid for the men as they passed through the cattle. They could easily be squashed by those huge bottoms, and surely the beasts kicked? The cattle were making an awful din, bellowing as if they were being butchered, but Caleb had already explained that the workers had to separate mothers from their calves, and that was why they sounded so unhappy.

"Amanda, can you see where it's gone?" Caleb's voice could barely be heard above the noise of the hundred or so head of cattle between them.

"They all look the same to me," Amanda bawled back, looking around her for a place to get a better view. Climbing onto the gate, she pulled herself up until she was standing on the middle rung, keeping her balance by pressing her shins against the top bar.

"Its light brown," Caleb yelled, arms waving, "about this high."

"Well if you had my view you'd see just how many light brown cows there are," Amanda muttered, staring out at the sea of cattle. "What does it matter which blinking cow gets chosen? I'm sure no one will complain if they get a cow that's not quite the right colour."

"There it is Boss!" One of the men suddenly let off that shrill whistle which modulated up and down. The cow seemed to respond, for it slowed its pace and seemed hesitant as the men darted around it and started herding it towards the truck.

"Not bad!" Amanda clapped her hands softly to herself, turning warily to watch a huge cow that was approaching her very decisively. "Hey, don't come here. Go away!" Amanda hissed, slipping down off the gate. "Go over there, to the guy in the big hat; he's the one selling you all off. I'm just a spectator."

The cow kept coming closer until it stopped about two metres away and lifted its head to smell the air, its huge brown eyes watching Amanda's every move. It was taller than Amanda, and the enormous bump on its shoulders flopped slightly to one side. Almost like a cross between a cow and a camel, Amanda thought nervously.

"Caleb, there's an unhappy cow here, and I don't think it likes me," she called, easing slowly along the fence in the direction of Caleb.

"She's just curious," Caleb called. "It's a cow trait." He didn't look her way as he slapped a beige cow's hide and urged her up the gangway and into the truck, before turning to watch one of the men usher another cow along in his direction. "Hey, Themba! Let that be the last one and then we'll go."

The man nodded, guiding the cow along with a thin stick which he gently rapped against it every now and then to get it going the right direction.

"Where are you, Amanda?"

Amanda looked up just in time to see Caleb's horrified expression as he spotted her and the cow.

"What's wrong Caleb?" she asked fearfully, backing away from the fence. Was the cow diseased? Or—it didn't have any horns but that didn't mean it couldn't gore her, did it?

"Who let the bull in with the cows?" Caleb roared, his face turning bright red.

"It has been there for many days," one of the men called as he jogged over. "You did not want it so?"

The men abandoned English to jabber away in the local language. Amanda stared at them, and then at the cow that was actually a bull. This didn't look good.

She peered past the animal to see Caleb listening intently to the worker. He looked furious.

"Okay, well, you've been discovered, now you can go." Amanda flicked her hands at the animal encouragingly.

Caleb came over. He looked exhausted. "Well, we won't be taking any cattle to the market today."

Amanda stared at him incredulously. "But we've been here for *hours*!" she exclaimed. "We've carefully picked out the cows, chased them around the field, smacked other eager beasts out of the trucks—why this now?"

"The bull," Caleb said, leaning against the other side of the fence and gazing at the culprit, "has been in with the cows about four days. We don't know how many cows he's impregnated."

"And so?" Amanda shrugged. "Just because they're pregnant it doesn't mean they can't be sold, surely?"

"But we'll be losing money if we sell pregnant cows. That's why we were separating them. We knew which ones were pregnant, which ones we want as mothers this year, and which ones are getting old and need to be sold. But to sell a pregnant cow means losing out on a calf that could potentially be sold at a later stage. It's just not worth it."

Amanda felt her heart sink as a farm hand opened the truck door and the cows poured back into the field to join the others. All their hard work and hours of careful selection, and this is what happened!

"So now what?" she asked, her heart going out to Caleb.

"Well, all we can do now is separate the bull from the cows and keep an eye on the cows to see which are with calf and which aren't. Only once we know that can we make our next move."

Amanda gripped the edge of the wire fence, avoiding the barbs, and watched as Caleb cautiously guided the bull into the next field, and then on into a field beyond that. The men drove the trucks out of the pasture and one got out to close the gate behind him before they drove off down the road.

Amanda sat down on a rock in the shade to wait for Caleb. "There's just such a lack of organisation and good management," she complained, eyeing the cattle angrily and feeling that somehow they were to blame. "We could have had them already on the way to market, but because of one stupid bull the whole afternoon was wasted!"

She leant against the tree and a fresh wave of cow-smell hit her. Wincing, she briefly covered her nose before lowering her hand in resignation. There was no point blocking the smell out, it was getting through her hand anyway, and besides—it wasn't actually *that* bad.

It's just cow-smell, Amanda told herself, looking up at the blue sky with its unmoving cotton-white clouds. She closed her eyes and listened. It was so still. Even the restless movement of the cows couldn't detract from the peacefulness of the late afternoon. A step crunched nearby and her eyes shot open guiltily. She didn't want Caleb to get the impression she was enjoying this.

Caleb was just shutting the gate nearest to her. The walk across the fields had obviously brought him to terms with the situation; his expression was resigned, possibly even content.

"You're looking too cheerful," Amanda frowned, standing up. "The bull may be in his own field, but your cows are also still in theirs," she reminded him.

Caleb ruffled his hair. "They sure are." He pulled a face at the cattle before nodding at the old Bedford. "You ready to head home?"

Home?

Amanda nodded, following curiously. "So did you come up with a big idea of how to solve the problem while chasing the bull to his own digs?"

"Nope." The truck shuddered into life.

"Well, what then?" Amanda persisted, strapping her seat belt on. She noticed that Caleb didn't strap his on. No laws? Different laws? Or just a Zimbabwean thing?

"Well what?" Caleb responded, before shrugging: "There's nothing that can be done now. What's happened has happened."

"But your staff showed negligence. If I were you I would fire them. You put them in charge of your herd and they clearly didn't do their job."

"What are you—a law enforcer?" Caleb half-joked.

Flushing, Amanda glared at him. "No, but I do see where there is a problem and what should be done."

"So if I fire my men are you volunteering to take their job? And to feed their families?"

"Augh! You're just trying to be difficult!" Amanda gave up in disgust.

"I'm just seeing that there is nothing to be done now

except wait. I've given it to God and I'm going to trust Him to carry my family through this period while we wait to sell the cattle."

"Hah! So *that's* what you were doing while you walked the bull home," Amanda said, leaping on his words. "Back to this prayer thing. You were praying and now you think God is going to sort everything out neatly and you don't have to do a jot more."

"That's not what I said," Caleb disagreed. "Just because I have given this situation to God does *not* mean I do nothing, but it does mean that God and I are working together, rather than me against God."

"Does your whole family think like you?" Amanda queried with a scowl.

"To different degrees," Caleb acknowledged. "Except Andy. I think I can safely say that Andy is anti-God."

"Oh? And how did that happen in such a devout family? Too much excitement for him?" Amanda asked sarcastically. She ignored Caleb's scrutinising glance, pretending to be distracted by the scenery.

"Is that a genuine question?"

Amanda glanced back at Caleb, and the tension in her eased as she saw his clear-eyed honesty.

Sighing, she unbuckled her seat belt and pulled her knees up against her chest. "No, not really," she admitted. "Although now that you ask, I am curious to know."

She noticed Caleb's hesitation. He took so long to respond that she wondered if he would answer.

"First, I have a question for you," he said finally. "Why are *you* so against God?"

The constriction across her chest immediately tightened and Amanda hugged her legs closer to her body. "I'm not *against* God," she corrected, "I'm just not *for* Him."

"'He who is not for Me is against Me'," Caleb murmured.

"What was that?"

He shook his head, "Just a Scripture. Go on, what were you saying?"

Reluctantly, Amanda turned back to the road. How much should she say? How much could she answer?

"Well...I just don't have much time for God. He hasn't really had much time for me, either." She averted her gaze to the left, trying to hide the tears that sprang into her eyes, surprising her with their speed of arrival.

"Why do you say that?"

"Why?" Amanda frowned, clutching her toes tightly, before answering stiffly: "I've just seen that's the way it is."

"Is there anyone in your family who is a believer?" Caleb asked, trying a different tack.

"My younger sister, Polly, is an outright Christian. The other three of us go to church when we can—well, at least Ruth and I do—she's my older sister. I don't know about my brother. I haven't seen him in a while."

Ten years and two months to be exact. She hadn't seen him since the day she had come home and found him weaving around the kitchen, absolutely drunk, a knife in his hand, chasing a frightened Kari around the kitchen table. That day, she had barely recognised him. Alcohol, drugs and whatever else he was into was already beginning to take a toll on him. The bleached hair, black clothes and hollow eyes had frightened her. Kari said he was trying to find himself. Along the way her close relationship with Cobs had become seared. He was no longer the loving brother she had grown up with and absolutely doted on.

"Enough about me," Amanda ordered. "Your turn now." She tried to discreetly clear the tears from her eyes before glancing across at Caleb, his profile almost a silhouette now in the setting sun.

"Well..." Caleb rubbed the bridge of his nose. "Andy and I haven't had much to do with each other for ages. I honestly couldn't give you a certain answer about why he is anti-God, but I can guess part of the reason. A big part."

Amanda wriggled in her seat. Caleb reached over to fiddle with the radio but only got a crackle of response out of it.

"Stupid thing," Caleb growled, glancing uncomfortably her way.

Amanda resisted a giggle, grateful for the first time that something wasn't working as it should be here. She was determined that Caleb should answer her questions, and having the radio on would only be a distraction.

"So?" she asked pointedly.

It was with great anticipation, and relief, that Amanda finally heard Caleb clear his throat.

"Andy and I are a year apart in age. We barely did anything without including each other, somehow, when we were growing up. Dad and Mom sent us off to boarding school when I was starting Grade 3. I hadn't yet turned eight. We would come home only for half term."

"No surprise then that you and Andy were so close," Amanda put in softly. The image of two lonely little boys buried in some boarding school had her squirming inside.

"Yeah," Caleb nodded. Voice thick, Caleb continued, "Well, we got into a bad crowd in my senior years of school."

"Drugs?"

"No," Caleb growled, "not drugs. It was worse in some ways. We were cocky bullies basking in the warmth of our power. We would never have called ourselves that, of course. We thought we were 'responsible leaders of the school who were maintaining tradition and order'." He let out his breath sharply. "The power got to our heads. We were physically and verbally abusive. We bullied the younger boys, ordering them around like slaves; making them do things that we'd had to do when we were juniors, stupid things that were fun for us and a nightmare for them."

"Like what?" Amanda asked nervously, wanting to know, yet afraid of what she was going to hear.

"Oh, I don't know..." Caleb hit the steering wheel. "Anything from spending the night in a tree to warming the toilet seat for us in winter, or sometimes making them swim until we told them to stop. Whatever popped into our thick numb-skulled heads. Us seniors, both black and white, were also racially abusive at times. It was like a gang mentality. Whatever was the 'in thing' was what we all did."

Memories of her own boarding school sprang to mind, but Amanda disposed of them as quickly as they came.

"And then?" She pressed Caleb to talk, despite hearing the catch in his voice. She wanted to know what had happened. It must have been bad, for Andy to choose not to follow in the faith-footsteps of his parents.

Caleb sighed heavily again, "Well, we always grilled the juniors when they started school. Their initiation into high school was tough. Sometimes we put them in trunks and rolled them down the stairs. Other times we made them keep swimming until they were on the point of drowning, and we loved every moment of it. We thought we were tough-ening them up."

His hands were clenched over the steering wheel, his teeth gritted with the agony of the memories.

"I had to go through it as a junior. Andy had to go through it when he entered high school. It was just the way things were done. It was a tradition. The juniors at the mercy of the seniors, at the mercy of those who should have been protecting them, leading them, guiding them." He shook his head. "We messed up big time."

For the first time Amanda wondered if she should stop her relentless pursuit of knowledge. Caleb was speaking strangely, as though commentating on a scene before him, like this was a documentary.

"He was a small kid. It was his first time at an all-boys' school, never mind at boarding school. He hadn't been toughened up like I had. Well, I had a new idea. I could see this kid was soft and wouldn't cope with the vigorous intensity of the usual initiations, so I thought a good idea would be to have him spend a night out in the bush alone. A night in the bush seemed the perfect initiation for this particular kid." Caleb glanced over at Amanda, his eyes beseeching her to understand. "It's something that *I* would have enjoyed and easily coped with, but it was supposed to be an ideal challenge for him," he explained. "It wasn't like he wouldn't be safe. It wasn't a game park, there were no dangerous lurkers nearby. It was *safe.*"

"Except it didn't turn out to be," Amanda guessed, the turmoil in her growing as she saw Caleb's heightening anxiety.

"We were psyched up. We were ready to shower praise on this kid if he pulled his initiation off, and threatened him with punishment if he didn't. We drove him and two other boys, all blindfolded, into the bush and randomly dropped them off at different spots just before sunset. I had a rugby game the next day, so Andy went to pick them up with two of our mates. They were joking and laughing, ready to pat or slap the boys, depending on how they had coped. They picked up two of them."

Caleb's voice choked up. The truck slowed and stopped, the engine dying with one final shudder as Caleb leaned hard on the steering wheel.

Amanda breathed deeply, her insides churning as she desperately hoped that the story would not end the way it was going. Tough Caleb was a broken man beside her.

"But when they found James Stewart—that was this kid's name—he was dead."

Just like that, the horrific truth was simply stated.

"I was just coming back from winning the rugby game when they pulled up in the car park." Caleb shook his head, eyes glazed. "Andy's face—it was so—so hard. He looked right through me, like I was a stranger. And the kid—he was laid out on the back seat, two traumatised boys beside him. A scorpion sting—that was all it took. The kid must have been dead within an hour."

"A *scorpion* sting?" Amanda echoed, staring at Caleb.

"Yeah, the kid must have sat on it or something. He just didn't know the ways of the bush."

"And the other two boys?" Amanda whispered.

Caleb shrugged. "One of my mates said that the boys were as proud as anything when they were picked up in the morning; that is, until they found Stewart. Andy has barely spoken to me since then, thirteen years ago, because I was the one who thought up the idea."

"But it was more appropriate for what this boy could handle!" Amanda argued. "You were trying to *help* the boy!"

"Obviously not," Caleb answered through clenched teeth. "Anyway, I stayed and finished my A-levels. People thought I hadn't an ounce of repentance in me, that I was a remorseless murderer." He ran his hand through his hair. "It was one of the hardest years of my life. I just dove into my studying and blocked the rest of the world off."

"And Andy?"

"Andy? He stayed on at school but he wasn't focussed. The rest of our mates were either expelled or left the school of their own accord."

"Why weren't *you* expelled?" Amanda cringed at the audacity of her question.

Caleb shrugged, "I was allowed to finish the year out. I explained my part in the whole thing and how I had reasoned it all out – I guess they saw how genuinely sorry I was. Honestly, I don't quite know how I was allowed to stay, but I was."

Amanda sank back against the seat, stunned. She had no idea what to say. A boy killed during high school initiation. She knew she would have been scared stiff to be abandoned in the bush on her own for the night, but from Caleb's point of view such a thing would have been peanuts to handle.

The story of Joseph suddenly dropped into her mind. Massaging her temple, Amanda tried to rub the thought away, but it stuck: an image of Joseph's brothers as they plotted to kill him. One brother disagreed with the others—Reuben, the eldest. Wanting to save Joseph's life, he suggested they deal with their brother's pride issues by putting him in a dry well, at the mercy of the wild animals.

He planned to rescue Joseph later, but it all turned out wrong, Amanda thought. *Horribly wrong.*

Wasn't Caleb like Reuben? Hadn't he tried to save James Stewart from the planned initiation that the child would never have coped with?

"Oh, man!" Amanda pressed her fingers against her eyes, trying to blot out these thoughts. Where were they all coming from? *I'm getting like Mrs May—a Biblical story to accompany every life situation!*

When the truck suddenly jerked forward Amanda realised that Caleb had re-started the engine and was heading on home. Neither said anything for the rest of the ride, and on reaching the homestead Caleb climbed out without a word and disappeared round the corner of the building.

Numbed, Amanda grabbed her kitbag and made her way into the house, where she collapsed limply onto the couch. What a nightmare for Caleb and Andy to be living with! And she thought her boarding school life had been tough!

"Hey Amanda!"

She woke suddenly to a high-pitched voice and someone bouncing onto the couch, a pair of bright eyes looming over her. "Hi Penny..." Rubbing the sleep from her eyes, Amanda tried to clear her vision. "You're home early."

"It's almost seven-thirty," Penny giggled. "You've been sleeping."

"Seven-thirty!" Amanda bolted up into a sitting position and gazed around the empty lounge, then back to the bright-eyed Penny. She could hear voices in the kitchen, but none sounded like Caleb.

"Caleb's gone back to work," Penny informed her, as though reading her thoughts, "so I'm really glad you're here still. It's lonely when Caleb goes."

Amanda didn't try to understand the young girl's logic. All she heard was that Caleb had gone—run back to the bush at this late hour without saying goodbye—without a chance for them to properly close their conversation.

She smiled weakly at Penny. "Well, I hope I live up to your expectations."

What she really needed to do was go and find her research file and spend some time working through that. Working on a research project was the most effective way of getting rid of a worry. It was just unfortunate that right now she had no data to research!

Amanda looked up at the young girl, who was still watching her expectantly. What had she missed? Was there something she was supposed to be doing?

But the child's attention was abruptly drawn away as she spotted something outside. "Amanda, come and look at this!" Penny squealed, dashing to the window and then abruptly spinning around and skidding out through the lounge door. "Hurry!"

Interest piqued, Amanda ran a hand through her ruffled hair and hurried after Penny. She found the young girl crouched down gazing at the hard dirt.

"Look, flying ants."

Amanda crouched down beside her. The air was still hot and humid. It was still light enough to make out the tiny hole that Penny was pointing out. Slender white bodies with delicate transparent wings were pushing out through the hole, taking time to stretch their moist looking wings.

"This means it's going to rain!" Penny's eyes sparkled up at Amanda. "They only come out like this before it rains, or soon after." She tilted her head back, her peaked little nose breathing in the air. "Can you smell it? That's the rain smell." Almost immediately she was engrossed in the white ants again, but Amanda took her time savouring the scent. She could see the darkness of the clouds turning heavily in the sky, and the shadowy figures of people beyond the fence.

"See them go," Penny whispered, clutching Amanda's arm. They watched as the white ants flew up into the sky heading off in all directions—a cloud of fluttering wings.

"And see how many wings are all over the ground," Penny pointed out. Amanda noticed for the first time how many white ants were left stranded on the ground, running around in circles over the delicate wings. Above her the birds were having a heyday, swooping down and plucking the flying ants out of the air.

"Do you have friends who are hungry?"

Penny's question caught Amanda off guard. She stared at the girl, stymied. She thought of Kari; Kari was probably always hungry, and definitely hungry of spirit, but she didn't think that was what Penny was asking.

She shook her head slowly. "No, I don't have any friends who can't buy food." Amanda studied the intense young face before her. "And you?"

Shrugging, Penny nodded. "Yeah." She shrugged again, her young brow furrowed. "I feel so bad Amanda," she admitted, her voice just a whisper now. "I have all my family who are alive and love me, I have food, I have a safe place to go." A lone tear trickled down the child's face, a sob catching in her voice, "And Ji—" she gulped, "and some of my friends' don't have a dad, and they have to look after their brothers and sisters all day, and they only have one meal a day."

The tear-streaked face turned up in her direction and Amanda felt her own vision blurring. "I'm so sorry Penny," she whispered, catching the girl's hand and soothing it with her thumb. "It must be so hard."

Penny sobbed again and nodded. "I feel so guilty. I wish there was more I could do."

For a moment the two stared at the now almost invisible hole, the darkness closing in on them, and then Penny asked abruptly: "Do you want to play Chinese Checkers?"

"Uh...sure," Amanda nodded. "That sounds good to me."

She sighed heavily as Penny dashed into the house, her bare feet thudding dully on the hard dirt. Growing up, she and Kari had always been worrying about their weight and figures. They had watched their calorie intake and flipped through fashion magazines for hours, not crying over the pain of those around them.

"Self-imposed hunger versus the real thing," Amanda breathed, her chest squeezing tight. How much was she responsible for Kari's anorexia?

Almost unable to breathe past the crushing tightness around her chest, Amanda stumbled after Penny.

Chapter 10

Penny was right: with Caleb gone it was very quiet. Jeff and Andy were usually leaving the house when Amanda got up for breakfast. Sophie was as usual just like the bunny in the battery adverts: if she wasn't chasing Mick and Penny out of the house for school, or attending to their guests with such gracious warmth, then she was running some other mission—anything from caring for their farm workers to supporting some charitable cause.

It was so quiet during the day!

There'd definitely be more action if Mickey didn't have to study, Amanda thought wistfully, pushing aside the hope that Caleb would return.

She wandered through the silent house and eventually found her way to the kitchen. *Funny how just one afternoon with a fellow can disturb the peace.*

Amanda stared around the abandoned room. Even Rosie was off doing other things.

I should try and do some research work I suppose, she thought, amazed at how uninspired she felt. Usually the thought of her research got her all fired up. And then Kari would be there, nagging for her to stop working and come and play squash or watch a TV program.

*Kari...*Amanda smiled wistfully, and retraced her steps to the telephone table.

"Make today my lucky day, phone! Just *work!*" she said sternly, picking up the receiver. She tapped in the number, international codes and all—now firmly branded into her mind after several attempts to get through to Scotland— and waited with bated breath. She listened to the musical rhythm of the numbers being processed, then a pregnant pause before the sound of a busy line beeped in her ear.

"No!" Amanda slammed the receiver down before picking

it up again: "I *will* get through to Kari today. I *will!*" She determinedly punched in the numbers again. And then again when the phone still sounded engaged. Finally, after the eleventh try, she heard the sweet sound of the phone being answered and Kari's bright, "Hello?".

"Kari! Yayee!" Amanda clutched the receiver with both hands, absolutely amazed that she had finally got through. "Thank you God!" she breathed, and meant it. Kari sounded way better than she had hoped. Perhaps she had been worrying for nothing.

"Amanda, is that you? Amanda! Where are you, you lunatic?"

Laughing in relief, Amanda cradled the receiver, absolutely thrilled to be connected to her friend once more.

"Kari, I am *so* glad to hear you. You don't know how often I've tried to get through to you. I'm in Zimbabwe."

"So you *are* in Africa then?" Kari confirmed. "We were trying to trace your movements."

"Zimbabwe," Amanda corrected.

"Zimbabwe, Africa—what's the difference?" Amanda rolled her eyes at Kari's uninformed thinking. "At least I now know where you are, and that's what counts. Now tell me what's going on. Why didn't you phone your parents or your sisters and let them know where you are?" Kari demanded to know.

Amanda brushed over the question: "Kari, can you phone me back? The people I'm staying with have a tight budget and its costing a fortune to phone out of the country. Here's the number."

Kari noted it down and Amanda reluctantly lowered the phone, feeling like her life-line had been cut as she heard the receiver click into its hold. She stood and paced anxiously, stopping to peep at the clock in the kitchen every few minutes. Almost quarter of an hour had gone by. What was taking Kari so long to phone back?

When the phone finally rang Amanda pounced on it. "Hello—Kari?"

"Hello..." The person on the other end suddenly broke into a babble of words that Amanda couldn't understand.

"Who do you want to speak to?" Amanda interrupted, fidgeting.

In the string of words that followed she thought she heard the name 'Mavis'.

"Look, there is no Mavis at this house. You have the wrong number." Amanda hung up and tapped her fingers anxiously together. "Come on, Kari."

The phone rang again. Amanda grabbed the receiver and lifted it to her ear, eyes scrunched shut as she said cautiously, "Hello?"

"Amanda? Finally!"

Almost sobbing in relief, Amanda hissed, "Don't you get off this line until we have absolutely finished everything we have to say. What took you so long?"

"Engaged; dial tone; a Chinese automated voice response..." Kari listed. "Now talk girl! I want answers. What happened?"

Amanda poured out the events of her journey, ending with: "And it's now been ten days and there is still no sign of a flight out. It's crazy Kari—I wish you were here."

"Well, by the sounds of things I'm glad I'm not," Kari retorted. "So now what?"

"I wait." Amanda laughed as she heard herself repeating the words of almost every single Zimbabwean she had spoken to; everyone was waiting for something.

"Well, should I let your parents know where you are? I must at least tell Polly, she's been phoning me twice a day, absolutely frantic with worry."

"Would you mind? Thanks Kari." Amanda let out her breath. "You have absolutely no idea how wonderful it is to be found. It's like living on an island—a desert island. I am so lonely, and absolutely bored stiff. I am helping out a bit but tend to be avoiding the other tourists if possible – just in case I spark!"

Kari laughed, "Oh, I wish I could see the sight of the driven Miss Amanda McCree at a loose end. This is so not what you had planned."

"You got that right," Amanda answered gloomily. "But there is one thing that I'm trying to sort out. There have been some poaching incidents. Three impala—they're like deer," she said, then wrinkled her nose: "sort of anyway— have been found wounded or dead. There's the tourist living in one of the cabins; he's a really cocky character and I think he's the one doing it. The poaching seems to have only really started since he arrived. One woman in his tour group has wanted to speak to me privately. We did go for a game walk early one morning. Jeff, my host, took the tourists and me for the walk. I tried to talk with this woman then but she just shook her head – maybe she changed her mind?"

"Have you come up with a plan, then?"

Amanda shook her head unhappily, "No, not yet. And you—what have you been up to, Kari?"

"Me?" The pause was enough to tell Amanda that her friend was not in a good place, after all.

"Have you been eating properly?" she queried.

"Of course!"

The answer was too quick. Amanda rolled her eyes but there was nothing she could do from here. "Okay, well... make sure that's true, or I'll hunt you down! Hey Kari, when you phone Polly would you be sure to give her this number please? Thanks." She would get Polly to go and check on Kari.

"Kari, thanks so much for phoning. I really miss you, and the greenness of Scotland, and the way the system works properly, and being able to run down to the shop and grab a Diet Coke. There's just so much I took for granted..."

"Well, maybe I can phone Mrs May and see if she'll pray you out of there," Kari joked.

"No!" Amanda's heart leapt in fright at the very thought. "Don't do that. I'm convinced Mrs May's prayers had some part in landing me up here, any more praying from her and goodness knows where I'll end up."

"It sounds to me like you think prayer works." Laughing, Kari said good bye and moments later hung up.

Amanda sat listening to the dial tone, wondering if Kari could ever begin to fathom how she felt right now; cut off from the world she knew and loved.

She slid the receiver back onto its holder and drifted back into the kitchen. Kari's words echoed through her. *Did* she believe that prayer worked?

Of course not! Amanda's nervous laugh died almost instantly. Then why was she so worried about Mrs May praying for her?

"Enough thinking," Amanda muttered, peering out the

back door. Where *was* everyone? Not even the maids could be heard singing somewhere around the house. The dishes were stacked neatly into the rack, all clean and shiny. The speckled black surfaces were wiped bare, and the back door was open, allowing the hot breeze to swirl around the kitchen, bringing leaves in with it.

"Absolutely nothing to do," Amanda complained, her gaze fluttering over to the computer in the corner. Not many people kept their computer in the kitchen, even one as big as this. But then again, the Jacobs barely used their computer, what with all the power cuts. The generator was used a fair bit to cover the basic needs around the place, such as for lights and cooking, but to use the computer was more of a luxury.

I wonder whether Caleb uses this one, or has a laptop? Amanda mused, absently also wondering why she had not told Kari about Caleb. She stared down at her sweaty hands and ambled over to the sink. "The heat is unbearable," she complained, twisting the cold tap with her left hand, her right hand poised beneath it.

"Nothing!" Amanda groaned, tightening the tap again before trying the hot tap. A thin trickle dripped out of it. So these were the infamous water shortages the family had been talking about just last night.

"'We haven't had water cuts for almost two weeks; perhaps things are improving'," Amanda mimicked Sophie, banging the top of the tap with her palm in frustration. "Come on, work!" She dribbled the resulting water over her hands before it stopped altogether. "No water, dim generated lights—and, lucky us, infrequent phone calls. Great life!"

Amanda slumped down onto a stool and stared bleakly out at the chickens pecking hopefully at the dusty ground. *Poor stupid creatures,* she thought, pushing off the stool. Where was that little white hen she had taken a fancy to? Surely it hadn't been the one chosen for the pot last night? *It must be in the hen house,* Amanda guessed, not wanting to go and check just in case it wasn't there.

"I wonder if Dad and Mum have even realised that I haven't arrived?" Amanda sighed aloud, filled with self-pity for her plight.

Bored out of her mind, she got up and started flicking cupboards open. Pots were in the cupboard beneath the sink and next to the forgotten dishwasher. She shifted over to the next cupboard. More pots. Then, opening up the cupboard above the kettle, Amanda discovered an archive of recipe books.

Pulling the stool over, she scrambled up and fished out a couple. Sitting on the counter, she flipped through the pages and came to a halt when she was confronted with a picture of a mouth-watering vanilla biscuit with cherries in it. Perking up, Amanda skimmed down the recipe. Simple enough; it was likely that they had all the fixings. She'd surprise them all with a treat when they got home!

Excited, she began pulling the ingredients out of the cupboards and after some hunting around found the mixing bowls. She could do this. It couldn't be too hard to make biscuits, could it?

An hour and a half later Amanda was sweeping up the last of the spilt sugar, a tray of picture-book biscuits cooling on the metal racks.

Humming softly, she took the baking sheets to the sink but remembered there was no water with which to wash them. Scooping up the dish towel, she brushed flour off her hands as she hovered proudly over her round little masterpieces.

"Might as well sample one."

She carefully studied the cream coloured biscuits before delicately extracting one from the pile that seemed to beckon her. It melted in her mouth, leaving only the cherry to chew.

"Hmm-mm..." Amanda licked her lips clean of crumbs and gazed around the tidy kitchen once again. Only the beautiful smell of fresh biscuits, as well as the cookies themselves, bore witness that anything had happened. Otherwise, the kitchen was just as she had found it.

Glowing with pride, Amanda was still hovering around the vanilla biscuits when Sophie sailed in, a bright smile on her face.

"'Mmm, smells good in here."

Nodding excitedly, Amanda watched Sophie look around the kitchen expectantly, and then the corners of her mouth drooped.

"Do they not look good?" Amanda croaked out, eyes flicking anxiously between Sophie and her beautiful biscuits.

"Oh Amanda," Sophie faltered, "they look yummy."

Amanda nodded uncertainly. "But?"

Sophie looked up and must have seen Amanda's disappointment at her response, for she smiled suddenly and rushed over to embrace her guest. "They are honestly beautiful." This time her tone left no room for doubt.

Smiling in relief, Amanda settled on a stool and watched Sophie tug off her gumboots and prop the spade up against the back door, wet mud still smeared over it.

"I'm—I'm going to have to go into town later, Amanda," Sophie said, flipping open the sugar cupboard.

"Oh, I spilt some sugar," Amanda admitted, "but only a cup or so. Most made it into the bowl," she added cheerfully, "and I swept it all up."

Sophie just nodded, her back to Amanda. Something about Sophie's posture and strange silence set warning sirens off in Amanda. She shifted uncomfortably. Perhaps she should not have made the biscuits. Sophie didn't seem as pleased as she'd hoped...

"Sophie, what is it?"

Sophie turned and smiled weakly. She looked strangely old and tired.

"Oh Amanda, I know you were trying to help. It's just that we have no more sugar for Mickey's birthday cake that I was going to make, and the cherries..." her voice grew faint and then slowly louder again: "It's not your fault, you didn't know."

Amanda stared at Sophie, aghast as it dawned on her what Sophie meant.

"Oh Sophie!" She slid down off the stool and tentatively touched the other woman's elbow: "I'm so sorry, I didn't even *think* about the sugar shortage..." Amanda stifled her own tears when she saw Sophie's drowned brown eyes. She was devastated that Sophie was taking this so badly.

"I'll go and get more sugar from town, or the airport. Do you mind if I borrow your Land Rover? I'll give you money for the fuel I use."

Amanda wondered at Sophie's broken laugh, but she left

117

with the keys and moments later was bouncing along the dusty road towards town. The rain still had not come. There had been lightning, thunder and a few drops but it was as though the sky was reluctant to release its life-giving water. The land was cracking under the heat.

It was Amanda's first time into Bulawayo, and after spending just under two weeks in a fairly remote area, it was almost a shock to see the crowds of people. Pedestrians were walking along the sides of the main highway long before she reached the actual town. No one seemed in a particular rush (no surprise there, considering what she had seen so far of Zimbabwe). They whistled and flapped their arms at the truck as she passed by.

One bent sign with 'Bus Stop' printed on it had about twenty people clustered around it. At least five women leapt off their bags to call and wave at Amanda as she sped past. Amanda knew that they were flagging her for a lift, but fear of an unknown country and people made her press the accelerator down slightly more while she waved back with false brightness at the women. Glancing guiltily into her rear view mirror Amanda saw that they were once again blending back into the crowd..

Well, they're strangers, she reasoned defensively against the unseen accusers. *They could have had a gun or...something.*

The image of the middle-aged women propped up by their colourful bags and surrounded by small children did not support the gun theory. Sighing, Amanda tried to forget about them and instead watched the barbed wire fence race along beside the truck. In the distance she could see the shapes of buildings forming. One or two were high rise. Her heart was unexpectedly stirred at the sight. Was there a chance she might be able to connect with someone in Bulawayo who could help her on the cultural aspects of her research?

Hope urged her forward. The main road was a single lane either way, but it was wide, with a broad yellow-lined hard shoulder. Up ahead, on the right, was a BP garage.

"I'll be able to get sugar there, as well as fuel." Amanda swerved across the road and jerked to a halt in a parking space, feeling pleased with the simplicity of her mission.

With a cautious glance at some nearby lurkers, Amanda jogged across to the station shop.

She faltered as she gazed around at the empty shelves, and then at the empty fridges. Only one shelf in the fridge had anything on it, and that was bottled water. An elderly man was leaning against the till watching her, his shrunken eyes curious.

"Are you closing down?" Amanda stayed where she was, just inside the glass door.

"Eh?"

"I said, 'Are you closing down?'" Amanda approached the till, speaking slowly so that he would understand her accent.

The man smiled with the same weariness that Sophie had. "Because our shelves are empty? No, we are not closing down."

"Then what?" Amanda was baffled. This was more derelict than the airport shop.

"No supplies," he shrugged.

"So where can I get sugar?" Amanda persisted determinedly, pushing dark hair away from her hot cheeks.

"You are a tourist?"

It was asked as a question but it was obvious the man knew she was. Nodding, Amanda waited, glancing warily behind her. The old man folded his hands together, his thin face earnest as he tried to make her understand.

"This is how it is now. Everywhere people are searching for food. Everywhere people are hungry." He studied Amanda until she fidgeted uncomfortably. "If you find sugar then know that God has blessed you today."

Amanda's heart stilled at the words and she looked up to meet the old man's watery eyes again. He sealed his words with a firm nod, eyes never wavering. Disturbed, Amanda tried to regain control of the situation, wondering how God had got into her shopping-for-sugar plans.

"Well, I'll just get some diesel then, my tank is low," she asserted.

The greying head shook, a slight chuckle catching Amanda unawares: "No diesel. Come back next week or the week after. Maybe we'll have some then."

It was with trepidation that Amanda pulled back onto

the road and continued in to the town centre, the man's words lingering with her.

"God's *blessing* to get sugar?" Amanda shook her head in disbelief.

Sweat streaming down her face and her long sleeves rolled up to her shoulder, hair scrunched into a haphazard bun with a piece of black string she had found, Amanda took her place in the third queue of the day.

Gone was her discomfort with the pushing bodies and smell of stale sweat. Gone were her scowls at the loud voices blaring in her ear and blethering people crammed around her. Gone was her concern with her appearance, and the awareness that she was the only white person around and stood out like a sore thumb. This was *war!* Five hours of bickering, pushing, and searching for sugar had broken Amanda. She had waited in the last two queues, even reaching fifth from the front in one, only to be told the sugar was sold out. Would this be a repeat?

A bony elbow shot into her back from behind. Turning around, Amanda scowled and her fury only grew when she saw that the laughing man was apparently not even aware that he'd gouged a hole out of her, as he elaborated on his story with big gestures.

Sighing, Amanda stared into her shopping basket, drawing it up close to her chest lest anyone got the bright idea of sneaking something out of it.

"I would honestly beat anyone up who tried to take anything out of here," Amanda muttered intransigently, frowning in consternation as she realised that would mean leaving the queue to do so.

Enfolding the basket in protective arms, Amanda determined that no one would get to her hard-won goodies in the first place; then she wouldn't face the certainty of losing her place in line while she retrieved stolen supplies. She shuffled close to the person in front of her as the line moved forward, leaving no gaps for any opportunists.

There were two tubs of cherries in the basket, three loaves of fresh white bread, one tin of strawberry jam, two packets of currants, and a packet of peppermint sweets. Each item had been achieved through endurance and excruciating patience.

"Hey, I was here!" A young woman began to push into the line in front of Amanda.

Two hours ago Amanda would have been intimidated by the move, but now she pushed back with her shoulder, glaring firmly at the woman.

"You were *not* here."

"Ask my friend!" The woman pointed at the man in front of Amanda, who turned around to see what was going on.

Amanda did not budge. "I have no time for this nonsense— go and stand at the back."

Their eyes locked in silent challenge, and then the woman reluctantly moved down the line to try her luck somewhere else.

Twenty minutes later Amanda was given her ration of three packets of light brown sugar. She could have kissed the store assistant who was handing it out.

"Thank you. Thank you so much!" she beamed at him, gratefully basketing the sugar and smiling as she weaved through the sticky queue and towards the pay-tills.

On a flat board, just before the pay-counter, lay two white 5kg bags with 'Mealie-Meal' printed on it in big blue letters. Amanda had no idea what it was for, but grabbing one of the bags, she headed for the till to pay. Whatever 'mealie-meal' was it had to be useful, because there were only two bags left.

"Eh, you've done well," the teller whistled as he scanned Amanda's shopping through. "You were lucky today."

"Blessed," Amanda whispered without stopping to think.

"Eh?" the hand paused over one of her sugars as the man looked up.

Amanda lowered her eyes sheepishly, staring at the sugar packet that lay between them. Raising her voice just above a whisper she repeated with conviction, "Today I am blessed."

Her heart stilled at her confession. Through her eyelashes she watched to see what the man's response would be.

To her surprise, the teller merely grinned and agreed cheerfully, "Yes, you are blessed." His conversation flowed on as Amanda slid her shopping carefully into the plastic shopping bags, her thoughts on the old man at the BP garage and his words of truth.

The revelation that God could bless someone's shopping trip stayed with her as she floated out of the double doors and passed obliviously by the street vendors and street children she had so nervously avoided on her way in. Tucking her shopping bags under the front seats of her vehicle, Amanda was just about to reverse into the road when she was stopped by a tap on the truck door and a keen face leaned in close at her eye level. Amanda kept a careful eye on the passenger seat lest someone slip her shopping out from its hiding place while she was being distracted.

"Yes?"

"Diesel at the garage three streets down," the man informed her, and gestured with his hand for a tip for his information.

Amanda scrutinised him thoughtfully a moment and when he held her gaze she decided he was telling the truth and obligingly dug out a $5000 note.

"Thanks," she said, trying to ignore his disappointed look as he stared at the note. "Sorry, it's all I can spare."

The man shrugged and drifted away unhappily while Amanda reversed into the road and guided the Land-Rover around the block in search of the garage with diesel.

It was almost eight o'clock when Amanda watched the diesel attendant snap the shutter closed and prop the dripping pipe back into its slot. Tank full, she drove slowly past the waiting line of cars that circled at least two blocks and then queued up along a stretch of the main road; she almost felt guilty—it was likely that many of them would not be getting any fuel tonight.

Amanda was relieved to find her way back onto the road leading out of town after a couple of false starts. Without working street lights it was very dark; the only light on the road was the beam from her headlights, which illuminated the stretch of road ahead of her—now deserted.

On the outskirts of town the BP garage was all lit up. Perhaps it had a generator. On an impulse, Amanda flipped her left indicator on, drove up beside the shop window and peered in. "Yip, he's still there." Amanda waited for the aged head to turn her way and then waved for him to come out, unwilling to leave her truck.

He smiled when he saw her and immediately shuffled out of the door. "You are on your way home?"

Amanda nodded as she dug under the passenger seat. "I want you to have this," she said, handing him one of her precious sugar packets. She did not wait for his thanks as she saw his eyes grow suspiciously watery. But just as she pulled away from the curb she said thickly, "You were right—about God and the sugar, I mean."

Chapter 11

The stars were bright against the dark sky and the moon was high. It was a warm night and even above the engine Amanda could hear a night bird calling. Tears of exhaustion welled up, blinding her vision, as she got out to open the main entry gate to Shamwari Ranch.

Home seemed such a long, long way away. She missed Kari's crazy jokes, and Sally's soft voice. She missed her own cups and plates and she missed seeing her breath fog up in front of her on a cold day. She missed her piles of organised papers on her desk, and walking under orange-lit street lamps on a winter's evening.

"Everything is so *foreign* here."

The night was so dark and the stars so white. Strange night calls filled the air and something was coughing really loudly close by—and not a human cough, either!

"Foreign, foreign place," Amanda whispered, feeling extremely vulnerable and exposed in the open-topped vehicle.

Above the sound of the engine Amanda heard the noise again, that strange coughing, and as she rounded the bend her headlights lit up the road ahead. Sprawled out in the dead centre of the dirt road were two lions.

"Oh—*help!*" Amanda yelped, slamming on brakes.

Both lions—*lionesses*, she had time to correct herself—blinked their yellow eyes in her direction. One opened its mouth and gave an enormous yawn, white teeth gleaming in the headlights.

Heart pounding, Amanda shifted into reverse as quietly as possible and began backing slowly up the road.

A snuffle just beside her sent chills down her spine as she turned to her right. Metres from the Land Rover lay a huge male lion, its thick tawny mane raised up as high as the sides of her vehicle. This was no zoo lion. Its paws were at least the size of her head.

Feeling incapacitated, her bones turned to water, Amanda finally managed to jerk the Landie backwards, her heart throbbing in her throat as the huge animals stretched and then sat up to watch her retreat.

"God, help! Please!" Dry-mouthed with fright, Amanda kept reversing until the three lions were at the far edge of the beam of her headlights. She wasn't going to risk letting them out of sight so that they could circle round behind her and spring up onto her back, crushing her neck between—

"Stop it Amanda!" she hissed, trying to halt her spiralling thought patterns.

"Jesus, I'm sorry..." Amanda hugged her knees to her chest. "I know I've been running away from You. I know Mrs May was right, which is why I couldn't stand seeing her. I have put everything in my life before You, I freely confess that..." She stared at the three lions staring back at her. "I'm scared, God," she whispered.

The night sounds didn't change but the two lionesses pushed off their haunches in unison and padded silently over to the male.

God, You were able to help me get sugar today against all odds. I know that. Amanda licked the dust off her lips as she considered the day. *If You could be bothered to get me sugar, then hopefully I get to eat the sugar, which means I don't get to be mauled to death tonight,* she reasoned, a spark of hope rising in her. *And if You could be bothered to help me get the sugar, then surely it'd be nee bother for you to protect me from these lions and get me home somehow?*

She suddenly recalled the letter Mrs May had given her that night in the car park, and wondered what was in it. "Bad timing," Amanda whispered. "That's like a last minute death thought. Just when normal people would think of everyone they should have told they loved, *I* think of a letter from Mrs May! Just great."

For over five minutes Amanda sat watching the lions, waiting for God's answer. There was no thought that He wouldn't answer her prayer, so when she heard the rattle of an approaching vehicle behind her she gathered up her shopping expectantly. Headlights glared into her face as she hopped out, and she had already scrambled up into the big jeep before it had fully stopped. Only once the door was closed and locked—not that it would actually make any difference, as this was also open-topped—did Amanda look up at her rescuer.

"Caleb?" For a moment she was taken aback; then she smiled and settled her shopping more comfortably on her lap.

"Amanda?" Caleb's voice was low. "What are you doing out here by yourself?"

"Playing with lions, what else?"

"Amanda!" Caleb was insistent.

Shrugging in embarrassment, Amanda said, "I wasted all your mother's sugar which she had specially kept for Mickey's birthday cake, so I had to go and get some more."

Caleb said nothing, but the moonlight was bright enough to give away his thunderous expression of disbelief.

"Tough day?" Amanda asked sarcastically, eyes fixed on the lions. She nodded her head at them, then relented and humbled herself to admit to Caleb: "I'm glad you came, I was really scared."

"So you just jump into the first vehicle that comes along?" Caleb shot back, his voice shaky. "For goodness sake woman, I could have been *anybody*! What were you thinking?"

Amanda stared at him, looking at him properly for the first time. In the moonlight she could make out the fear in his face. His eyes were wide and his mouth was tight.

"Think woman! What's worse, lions or a stranger?"

"But God sent you," Amanda whispered, trembling, thinking that Caleb's question was a ridiculous one considering she'd already had to make that decision. He was the one who had encouraged her to pray. She had prayed, and God had heard!

"God sent me?" Caleb sounded bewildered.

"Yes," Amanda nodded. "Don't be angry with me Caleb, please." She was absolutely exhausted—she had no energy left to handle an angry Caleb.

She watched his hands tighten on the steering wheel as he said in a strained voice, "I'm scared, not angry. Anything could have happened to you."

"Why?" Amanda stared innocently at him. "God told you to come."

"God didn't *tell* me to come," Caleb corrected. "It's Mickey's birthday. I couldn't get away from the Mission any sooner to get here."

"Oh?" Amanda took a moment to absorb his words. "Well no-one told me that's how it works. I thought God spoke and people obeyed." She shrugged happily. "Anyway, now I know."

"Know what?" Caleb shook his head in confusion.

"Well, that God heard me and delayed you until the right moment. It makes sense in some way, even though it's not the way I thought He worked." Amanda smiled at Caleb, and then nodded at the lions. "So how do we get around them?"

She waited trustingly for Caleb's answer. She might be angry that he had disappeared before they finished their conversation, and that he could be exasperating, but she trusted him implicitly. That in itself was huge for her—she did not readily trust anyone. At least her parents had taught her that much, even if only indirectly!

Caleb's straight nose and defined jaw line were still stern. He really didn't look very happy.

"Well, it's not my fault that there were lions on the road!" Amanda exclaimed, annoyed that he wasn't moving on. "Do you think I ordered the blithering things to be waiting for me in my *topless* Land Rover so that I could wait, exposed, for them to have a good feast?"

"Sshh!" Caleb waved a hand, but his tense profile eased into the slightest of smiles.

"Well, do you?" Amanda hissed, shaking his arm. "Do I *look* like a crazy tourist?"

His smile broadened as he swivelled around to have a good look at her. She fidgeted, growing uncomfortable under his lingering gaze.

"Maybe I should have been more specific about how I wanted to be rescued," she muttered. "I'll remember that for next time."

Caleb nodded agreeably. "Perhaps." He gestured at her packets. "And what is that you're clutching with such devotion?" Amanda glanced down and realised she was still clinging to her shopping.

"Oh, this? This is my hard-fought-for shopping. Bread, cherries, jam, currants, and sugar—" she nodded across at her car "—and some big sack called 'Mealie-meal'. It beats me what it is but it looked important so I bought it."

"Uh-huh."

"You're laughing at me," Amanda accused, peering at his face.

"And what will you use this mealie-meal for?" Caleb asked, grinning broadly.

Hackles up, Amanda glared at him, but his disarming smile soothed her ruffled feathers. She leaned against the head rest and grinned back.

"I'll let you decide how you want to use it, if we can convince your mother that it is edible. Uh...it is, isn't it?" She sighed in relief at Caleb's nod.

"Do you know that—"

"Sshh!" Caleb waggled a finger suddenly.

"What?" Amanda matched his whisper instinctively. She stiffened, peering into the darkness ahead of them. The lions were no longer in the beam of the headlights.

"Oh no! Caleb—what now?" She swung around to probe the darkness behind them, expecting a massive face of teeth right next to her.

"Don't stress," Caleb whispered easily. "This is an experience to be treasured, not one to fear."

"You're crazy," Amanda hissed.

"It's like a thunderstorm," Caleb said. "Some people really fear thunderstorms, yet they can be the most beautiful experience ever. The same goes for lions." Caleb started up the engine and edged forward. "We'll follow their tracks."

"Caleb, I want to go home." Amanda's voice was low and firm. She could feel the sweat sticking the palms of her hands to the shopping bags. She didn't turn when Caleb looked her way. "I mean it, Caleb."

The Jeep slowed and came to a stop. "Is this about the boy? James Stewart?" The pain in Caleb's voice was unmistakable.

"James Stewart?" Amanda stared at Caleb incredulously. "James Stewart!" she repeated, shaking her head at the thought. "This is about *me*, Caleb! I'm too selfish to be worrying about *James Stewart*. I'm deathly tired, but on top of that I'm plain scared of lions, scared of the bush, scared of—the unknown," she flared at him, glad to finally have something tangible to vent her emotions on. "I didn't even want to come to Africa, never mind be stranded out here in the wilderness where no-one can find me. It's scary!"

She turned away from him back to the darkness. "I'm just scared Caleb," she admitted softly, "but if I had to be stuck with anyone at all with lions prowling around me, I'd choose to be stuck with you first." She glanced across at him and said dryly, "Lucky you."

It was a hot night and there was no wind to ease the discomfort of the dry air that settled over them. Her face felt flushed and her lips were cracked. It was all so...so *discouraging!* She was trapped. She could do nothing to change her circumstances. She was stranded in a world she did not understand, and was at the mercy of strangers who had rapidly become the closest thing she had ever known to a family. It was all so ridiculous! Her triumph of today was getting sugar and bread. What had happened to the thrill of leaping upon some nitty-gritty detail after digging and sifting through mountains of research papers? Sugar and bread would have been her final stop at the little corner store on her way home at night, not a day's mission.

A soft touch on her hand stirred her. She looked up and was enveloped in eyes full of compassion. Caleb. Who would have thought she would land up on the African doorstep of some guy she spotted on a Christian singles web page? It had been fun to laugh and flick through the catalogue of men, so distant and removed from her. It was a whole other matter to get to know one of them, a person with flesh on him, with a heart that was easily moved with compassion, and yet a will of iron. He had so much love to give, and yet such uncertainty about how to do it.

Amanda sighed softly, her gaze flitting down to the roughened masculine hand that enclosed her own. Perhaps it was true that one had to have been broken and hurt before they could really understand someone else's pain.

"Amanda." Caleb's voice was husky. "Thank you."

Amanda tilted her head up, "For what Caleb?"

"For trusting me." He gazed down at her. "It's been a long

time since I have known that someone truly trusts me, even among my own family."

"Oh Caleb..." Amanda wriggled her hand around until she was able to give his a quick squeeze. She shook her head soberly, laughing inside, "It took lions to do it."

The seriousness of the moment was lost, but both were smiling.

"Amanda, can I show you the beauty of Zimbabwe? Can I show you what I see amongst the pain and what I believe I am called to do to make a small amount of difference here?"

Amanda hesitated, searching his eyes. The words "beauty for ashes" leapt to mind.

"I don't know," she said, rubbing the plastic bag between the thumb and forefinger of her free hand nervously; "what if I'm not able to see it?"

She expected him to laugh at her. Instead Caleb responded with: "Well, how about we give it a try?"

Amanda still stalled as she scanned the night for the lions. What was beautiful about the dust, the heat, the shortages, the hungry people, and the scariness of this unknown place?

"Alright." She shrugged. "I'm stuck here anyway, so what is there to lose?"

"Okay!" Caleb gave her hand a quick squeeze before re-starting the engine once again without yet shifting into gear.

Amanda hesitated. She really should be getting back to Shamwari. She had promised to be back with the sugar. And Mickey would be expecting Caleb. And they'd probably be worried about her by now...

Amanda glanced at Caleb and felt a bubble of excitement rise in her. It would still be Mickey's birthday when they got back, and Sophie would probably not bake a cake this late at night—surely!

Amanda hid a nervous laugh at his boyish excitement and leant forward, hands squeezed together. "So—what's your big plan?"

Caleb grinned. "Night-tracking. You can see the lion tracks there. We'll follow them."

"How, Einstein? It's dark," she reminded him dryly,

though she wouldn't admit that she couldn't see the tracks he'd seen.

"Spotlight, Einstein-*ess*," Caleb shot back, his expression eager. "Let go of your shopping and hold this."

Amanda reluctantly released the packets, settling them on the floor. She felt a little bereft as she let them go, but took the huge spotlight that Caleb handed her.

"Shine it on your side and look for prints."

"You make it sound so simple," Amanda grumbled, pushing aside a strand of hair that kept falling across her eyes. As far as she could see there *were* no prints.

Caleb pushed up off his seat and leant against the hand rail behind him, craning his neck to follow the spotlight.

"There!" he called. "Wait—shine the light back a bit. To the left. That's it. Stop." It was a soft indentation in the dusty ground; only half a print was visible.

"If you look carefully you can see the toe prints are facing towards the car which means the lion was headed toward the right. Here, pass me the torch, we'll look over here on my side."

It was Amanda's turn to crane past Caleb to follow the light. She grabbed the thick metal rod behind her head for support, loving the coolness of the bar. If she hadn't been afraid to be alone up there, she'd have sat on one of the tiered seats behind them where she'd have had a better view.

"See it?" Caleb half-glanced over his shoulder and swung the torch, lighting up a skinny bush track heading off into the grass. Amanda could just make out a couple of tracks.

"So we lost them?" She settled back down, not sure if she was disappointed or relieved.

"Lost them?" Grinning excitedly, Caleb handed her the torch. "No, we've *found* them. This baby is a tough cookie—" he patted the steering wheel "—she was made for bundu-bashing."

At Amanda's curious glance he explained, "Driving through the bush where there are no roads."

"Ah!" Enlightened, Amanda watched Caleb shift into first gear and gently pull the wheel to the right. Her heart lurched as they left the relative safety of the main road.

"I don't think we should leave Sophie's Landie. It's got a

full tank of diesel," she explained lamely.

"You have the keys, don't you?"

At her nod, Caleb shrugged. "She'll be okay for a bit."

Every now and then they hit an anthill and Amanda was either flung against Caleb or slammed into the door. And when they weren't climbing anthills they were careering over holes which bounced Amanda high off her seat.

"These rabbit burrows!" Amanda exclaimed, clutching her bruised arm. "It's like you're *trying* to hit them."

"Don't give the hares all the glory," Caleb said. "They could be snake holes, or ant bears, amongst other creatures."

"A very encouraging thought," Amanda remarked dryly.

The long grass scraped against the sides of the Jeep and Amanda could feel it scratching under her feet as they drove over it. A glance behind showed that most of it straightened up again once they had passed by.

She could sense Caleb's excitement as he dodged another anthill and grinned at her.

"Very good," she praised, wrinkling her nose at him as they hit a rock. Up ahead were trees. "I'd like to see how you manoeuvre around this one!" Amanda smiled smugly.

Without a word, Caleb drove directly into the clump of trees. Gasping, Amanda shielded her head with her arms as a small sapling was sucked under the chassis. She clutched at the seat as they bumped between trunks and branches, only letting out her breath as they came into the clearing beyond. She had an acid comment all ready, but it evaporated as her ever-shifting eyes were drawn to a dark shape.

"Caleb," she whispered, leaning fearfully closer to him, "what's that, there on my left?"

He leaned forward. "Giraffe, a mother and a baby by the looks of it."

It was very quiet when Caleb turned the engine off, but after a while her ears began to adjust to the silence. Amanda could hear the soft crackling of twigs or leaves being broken off.

"They're feeding off the tree." Caleb's voice was so low that his words were only just audible.

The shape moved so that the moonlight shone from

behind it. The silhouette that formed was beautiful: a long graceful neck and head extended up into the tree and elongated legs stretched down to the ground. Something reached out of the giraffe's mouth and wrapped around a bunch of leaves.

"What is that?" Amanda was horrified.

Caleb caught on immediately. "Its tongue. Really long, hey?"

Nodding, Amanda gazed at the animal in fascination until the truck vibrated into life.

"We'd better go."

Amanda swivelled around in her seat in disappointment as Caleb drove on. She watched the dark shadows of the giraffe until she could no longer distinguish them from the trees. When she turned around she could sense that Caleb was driving with purpose. He had some goal in mind.

"You're cheating, aren't you?" Amanda accused. "You can't possibly be following the lions' tracks at this speed."

Caleb glanced her way. Amanda couldn't see his features but she knew he was impressed with her observation.

"Got me there," he admitted. "But if I've got the right pride of lions—and I think I do—then they should be heading for their favourite waterhole. If we get there first we might see some action."

Amanda nodded, the excitement in her growing as she latched onto Caleb's idea.

"We'll park here between these bushes. We'll have a good angle on the waterhole and the plain."

Amanda wasn't certain how long they waited, but the time sped by quickly. The air was thick and heavy. Caleb pointed out lightning on the horizon. It flashed strong and white against the darkness.

"I can smell the rain..." Amanda tilted her head to sniff the air. She smiled across at Caleb. "The promise of rain! We need it. Everything is so dry and hot here. I saw a lot of burnt land on the way into Bulawayo today." She frowned at a sudden thought. "Wouldn't many animals be killed if there was a fire in the game park? The lightning could do that?"

"It is a worry," Caleb agreed, "but that's where we give this worry to God and pray for rain."

Amanda studied him thoughtfully for a moment before turning back to watch the distant sky light up again. Praying did make a lot of sense; she was beginning to see that. And in many ways there were few alternatives here in Zimbabwe. Day to day living was so difficult.

Maybe that was why she hadn't bothered to pray much back home. She had always been in control of every situation. There just had not been much room for God in her life—no need for God.

"Here they come!" Caleb nudged her as four dark shadows separated out of the long grass.

Amanda re-counted them. Where had the fourth lion been hiding when she had crossed between her car and Caleb's?

A soft touch on her elbow directed Amanda's focus to a small herd of buck by the waterhole. What had Sophie called them? Impala, was that it?

Sure enough, Amanda watched three of the lions slink silently back into the grass, splitting ways so as to cover all possible escape routes the impala might take. One of the lions remained where she was, the biggest lioness of the lot, pressing her body close to the ground.

Caleb reached for the torch but Amanda held onto it.

"The moonlight's quite bright," she whispered. "Can we rather watch them by that?" Nodding, Caleb's hand dropped back onto his leg.

Did he know that he looked like a little boy released from the imprisonment of a classroom into a sunny playground? Smiling to herself, Amanda tried to follow the movement of the lions, guessing where they would all place themselves for the strategic attack. She noticed that the unsuspecting impala were continuing to drink at the waterhole. Not even the impressive male with his spiralled horns was on the look-out for a possible attack.

The big lioness was the only one of the pride Amanda could now see, and if the shadows weren't playing with her eyes, Amanda thought she could see the haunches move slightly, as though the lioness was edging forward.

In the distance thunder rolled, and the smell of rain grew stronger. The impala were also growing fidgety. Was it the thunder, or did they sense the lions?

From the left, just below where they were parked, a dark shape sprang forward. Almost immediately the two other lions reared out of the shadows, scattering the impala. The buck were in full-tilt panic, their frightened calls blending together in a cacophony of confusion as they bumped into each other before following the ram straight towards the big lioness that lay in wait for them. The male dropped back, letting the two chasing lionesses close in behind the impala, steering the herd straight on.

"They have no hope," Amanda whispered as the huge female sprang up, startling the lead buck into a frenzy of panic as he bounded and twisted in an attempt to dodge the lioness.

The big cat leapt into the air and swiped, one huge paw knocking the buck up in the air as the rest of herd darted into the grass. The ram was up and running, leaping from side to side as he tried to weave through the lion pack that had now closed in on him. Another lioness flung herself at the buck, her claws piercing his hide. After that the end came quickly, for the big lioness lunged at the ram's neck, breaking it as she pulled the struggling creature to the ground.

Only as it gave a few last feeble kicks did Amanda become aware that she was clinging to Caleb's arm, her heart pounding. Sheepishly, she prised her fingers off him and handed him the torch, absolutely speechless.

Caleb flipped the switch on and lit up the scene. The lionesses had backed off under the warning roars from their master, leaving him to eat first. Later, they would move in for his leavings.

The big lion raised his head, blood smeared across his muzzle and magnificent mane, and then buried his face again in the rib cage of the impala.

"Well, that's that then." Amanda tried to sound matter-of-fact. In truth the sight had been splendid and fearsome, and absolutely heart-pounding.

"Are you alright?" Caleb checked. "My arm is feeling a mite bruised." He touched his arm tenderly.

"Sorry..." Amanda grimaced, but once again she felt a strange urge to express her feelings. It must be because Caleb had been so open with his. There was no other explanation for her sudden honesty when he was around.

"It was exciting," she laughed self-consciously, "but I feel guilty that I found it exciting when one poor impala lost its life."

Caleb said nothing as they absorbed the scene. Did he think her callous?

"Are you ready to go?" he asked as the first of the lions drifted away from the carcass.

She nodded, ashamed at her emotions, and then, unable to bear the anxiety of not knowing, she asked, "But aren't you going to say something?"

"About what?" Caleb sounded surprised.

Amanda's brow furrowed. "Well, about what I said—you know, about feeling guilty about enjoying such a scene." She waved a hand at the last of the lions.

"Oh, that. You aren't unusual; most people have a similar response. And this is the way it works out here, it's nature. Sure it's sad, but everything has to eat to survive. Lions have to eat, you have to eat..." Caleb shrugged helplessly. "I'm not sure what else to say."

"So you don't think I'm callous?" Amanda persisted, wondering why she was not letting this go.

"Callous? No." Caleb ruffled the back of his head and stared at her.

Suddenly shy, Amanda gave a nervous laugh and flicked the torch off. "Alright then, now that's resolved I'm ready to go."

The thunder boomed again, louder this time. By the time they reached the main road leading to the house there were only two counts between the lightning and its sound.

"You'll follow me?" Caleb checked.

"Yeah, in your Jeep," Amanda answered quickly, judging the metres between Caleb's vehicle and Sophie's Land Rover. She wasn't going to cross any gaps again tonight, once was more than enough—especially considering that the first time, there had been an unaccounted-for lion somewhere nearby.

Grinning knowingly, Caleb gallantly hopped out and held out his hand for the key. "I won't use any more fuel than I can help," he promised, teasing her.

Flushing, Amanda was grateful for the darkness. She

slid across into the driver's seat and pulled it forward so that she could reach the pedals.

"You'd better not."

As she drove meekly behind him, Amanda noticed that Caleb drove with his right hand dangling out of the window, just as his grandfather had.

"Great bait for lions," she muttered darkly.

A quarter of an hour later they pulled up to the farm house. The dashboard clock read 10:45. Would anyone still be awake? They must surely have missed Mickey's birthday celebration...

She was still gathering her parcels when Caleb jerked the Jeep door open for her, his easy grin and boyish excitement now replaced with a pair of serious eyes and a quiet smile.

Amanda felt his heaviness as she meekly handed him the shopping bags and followed him up to the house. It puzzled her, but then the truth struck her so forcefully that Amanda staggered under its impact: *Caleb was uncomfortable with his family!* He was holding himself aloof because of James Stewart. He was still trying to pay for something that had happened over thirteen years ago. How sad that this lovely family should have to cope with the knowledge that the two eldest sons had been involved in the death of a boy—but why had they not sorted it out between themselves long ago?

At the door she tentatively touched his arm and stared at his chin, uncertain what to say. In the end she gave him a smile and hoped he understood, hoped that he knew that she felt his pain. Whether he did or not she didn't know, but his eyes did soften as he slid a key into the front door and stepped back to let her in.

Chapter 12

"Get in here and let me look at you!"

Amanda was yanked into the bright light of the kitchen and found herself under the surveillance of the entire Jacobs family, who were scattered around the kitchen. Empty coffee mugs were lined up beside a steaming kettle and the sweetener—a jar of strawberry jam.

"You appear to be intact," Sophie observed, cupping Amanda's face between her hands. "Sunshine, don't you ever come home this late again! Alright?"

Amanda nodded mutely, overwhelmed by the concern of the entire family.

"Oh 'Manda, we thought something really bad had happened to you!" Penny wrapped her arms around Amanda and clung to her.

Amanda awkwardly patted the little girl's back. "I just left town really late. I'm sorry I worried you." She squirmed guiltily. They should have come straight home.

"Well, you'll have to tell us all about it just now," Sophie said, "over a cup of coffee."

"Well, first of all, I took the road..." Amanda obligingly began. She stopped when all heads turned towards her looking curiously surprised. "You said to tell you just now," Amanda confirmed.

Sophie nodded, "Yes, I was meaning in a moment—I thought you'd want coffee first, but you can tell us now if you want."

"Oh?" Amanda tried to fathom Sophie's reasoning.

Jeff suddenly began to laugh, "Oh Soph, Mom's done this with me before. 'Just now' in Scotland means 'right away', not 'in a moment'."

"Oh!" Amanda's face grew long in surprise. "Well, that makes sense." She turned towards the door. "I wonder where Caleb has got to?"

"Caleb? Caleb's here?" Penny raced to the door: "Caleb!"

Amanda watched the youthful face light up, and dimpled to see the delighted embrace of brother and sister as Caleb came in. He'd dumped the shopping bags just inside the door in order to fully put his arms around his little sister.

"Caleb, you're back!" Penny bellowed, clinging to him.

"She's not short of lungs, is she?" Caleb grinned at Amanda over the top of his sister's head.

Amanda's worries evaporated at the sight of Caleb raising a quirky brow at her. Smiling, she looked away. If faced again with the decision of coming straight back to the ranch house or going with Caleb, she knew she would have changed nothing.

It was as if they had returned home from war. Everyone was babbling together in excitement, so glad to see them... So this was what it was like to be a family: Mickey and Caleb getting into a ruck of sorts, Sophie pouring the coffee, and Jeff rummaging around for biscuits. Only Andy sat aloof in his corner. He seemed determined not to be involved, but his eyes followed Caleb's every movement. Though she tried, Amanda was unable to interpret the changing emotions that played across Andy's face, but one thing Caleb had definitely got right was that Andy was hurting.

"So Amanda..." Mickey sauntered over, his face all red from his roughhousing, and draped a brotherly arm over her shoulder. "Where did you scoop the lone ranger up from?" He winked at her.

"Mickey!" Amanda nudged him indignantly. "I didn't *scoop* him up—" she looked around at the now listening family "—we just...encountered one another on the road."

Jeff was grinning at her, his expression suggesting that he didn't believe her story entirely.

Amanda glanced up at the straight face of Mickey. "Seriously."

"That's not the way I remember it," Caleb drawled, leaning against the counter by the kettle.

"Well, you tell us your version then," Penny said devotedly.

Ruffling her hair, Caleb eyed Amanda over the rim of his mug, his eyes teasing. Suddenly afraid of what Caleb might come up with, Amanda shook her head.

"His version is all wrong, whatever he says."

"Whoa-ho, this sounds interesting!" Mickey whooped. "Perhaps we all need a seat."

"Oh, wait a minute—" Amanda slipped out from under Mickey's arm "—I did succeed in my shopping expedition today...Caleb, where...?"

He indicated the parcels in a heap on the floor, and while Amanda plonked them on the table, Caleb reached out of the backdoor, swung the sack of "Mealie-Meal" into the house, and triumphantly waved it about.

"Way-*hey!*" Mickey lunged at the bag and cradled it in his arms, staring at it in awe. "Where did you find this baby? What a birthday present!"

Amanda giggled as Caleb lifted a brow in her direction. He looked as pleased as she felt.

"It was this wee Scottish lass that got it for you, she's the glory girl tonight."

Mickey swung on Amanda, his usually ultra-relaxed frame was alive with pleasure.

"You and God must have been talking, 'Manda. I've been dying for *sadza* for weeks. I'll be on Rosie to make her *lekker sadza* tomorrow for the *braai*."

"It's like stodgy porridge that's eaten as an equivalent to rice," Caleb explained, seeing Amanda's bewildered look.

"With onions and tomato relish poured over the top." Mickey inhaled deeply: "Mom, can you smell it?"

Sophie laughed, "Perhaps. How about we open your presents now, Mick, while everyone is together?"

"I also got the sugar and cherries," Amanda offered, holding up her precious catch.

She handed the bag over to Sophie with such pride and delight. The way her hard fought for winnings were being received was like the grand finale of God's blessing on an exhausting and very long day.

"And currants!" Sophie waved the bag: "You see that Andy? This woman was definitely in the groove today!" She tossed the bag over to Andy, who smiled slightly at Amanda.

"Oh! Did you hear that thunder crack?" Penny squealed, squeezing Caleb's arm excitedly. "It's wonderful!"

There was silence as the family sat and sipped coffee and listened to the thunder. The breeze blowing in the back door was fresh and cool and the scent of the coming rain was something beautiful.

Amanda, perched on a stool, drank it all in, savouring every second that went by as she gazed around at each member of the family and memorised the moment.

It was like she was part of them. It was absolutely wonderful!

"Well, I vote Amanda as the birthday cake baker for tomorrow." Jeff waved a vanilla biscuit at her: "These are delicious!"

"I thought you said you *wasted* the sugar?" Caleb interjected.

Amanda shifted guiltily and glanced up at Caleb beside her. "I *did* spill some—and the rest was used for a purpose for which it was not intended," she finished loftily.

"So it's decided then," said Sophie. "You bake the cake, Amanda. And Caleb, I heard Dad say that he needs—"

Caleb cut in quickly with, "I'll help Amanda, Mom."

Sophie frowned, "You'll only get in the way, darling." They both looked at Amanda consideringly.

Amanda had listened with bated breath, debating whether or not to speak. In the end she said, "I'd like Caleb's help, I'll find a way for him not to get under foot."

Amanda tried not to shuffle when she caught Sophie's sharp glance swing between herself and Caleb, as though she was putting two and two together—only Sophie was making five, because if Amanda interpreted her knowing look correctly, Sophie's conclusions were all wrong.

"Okay!" Sophie raised her palms in resignation. "He's your cross to bear. Don't say I didn't warn you when you discover him trying to bake water droplets in your flour, or fry apple pieces when you had other plans for the oil." She swung on the rest of the family and in the same breath said, "Bed time everybody."

Taking a sneak opportunity when no-one was looking, Amanda elbowed Caleb. "Don't you look so smug!" she hissed. "Your mother is as convinced that I *can* bake as she is that you can't. I *know* I could bake this cake without your help, but I also know you'd go scot free if you went to *help* your dad."

Caleb lifted a brow at Amanda, "And that would never do?"

Amanda smiled as she watched the brown head cock to one side just as the first sounds of rain drops bounced against the corrugated iron veranda roof. "Definitely not."

Only Jeff and Sophie were left in the kitchen with Amanda and Caleb. Jeff sat at the kitchen table; he suddenly looked old and strained, the grey at his temples more noticeable tonight beside the tired lines near his eyes.

"We found another wounded animal today," he said, his voice breaking through the clatter of mugs as Sophie slid them into the dishwater. "An impala. It had been shot through the stomach. When we found it, it was almost dead from loss of blood."

"Oh no, Jeff, the poor thing!" Sophie whispered, abandoning the dishes.

"Yeah, we had to kill it. Andy's hung it up in the shed." Jeff shook his head. "I just don't get it. This is the second buck that has been found wounded in two days. It's almost like the poachers don't know how to shoot." His eyes met his wife's, something silent passing between them.

Sophie let out deep breath, her brow furrowed with concern.

Brain racing and heart pounding, Amanda stared at them, wondering if they saw the connection as clearly as she did. That tall Allen Fairbelt had arrived just as the hunting problems started. Hadn't he been interested in game hunting? And it would fit his character that he was cocky enough to believe he could shoot when he couldn't; and mean enough to leave an animal in pain when he messed up and left it wounded. She glanced up at Caleb, wondering if he was thinking the same thing.

"Where was it found?"

"Georgie phoned. One of the workers passing through his place told him that they had seen it on the far fence. I sent Andy off to track it." Jeff glanced around the table and saw the serious expressions. "We'll sort this out sooner or later, it's not like we haven't had poachers before."

"But they are usually going for rhino horns or food, we've not had wounded animals being left to die a slow death."

Sophie rapped the table angrily. "This is different."

Sophie's words confirmed Amanda's suspicions. If only she could get a chance to talk to that woman, then she'd know for certain that Allen Fairbelt was a lowdown poacher and up to no good.

"For now, we'll have ourselves some impala *biltong*." Jeff made an attempt to lighten the air, but his eyes remained heavy. Sophie rubbed the back of his neck, her eyes as dark as his.

A plaintive voice carried to them: "Mom, I'm in bed!"

Sophie smiled tiredly at Amanda, "That's my cue." She moved out the kitchen and headed down the passage calling, "Have you brushed your teeth, Penny darling?"

The rain sounded loud and strong compared to home, maybe because there were so many windows open and the veranda roof was aluminium—or maybe because it just was harder rain.

Jeff rose and followed Sophie down the passage. In the distance Amanda could hear a dog bark. It must be one of the workers' dogs. Hopefully they were safe in their compound and not wandering through the game park at this time of night.

"So—are we still on for our deal?"

Amanda turned to find Caleb still standing close to her. "Deal? You mean the beauty-for-ashes deal?" She waited while her words sank in and registered. "I didn't realise there was more you wanted to show me. I mean, what we saw tonight was incredible."

Caleb filled up the kitchen doorway, leaning against one post as he watched her put away the shopping bags that Sophie had abandoned. His expression was unreadable.

"Well, if that's a 'yes' then yes, the deal is still on." Amanda smiled with excitement at the prospect of more adventures through Caleb's eyes.

Caleb didn't move while she finished putting away the jam. He seemed content to stay and watch. Perhaps he was tired and was unable to kick-start back into action.

"Well, if you two have finished whispering together perhaps you'd help me check the gates are locked?" Sophie appeared back in the doorway.

"Sure Mom, can Amanda borrow your rain jacket?"

"Wait, now that is something I *did* bring with me," Amanda grinned at Sophie. She dashed down the passage to grab it before dashing back to the kitchen, anxious not to miss out on any action.

"Mom, I think she'd like to see it."

"Just look after her Caleb, she's not used to our ways."

"I'm back." Amanda burst back into the kitchen pretending she hadn't heard the soft conversation.

Both turned and eyed her thoughtfully, Sophie with keen, searching eyes and Caleb with a smile.

"Goodnight 'Manda, we'll see you tomorrow; 'night Caleb." Jeff stepped into her vision from the left. He smiled at her before gently guiding his wife away from the sink. "It's time to hit the sack, my lady. I'll finish up the dishes."

Amanda ducked into the rain, an image of the couple branded in her mind. It was amazing how much in love they were after all these years, and all the little love actions they did for each other. She hoped when she got married it would be like that for her.

As she chased after Caleb towards the far gate she wondered how her own parents related to one another. But try as she might, Amanda just couldn't stir up any memory of her parents—together—at any time she'd been there with them.

It must have been about 2am when Amanda woke. The burglar bars at her window were still trembling from a loud crack of thunder.

"Hmm..." Stretching contentedly, Amanda snuggled down into her sheets, enjoying the freshness of the air that poured in through the window, bringing that beautiful rain smell with it.

Caleb had said the smell came mainly with the first rains of the season. It was rain mixing with dust that produced the unique aroma.

*Rain and dust...*Amanda stretched again. *Funny combination to make such a beautiful smell.* She closed her eyes, enjoying the sound of the rain bouncing off the gutter and the steady stream of water from what must be the overflow.

"God, thanks for today, or yesterday rather. And thanks

also for bringing me to this family who have just accepted me as one of them. I could have—well, anything could have happened to me. Maybe I'd still be sitting at that airport! Horrific thought."

Amanda's mind turned to the undercurrent of hurts that flowed through this family. Had she imagined it, or had Sophie been afraid that Caleb wouldn't take good care of her?

"And God, it's incredibly sad that such a wonderful family that loves You could be so confused about each other. I can see they love each other, but only Mickey and Penny seem to be able to truly connect with everyone. Maybe You could do something for them?"

A sudden image of her own ruptured family relations sprang to mind. Amanda winced, tempted to push such grieving thoughts out of sight as usual. Instead she tucked the sheet under her chin and stared up into the darkness, her voice now small and uncertain.

"There's also my family, God. Dad and Mum You know. They've been missionaries for years: missionaries in China, missionaries in Mozambique, missionaries in Romania, and now missionaries in South Africa. I know they're doing something beneficial with their lives, being doctors and all..." Bitter tears stung Amanda's eyes as she hissed: "but I've always *hated* their work!"

Amanda tensed, expecting a God-directed lightning bolt right onto her bed, followed by a resounding thunder crack, after that confession! But there was none; the rain continued to pour steadily down.

Taking that as a good sign, Amanda pressed on with her honest opinion, hoping God had enough patience to hear her through now that she was finally willing to get going and tell Him what she really thought.

"They just couldn't be bothered with us. They dumped us in some boarding school and galloped off to fulfil their 'calling'. They were never there on Parents' Day, when all the other parents were. They never saw my first colouring pictures or watched me win my first race. They weren't there to check what time I got home at night, or to love me when I hurt." Amanda choked over the pain.

"Most holidays we didn't even get to go home, God—we

went to Great Aunt Marie, usually." Amanda grimaced: "That great pillar of iron strength and immovable will."

She stared across at the silhouette of the green alabaster jar that was the cause of her journey.

"I don't think any of us really recovered. We're kind of like this family I guess, broken yet not knowing how to be healed inside, not sure we *want* to be healed," Amanda acknowledged. "Except the Jacobs family is one up on us when it comes to communication. My family barely talks."

Wide awake now, Amanda talked on.

"And then You'll probably know my sister Polly and her husband Sam; I think they're Christians. At least they go to church faithfully." Amanda frowned, wondering why she was even questioning Sam and Polly's faith. Pushing that uncomfortable thought aside she went on doubtfully:

"I'm not sure if You *ken* my eldest sister or not? Her name's Ruth. I think she's bossy and controlling and would happily manage the world if she could, but because she hasn't had a chance to, Polly and I have been her project. She's the cheapskate who bought me the ticket that landed me here." Amanda scowled, making a mental note to get Ruth in hand the moment her plane touched ground in Edinburgh, if that ever would happen.

"I think both my sisters keep in touch with the parents still. Cobs and I are the ones that don't. Cobs doesn't keep in touch with any of us." Amanda sighed, brushing a tear-dampened strand of hair off her face. "You see, God, we're really messed up. If You can be bothered with such a derelict lot, maybe You could do something about us too?"

She wrinkled her nose up at the ceiling sheepishly. "Sorry if I've bored You, but thanks for listening." She sighed again; it would have been nice if God had answered. Anyway, she felt much better for having finally talked to Him about her family.

"In fact, I feel close on peace," Amanda murmured, stiffening as she heard a deep coughing noise. *The lion grunt!* Amanda shivered with pleasure, reliving her night drive.

It hadn't just been the hunt that had been wonderful or the thrill of the unknown as they bounced along. There had also been the rain smell, the sound of tall dry grass against the Jeep, the night bird sounds, as well as the starry sky before the clouds had rolled in, that had all been so spectacular. And then there had been Caleb, a God-send after feeling so alone and lost in a strange land. Maybe Caleb was right, maybe there was more beauty here than she had given credit for.

And on that thought, I need a drink of water. Amanda slid out of bed, her nose wrinkling as she realised she was still wearing yesterday's clothes. She must have drifted off to sleep before she'd managed to get undressed.

"Too late to worry about that now," Amanda muttered, and grabbed the light jacket that Sophie had lent her. Using it as a makeshift dressing gown to hide her crumpled clothes—just in case anyone else was still up—she padded barefoot down the passage to the kitchen. As she softly pushed the kitchen door open she felt a flash of alarm at the eerie blue light that filled the room. It took a moment for her to realise it was the light from the computer screen.

Curious, Amanda silently closed the door and made her way across the cool tiles to the computer. Apart from once when Jeff was doing farm business, this was the first time she had seen the computer on. She supposed he'd left it on by accident before going to bed.

Glancing around and seeing no one, Amanda wriggled the computer mouse to get rid of the screen saver.

"Oh, man!" Amanda breathed, something spiralling down inside of her as she stared at the familiar web page—*the* Christian Singles web page where she had first seen Caleb.

So he was still looking at it.

Well, why shouldn't he? Amanda reasoned. *There's nothing wrong with stealthily sneaking into the kitchen at two-thirty in the morning to meet with other singles on your parents' computer!*

She cleared her throat unhappily, her eyes glued to Caleb's handsome face with that querulous smile.

"Amanda?"

She jumped guiltily, hands leaping off the computer mouse.

"I was just getting some water," she stammered, temporarily blinded as her eyes adjusted to the darkness of the room behind her.

The tall shape moved closer.

Oh *man!* Was this embarrassing, or what?

It took a moment for her to register that the masculine frame was more slightly built than Caleb's.

"Mickey?" Amanda let out her breath in relief. "What are you doing here?"

When he didn't answer Amanda fumbled for the light switch. The flood of light had them both squeezing their eyes shut. When Amanda ventured to crack her eyes open she saw the usually confident Mickey had red ears and was looking extremely uncomfortable. His eyes glanced past Amanda at the computer screen, guilt scrawled all over his face.

"It's you!" Amanda gasped in sudden understanding, and relief, "You're the one that put Caleb's profile up on the web page. Oh Mick!"

Shuffling, Mickey went to stare at the screen, his mouth working but no words coming out. Running a hand through her tangled hair, Amanda sagged against the counter.

This is just wonderful. Her joy was short-lived. "Oh, poor Caleb," she whispered, staring at Mickey in mortification. She poked at his arm. "You put your brother's profile on a singles web page! Oh, are you in trouble or what! If my sister dared pull that stunt on me—whoa-ho!" She shook her head at the thought. Polly wouldn't even get a chance to apologise. Except Polly wouldn't try that trick—that'd be a Kari-stunt, more like it.

Amanda shook her head to clear her thoughts, then padded over to Mickey and gently hugged his arm, staring down at Caleb's portrait, the relief in her mind curling down into her stomach.

"What were you thinking, Mick?"

Mickey rubbed the back of his head in the same way Caleb did when he was uncomfortable.

"It seemed like a good idea..." He glanced at her sheepishly. "Mom often cries over Caleb when she thinks no one is looking. There's stuff in the past...stuff you don't know, don't need to know. I just thought that if Caleb found a girl...well, he might get over it all."

Amanda's heart froze as she listened. So her analysis had been right; this family hadn't worked through its issues. Sighing softly, she leant her head against Mickey's shoulder, slowly digesting what he was saying.

"It was over a year ago that I put this up. I didn't do anything about it until some persistent girl kept contacting me a couple of weeks ago. In the end I replied." He coughed nervously. "After that I found it—uh—fun. The girl is a goner on Caleb."

Amanda rolled her eyes.

"So, you reply to her when no one is about? Shame for you the computer's in the kitchen," Amanda commented dryly.

"Well—this is also the time when she writes. She's on UK time. It's about twelve-thirty there, now—I guess she's a late owl." Mickey glanced down at Amanda. "Do you want to see her?"

Amanda shrugged. "Sure." She let go his arm while he clicked into Caleb's account.

"I have absolutely no desire to see some persistent man-hunter that won't leave a guy alone," Amanda mouthed at the computer, waiting to see what kind of girl had so little pride that she would stalk Caleb so persistently. It was all about the looks, it had to be.

"There she is—kinda pretty, huh?" Mickey flashed Amanda a cautious grin, "Caleb should be pleased."

Amanda wrinkled her nose dubiously at Mickey before leaning forward, curious. Her jaw dropped and then she giggled nervously.

"Well, wha-da-ya-know!" she exclaimed, her eyes dropping down to the name below the picture: "Kari MacArthur." Amanda began to laugh. So Kari had been taken by Caleb's picture and started contacting him—or Mickey, rather. Oh Kari!

She studied the familiar face of her friend. It was wonderful to see someone close and treasured again, even if it was only a photograph. Then she frowned as she peered closer at the screen. "Can you enlarge the photo, Mick?"

Mickey obediently did as she asked and Amanda's heart dropped as Kari's photo became clearer. The once gently curved face had become protruding cheekbones and a jutting chin. Huge eyes stared up at Amanda flatly; the dance in them was gone.

"Oh Kari!" she breathed, gently running a finger from

her friend's large brown eyes to the pointy chin. "You're so thin..." Her stomach heaved. So the niggling worry had not been unfounded. Kari needed help. Now!

"I need to get home!"

Waves of worry washed over Amanda, and her ears roared. She was trapped—trapped in this land with no way out. Kari needed her—she needed to get home.

"Amanda? Are you okay?" Mickey's concerned touch only dimly reached Amanda's thoughts. "What is it?" He followed Amanda's gaze back to the photo. "Do you know her?"

His voice pulled her back from the uncontrollable fear that seemed to burn over her body; that feeling of utter helplessness that had come and gone in the last weeks.

Amanda nodded, straightening, unable to pull her eyes away from the screen. She felt sick with fear.

"Amanda?" Mickey's concerned voice roused her.

Glassy eyed, Amanda swallowed, still staring at her friend's picture, "She's my best friend, Mick."

Mickey waited.

"Oh! She's so thin!" Amanda wailed, her words echoing over and over through her mind: "So thin! Oh Kari..." She turned and pressed her face into Mickey's shirt, trying to block out the images. "I must get home. Kari needs help. She's got no-one else. Oh Mick, do you think a plane will leave today?"

"Here, sit down Amanda." Mickey swung the computer chair around behind her. Amanda gratefully sank into it.

"She's just so thin, I can't believe it!" She took a deep breath and looked up at Mickey. "How long have I been here?"

He shrugged, "A week or two. I'm not sure. Definitely not more than three weeks."

"And this picture of her, how old is it?"

Mick shrugged, "A week at the most. Why?"

Amanda shook her head in despair. "Kari is anorexic, Mick." Amanda leapt to her feet and slid her hand into his, craving support: "She won't admit it, but it's obvious! Since I left home she's lost weight, and I've hardly been gone! This is absolutely crazy."

Mickey stared down at the screen, a different expression on his face as he studied Kari's picture through new eyes. There was such compassion in his eyes that it made Amanda choke up inside.

"So what do we do?"

His support gave Amanda strength to start thinking again.

"Well, she hasn't listened to me in the past..." Amanda looked up at the youthful face before her. "Maybe I didn't do enough? Maybe what I had to offer was not enough? I don't know..."

Could she lay such a heavy burden on such young shoulders? But dare she not, for Kari's sake?

They stared at each other, watching the same idea dawn in each other's eyes.

Amanda lifted her brow questioningly: "Are you up to it?"

In answer, he pulled up another chair in front of the computer.

"I'm not going to tell you what to say," Amanda whispered, staring at the huge eyes of her friend. Broken eyes. She didn't know what she would say anyway. "If she's kept writing to you then she likes you enough to be interested in what you have to say. Kari has no qualms about letting people know when she's not interested." Amanda laughed brokenly. "I should know."

She slid into the computer chair and rolled it back over to the computer, her heart stilling when she saw the sparkle of tears in Mickey's eyes.

"Mickey?" She clutched the edge of her seat. "What do you know about anorexia?"

Mickey ducked his head:. "I know it's serious." He swallowed hard. "There's a girl at school, she's suffering from it..." His voice cracked. Breathing in slowly, he flicked his gaze up at Amanda before focusing intently on the computer screen again. "No-one else sees what she's going through, but I do. She's consumed with this weight thing—it's all in her mind!" He shook his head despairingly. "I've tried Amanda, but even I can't get through to her!"

"Is she your girl?"

Mickey did not deny it. Instead he nodded almost absently, "Suzanne Stewart."

Fireworks exploded in Amanda. Was it possible, or was

it just a coincidence, about the surname? Her voice was controlled as she asked cautiously, "Stewart?"

Mickey looked up, his eyes connected with hers, and a flash of understanding passed between them.

"He told me," she said simply.

Mickey nodded. Nothing more was necessary.

Chilled through, Amanda tried to take this all in. Was Mickey suspended between the Stewart family and his own? Another family secret unearthed, another family member in turmoil.

"Suzanne sometimes talks about James," Mickey confessed. "I think she still misses him." He shrugged helplessly, "I've met her family..."

"And?" Amanda bit her lip.

"They're great. The fact they accept me is proof they aren't holding grudges, or hate my brothers. Suzanne's parents are so—free."

Amanda held her breath, waiting.

"It's my own—" Mickey stopped suddenly and glanced up at Amanda. And then the angry tension wheezed slowly out of him, his shoulders slumping forward. When he spoke again he sounded like an old man, tired and worn, "It's my own family that can't let go."

Amanda was horrified. "So...your parents haven't forgiven Caleb?"

Mickey dragged the back of his hand across his eyes. "No, it's not that. No-one in this place will forgive *themselves*. Everyone is living in cursed guilt!" He glared up at nothing in particular, his ferocious expression frightening Amanda, "What did Jesus die for except to forgive us? Huh?"

He was demanding an answer and Amanda didn't know what to say.

"Exactly! So either we don't really believe the Bible, or we're too high-and-mighty to humble ourselves and accept Jesus' death on our behalf—whatever the reason, we're surely not living as forgiven people!"

Amanda was finding it hard to breathe.

"My brothers never dreamed James would die. Sure, the whole initiation thing at the school is bad, but to live in torment, punishing themselves day after day with dark memories—that's not right. And my parents—" there was no stopping Mickey now, he was on the rampage; "—my parents blame themselves for sending them off to boarding school so young for so many years. No-one talks about it, but the whole thing sits with us at every meal, in every conversation—everywhere! And I'm sick of it!"

Heart thumping in her throat, Amanda stared at her hands. What now? She hadn't bargained for any of this midnight interlude. She didn't want to get involved. Sure, she had prayed the Jacobs family would have a breakthrough, but—but this was just too close to home.

"Oh, man!" Amanda groaned inwardly, vowing never to make generalised prayers again lest she find herself being commissioned as the one to bring about the change. She would have to learn to be specific when she prayed, and at the rate things were going it appeared she'd be praying more often than not.

The image of Mrs May in the church car park that night flipped into her mind. She couldn't remember what her teacher had said, but she was absolutely convinced Mrs May was somehow behind this all. The woman probably told tales on her every night to God.

Grimacing, Amanda stared heavenward. *What now God?* Her slender hand on Mickey's shoulder seemed so insignificant under the torment of emotions and built-up pain that she could feel coursing through his trembling body.

"Can we pray—together, I mean?" Mickey broke the silence, his voice barely audible.

Tense, Amanda nodded, "Uh—sure." She waited till Mickey had closed his eyes and then followed suit. When had she last prayed with anyone outside of church? And two prayers in one night! God must wonder what she was up to.

She listened to the young man pray. Apparently Mickey didn't see the need for any special God-tone, for he was praying just as he talked, simple and direct.

"Jesus, Kari and Suzanne are consumed with the idea that they're fat, even though they are like walking skeletons. And my family is a mess. Everyone blames themselves and no one will accept Your forgiveness. Jesus, I know Your death wasn't pointless, please help them to see that. So *ja,* all of us need Your help—please would You help us? And thanks for Amanda..."

Amanda wriggled uncomfortably, peeking an eye open to look at Mickey. His eyes were still shut and he looked dead serious.

"...Thanks for sending her to us, even though all her plans were messed up. You see what a difference her being here has made to all of us, Caleb especially. Thanks. Amen."

Amanda shot a quick glance at Mickey before pretending to open her eyes with him as he straightened. She felt relieved the prayer was over. It was one thing to pray for someone else, but another thing entirely to hear your own name in there.

Mickey stretched in his familiar way. "Well, that's sorted."

Amanda stared at him, he looked so at peace.

"So that's it?" She waved a hand: "You're not going to fast as well, or—or, I don't know..."

"You think I should shred my clothes like the prophets did in the Bible?" Mickey's eyes sparkled at the thought. "I can just imagine what Mom would say if I tried that."

Amanda flushed. "It's just that—well, *I* think it's a reasonable question," she answered defensively.

"So..." Mickey leaned forward seriously, chin resting on his fist. "What was it I heard you say when I came into the kitchen?" He frowned, pretending to rack his memory. "If I recall right, it was something like, *'Well, why shouldn't he?'*" Mickey gazed at his knee pensively. "And also about someone sneaking into the kitchen to chat with other singles." He tapped his knee casually. "You sounded real unhappy. I don't suppose I could have been the fortunate recipient of such affectionate thoughts?" He shook his head thoughtfully: "No—it couldn't have been me."

"Mickey!" Amanda grabbed a nearby book and playfully swatted his shoulder, "Your imagination is tremendous."

"Tremendously accurate," Mickey corrected, a dimple appearing in one cheek.

It was amazing how much like Caleb he was. Before the accident, Amanda could imagine Caleb being very similar to Mick. Up to now she had seen two sides of Caleb, one light-hearted and the other extremely cagey and defensive, especially around his parents.

154

"You're not denying it?" Mickey persisted, unwilling to let her off the hook so easily.

"Well, I'm not accepting your suggestions either."

"Alright," Mickey conceded, "you're not;" but his grin did not fade. Amanda found herself responding, against her better judgement, with a smile of her own.

"One last comment and then I'll let it go," he promised, "for now at least. Just so you know, I don't remember the last time Caleb came home so suddenly and within days of his last visit, or stuck around talking with the family for so long."

He let his comment sink in, and Amanda could feel her cheeks warm up as he watched her.

"Tea?" he offered abruptly. "We even have sugar." He winked.

Amanda grabbed at his offer, grateful for the change of subject. "Sounds wonderful." She swivelled the chair around and said slyly, "I know someone who's going to have a lot of explaining to do about an empty biscuit tin tomorrow."

Mickey pointed a finger at his chest innocently. "Me?" He waggled a finger. "Sorry lass, you're in this with me, both of us were up tonight. No one will be any wiser as to which one of us actually ate the biscuits. Anyway, how did you know?"

Amanda nodded her head at the biscuit crumbs spread across the table and then at the forgotten biscuit near the computer keyboard.

"Just guessed," she smiled sweetly, "and unfortunately for you, your Mom and I planned to bring out the rest of those biscuits for your birthday celebration today, so she'll know I never ate them."

Groaning, Mickey pushed the kettle switch on, before saying: "I'll take my punishment like the man I am. Now let's hope this kettle hurries and boils."

"Quickly," Amanda pleaded, laughing, "before the electricity goes out."

"Now you're getting into the swing of things!" Mickey sauntered over to the sink. "Let's just hope there's water."

Rolling her eyes, Amanda scrolled down the computer screen with the mouse. Kari hadn't said much about herself in her profile, or in her conversations with Mickey. She had kept her messages very generalised and open. In one place Amanda saw herself referred to. Kari hadn't mentioned her name but it was very clear that she was speaking about Amanda.

Kari had written, "If it wasn't for my best friend life would be really hard. She's all the family I've had after my parents died. It's just a pity she works so much, I don't get to spend time with her like we used to. We've known each other since we were eight…"

The message rolled onto other things but Amanda was left with a lump in her throat. She had always imagined that it was Kari who was always so busy that they didn't get to hang out like they used to.

"But how could it be her?" Amanda whispered, thinking of Kari's eight to four shift. "It *must* be my fault." The truth walloped her right in the stomach; it was undeniable. She was the one hiding, little by little backing away from the world and those closest to her.

"Afraid to trust…" Amanda breathed out the revelation thought that dropped into her mind.

"Okay, enough gloomy thoughts for one night." Mickey shoved a lumpy tea mug in her direction. "Snap out of it Mandy," he grinned, "though goodness knows you have every right to be gloomy, what with your infatuation for Caleb and all!"

"Mickey!" Amanda hissed, glancing towards the kitchen door, "someone might hear you."

Unperturbed, Mickey punched in a single line in reply to Kari: "Just hang in there Kari, I'm filling God in on you and something good is bound to happen soon."

Moments later the screen went black and the vibration of the computer faded away to nothing as Mickey shut it down.

"What do you think of our kitchen?" Mickey asked, perched the wrong way on the chair so that his arms could rest across the back of it.

"It's nice. Really nice." Amanda gazed around, taking in the granite counters, shiny black and white tiled floors, and the florescent light overhead. "Immaculate really. Your mom has a container for everything."

"That's Dad. He's the tidy fanatic." Grinning, Mickey

slugged down some tea and swirled the last of it around in his mug. "Andy carved all the sugar, flour, tea containers— all those."

Amanda followed his finger along the line of delicately carved containers all made out of a pine coloured wood, with the label carved out of each one's side and then highlighted in chocolate brown paint.

"They're absolutely stunning."

"Sure are. Andy's amazing when it comes to carving. He also made all the cupboard doors. Whenever we don't know where Andy is we can usually find him in the garage, carving."

Mickey rubbed his hands together: "And the rest of the kitchen is what Dad, Caleb and I did." He looked so chuffed with himself that Amanda laughed, then humbly apologised.

"And the curtains, table cloth, and tray cloths are what Mom and Penny did."

"Great team effort," Amanda praised, genuinely impressed. "How long did it take to do?"

"A couple of weeks. It was during the December holidays, so Penny and I were off school for about seven weeks."

Both suddenly straightened and listened. Above the sound of the rain on the aluminium veranda they could hear someone running. The footsteps slowed.

"Did you hear that?" Mickey checked.

Amanda nodded, looking around the kitchen for a weapon. She opened the cleaning cupboard and pulled out the broom, gripping it near the base so she had a good swing if she needed to use it.

Chapter 13

Amanda held her breath and listened as she watched Mickey slide over beside the back door and crouch down low. The sudden clatter and groan of someone stumbling startled them both.

"That's Penny's voice!" Mickey exclaimed, swinging the door open, the light from the kitchen pouring down onto the small form clutching her shinbone in the pouring rain. She gazed up at them, and made Amanda think of the impala caught in the headlights of the truck on her drive with Caleb.

"Penny, what on earth are you doing? Get in here," Mickey commanded.

Moaning, Penny hopped into the kitchen; a puddle forming around her feet as water poured off her soaking body.

"You better start talking," Mickey growled. "What were you doing out there?"

Tears pooled up in Penny's eyes at the anger and worry in Mickey's face. "I was only trying to help!" Her bottom lip trembled. "We have so much and—and Jimmy has to give his little sisters all his food." She looked from Mickey to Amanda and back.

"Oh Penny," Amanda breathed.

The child immediately came to her, clinging to Amanda's neck. Sobs racked her little body, soggy clothes soaking Amanda's as Penny sought reassurance.

"What were you doing then?" Mickey persisted grasping Penny's shoulder and pulling her back from Amanda so he could see her face.

She shot a nervous gaze between the two of them. "I was just—just giving them—food." She stumbled guiltily over her words.

"You were stealing Dad and Mom's food?"

"I wasn't stealing," Penny wailed.

"Sshh, stop crying." Mickey stepped back from her. "How long have you been doing this?"

"A while...I think the first time was the day Amanda arrived." Water dripped off the end of her nose and chin.

"Oh Penny..." Amanda's heart went out to the woebegone little face. She drew the child into an embrace and looked up at the stern face before her. "She was only trying to help, Mick."

Mickey shook his head but his expression softened. "Just don't do it again Penny, it's not safe to be running around by yourself outside, especially when none of us knew you were out there. Do you hear me?"

Penny nodded.

"Promise you won't do it again without telling me. Promise me, Penny."

Penny's lip trembled. For a moment Amanda wondered if she would fight Mickey on this, but then she whispered an almost inaudible, "I promise."

"Okay, go and get dry."

"I was only trying to help." Penny looked up at Amanda.

"I know." Amanda patted her back instinctively. "Come, I'm as wet as you are now. Let's go and get dry and then come and get something warm to drink."

Ten minutes later they settled into a companionable silence, warm and dry, Penny with hot chocolate and the other two with tea. Amanda was about to sip down the last dregs when she noticed that the sunflower clock above the stove read 04:40.

"Is that right?" Amanda checked doubtfully.

"Sure is. Due to your delightful company, time has flown." As Mickey held out his large hand for her mug, Amanda noticed blue ink spilled over the outside of his thumb.

"When's your next exam?" Amanda asked, watching him swish the mugs out.

"Last ones, you mean," Mickey corrected. "They're on Monday. I have three exams on Monday, but then I'm done—finally."

"I'm not sure if that's good or bad," Amanda frowned, glad the days of exams were over for her.

"Definitely good!" Mickey was decisive. "I'm sick of studying."

No one made any move to go; they all seemed reluctant to leave. Amanda rose and crossed over to the back door. The key turned silently under her fingers.

She paused. "Is your house usually alarmed?"

Amanda giggled at Mickey's squinted look. "I mean, does it have an alarm?" She glanced at Penny and then at Mickey.

"Nope, but maybe it should have." Mickey looked pointedly at Penny. Penny glared back, her defences securely in place once more.

They crossed out onto the back veranda. Amanda inhaled deeply, enjoying the rain splashing over her bare toes as it slipped under the aluminium roof.

"No point going to bed now, is there?" Mickey commented. Amanda shook her head in agreement.

The sky was growing lighter even as the rain seemed to ease up slightly.

"Might as well get comfy and watch the sunrise?" Amanda suggested, snuggling into the rocking chair and tucking her legs under her. "If it comes, with all these clouds around."

"It'll come," Mickey assured her confidently, stretching out on the basket chair, legs propped up on the low veranda wall. Penny cuddled up in the chair beside Amanda, one hand stretched out to loop through Amanda's arm.

This was the promise of a new day before them, but somehow, inside, Amanda knew there was a much bigger promise being birthed in her; a God sort of promise, of a new day or season in her life. Perhaps for the Jacobs' lives, too.

She closed her eyes, feeling deeply at peace. The fear and worry that had been plaguing her had dwindled away—round about the time that Mickey had prayed and she had released Kari into God's care.

The rhythmic glancing of the metal oar against the canoe faded away as her dream world was replaced by glaring sunlight. The clanging noise sounded again. Squinting into the sunlight, Amanda licked her dry lips and sat up slightly. A man was hoeing the ground nearby. Wiping her mouth, she propped herself up fully.

"You're going to have a double sunburn for sure," the man predicted, bending down to scoop up a shirt from the muddy ground. He tugged it over his shoulders.

Amanda tried to focus as he approached, her eyes still sleep-filled.

"What was this? A sleep-over?" Amusement mingled with curiosity made his voice sound thick, or maybe his mouth was just dry.

She shifted around to see if Mickey was still there. He was, stretched out languidly, arms behind his head. He hadn't changed his position much. Penny was a warm bundle snuggled against her.

"A picture of contentment," Caleb grinned.

"We came out to see the sunrise. What time is it?" Amanda asked through a yawn. She pushed back the dark hair that had fallen over her face.

"Just past ten—and we still have a cake to make before everyone arrives," Caleb reminded her. "I was just digging the veggie patch, waiting for you to wake up."

"Is that right?" Amanda raised a brow dubiously. "You were *just digging* the vegetable patch? From the sounds of it, I bet you made sure you hit every stone you possibly could in the hopes you *would* wake me up."

"That sounds very spiteful." Caleb clucked his tongue in mock disappointment. "There isn't a spiteful bone in my body."

"Hmm," Amanda grunted, giving him a dubious look. She smothered another yawn. "Well, cake it is," Amanda agreed, ignoring his curious look as he glanced over at Mickey again. It would all be too complicated to explain and anyway, she didn't want to explain lest he wanted to know what they had talked about.

"I'll be back in ten minutes once I'm ready for the day. And then we can bake the cake. But breakfast first, though," Amanda said firmly. "I'm starving."

She carefully eased away from Penny, tenderly brushing a stray piece of hair from the peaceful face. It was amazing how love seeds grew when one was least expecting them to.

A quarter of an hour later she was helping herself to

some cereal.

"What's Mickey's favourite cake?"

"I dunno." Caleb looked bemused as he kicked off his muddy boots. "I've never thought to ask."

Amanda flipped open the fridge. "Well, we've got carrots," she said, glancing up at Caleb and catching a curious look on his face. "What?"

He shook his head, a smile playing around his lips. "So, carrot cake then?" he guessed.

They worked in easy unity, as though they had been co-chefs for years.

"So—I'd like to take you to the Mission sometime," Caleb announced. "I'd like to show you what I do."

Amanda glanced over her shoulder, still grating the carrots. "Okay, I'd like that." She shrugged. "But I'm not sure I'm very good around sick people or children, I might give you some black marks."

"Oh, that's alright." Caleb kept his back to her. "All I'll ask you to do is give a couple of people injections, check temperatures, and clean up any messes that people make."

His laughter was deep and full when he turned to watch her reaction, "No I won't—really, I'll just introduce you to people, show you the hospital that the pastor and I built." He nodded to himself, cracking an egg on the rim of the counter: "It's good. I think you'll like it."

"Another beauty spot, then?" Amanda asked, watching Caleb's egg leave a gooey trail from the counter edge to the mixing bowl.

"Another beauty spot," Caleb affirmed, "smack dab in the middle of a whole heap of suffering."

"Well if it isn't my old arch-enemy!" a voice boomed behind them.

Amanda leapt round, startled. "Fabio! You gave me a fright."

The large farmer engulfed Amanda in a crushing hug. "It's been a long time since I saw you."

"Hey Fabio, are you trying to asphyxiate the woman? She can barely breathe."

Caleb's voice triggered Amanda's release. She gratefully drank in the fresh air and fluttered a hand near her face.

"Wow!" she gasped, looking at Caleb.

He grinned sympathetically, "Perhaps there is something worse than Fabio's handshake after all."

"Hello-hello!" Fabio peered over Caleb's shoulder into the bowl he was mixing; he stepped back and winked at Caleb. "Now this is a side of the man I haven't seen—a domesticated Caleb."

"Where's Georgie?" Amanda asked curiously, glancing towards the kitchen door expectantly.

"His kid has a swimming gala today. He'll be in for lunch, for sure."

"Georgie wouldn't miss lunch," Caleb agreed, putting his bowl down beside Amanda.

"Any news on the poaching?" Fabio asked, helping himself to a biscuit from the tin near the kettle.

"No." Caleb shook his head. "If they have shot any game then they must have taken the evidence with them."

"One more carrot to grate," Amanda said, soaking in the sunlight that streamed through the kitchen window. Mickey had been right—it was a beautiful clear day today, perfect weather for his birthday party.

"So Caleb, it's obvious who *you* think will win the football match today—hah! I just want you to know that I admire your persistent belief in your team. It's quite pitiful really, but I do congratulate your devotion." Fabio perched on a stool and completely obliterated it from sight.

Amanda tried not to stare, but it was hard not to. The high stool was completely dwarfed under Fabio.

"Amanda, there you are!" Sophie burst into the kitchen looking all flustered, "I'm so glad I found you in time. I have a confession."

"Oh?"

"Yes—I was dropping off some meat at Black Rhino Lodge and happened to mention we were having a birthday party for Mickey." She fiddled with her keys unhappily. "I don't know how it happened, but before I knew it all five of the guests were piled in the Landie and coming back with me. I think it was the blonde woman who somehow invited herself, and everyone else too. I'm so sorry."

Sophie was gazing at her so beseechingly, pleading for her to understand.

Amanda glanced at Caleb but he was engrossed in

conversation with Fabio. So Caleb had told Sophie about her most ungracious welcoming of the guests.

"Oh Sophie, you needn't worry about me, I'll do my best to behave," Amanda promised, shifting guiltily, wondering if she should apologise.

"Behave?" Sophie's peel of laughter startled her: "You are funny Amanda, and you say it with such a straight face! I'm just sorry that all your sugar will be used up with so many guests!"

Before Amanda could answer, Sophie had breezed on. Amanda could hear her snapping out brisk instructions to Mickey about firewood for the *braai*.

"Caleb?" Jeff wandered into the room, looking as if he was in another world.

"Dad?"

"Caleb," Jeff repeated, his brows drawn together, "have you been hunting lately?"

Caleb shook his head, looking puzzled, "No. Why?"

Jeff shrugged, "It's just that I seem to have fewer cartridges than I thought I had." He ran a hand through his hair. "Perhaps I counted wrong. I don't *think* I did, but you never know." He drifted out the back door, head down in thought.

Amanda stared after him. Caleb shrugged.

"Grandpa! Grandma!" Penny's clear voice pierced the morning air, startling a couple of buck that were grazing near the fence. They bounded into the shelter of a nearby tree.

"Oh, man..." Amanda sighed. She had forgotten that the grandparents would be coming. They would want to know why she hadn't visited them after all this time. "They must think me so ungrateful."

She tipped the carrots into Caleb's bowl and stirred it in, only half paying attention as she looked up to watch the five tourists make themselves at home around the *braai*. The big leader, with his safari outfit and black hat, was bellowing out his knowledge in a loud voice as usual. His flashy little friend picked her way daintily across the soft ground with a series of squeals as her high heels sank into the ground.

"Hey Amanda, can I buy you some high heels for your birthday? They seem to be quite exciting."

Amanda turned to see both Caleb and Fabio grinning at her. Smiling, she fluttered her eyelashes and answered in a high-pitched falsetto, "Oh Caleb, what a delightful thought, thank you." She turned away, ears red at the image of the two pairs of high heels lying unused in her suitcase.

With the carrots stirred into the rest of the cake mixture, Amanda retrieved the greased tin from Caleb's hand and poured the mix into it. He absently followed and grabbed a wooden spoon to scrape out the dish into the tin.

Mickey burst into the kitchen. "Matches, Mandy, chop-chop!"

Amanda shrugged, "Don't ask me, I just work here."

Caleb spread out his hands when Mickey looked his way.

"Oh, you guys are useless," Mickey muttered, rummaging under the stove.

"Try the broom cupboard," Fabio suggested. "You guys usually keep them there."

With no other ideas to go on, Mickey opened the broom cupboard and pulled out a box of matches. All three turned to look at Fabio curiously.

He grinned sheepishly and shrugged.

"Oh no! Trouble," Amanda muttered under her breath, watching through the window as the blonde guest approached the house. Amanda turned to the sink and began to wash dishes, hoping to escape detection. In spite of her note to Amanda, the woman had not been overly-eager to chat on the game walk—was she coming in to talk now? This surely wasn't the right time, with Fabio here as well?

The woman looked just as harassed and fearful as the day she had first come.

Perhaps now is *as good a time as any,* Amanda thought, scrubbing the mixing bowl vigorously as she remembered how the woman had darted nervously out from the lodge and thrust the note at her before dashing back inside.

"Hello, good to see you again."

Amanda listened to Caleb's warm greeting and sighed. How did the man always appear to be genuinely pleased to see people? It was a skill she definitely lacked, and wasn't sure she had the patience to develop.

"This is Fabio, our neighbour. Fabio, this is our guest,

uh—"

"Michelle," the woman softly supplied her name.

Amanda could feel the woman's eyes on her back. She dove deeper into the soapy water, hoping the woman would go away. She wasn't ready for this. Memories of her own unpleasant behaviour plagued her.

There was an awkward silence. No one appeared to be moving.

"Would you like to join us?" Caleb offered.

At the ludicrous offer, Amanda glanced over her shoulder to see the blonde woman settle down on a stool shyly. What on earth was Caleb thinking? Surely he knew how uncomfortable Amanda must be feeling!

He glanced her way, his eyes saying "What else could I do?"

Sighing in resignation, Amanda dumped the last spoon into the rack and dried her hands.

This was called 'Eat pride'. Taking a deep breath, she forced a smile to her face, and turned around. The woman was already watching her, her eyes large.

Amanda approached and held out her hand, "Hi, I'm sure you remember me. Amanda."

Smiling tentatively, the woman grasped her hand and shook it, "Michelle Tanner. I'm married to the short blonde man. Eric Tanner."

Amanda nodded politely, glanced at Caleb, and then said, "Would anyone like anything to drink?"

"Coffee. Three sugars." Fabio immediately ordered.

Three sugars! Amanda stared at Fabio in disbelief. Did he realise what a precious commodity sugar was?

"Three sugars Amanda," Caleb said with a straight face, "you heard the man."

"Ha! And what will you have?" Amanda demanded to know.

"Just one," Caleb answered meekly. "And you Michelle?"

"Black tea please, no milk or sugar," Michelle answered, her eyes following Amanda until Amanda began to grow uncomfortable.

Caleb grinned at Amanda, flashing an unspoken message with his eyes: *Well here is one person you should be pleased with.*

He turned to Michelle. "So Michelle, what made you choose Zimbabwe as a holiday location?" Caleb asked conversationally.

Amanda paused to glance at the visitor and was surprised at the confusion in her face.

"Umm, we've been doing some touring...I know my husband and I are planning to end our tour in Johannesburg." She hesitated nervously and glanced towards the back door just as the tall lean guest strode into the room and looked around as though he owned it.

Amanda stiffened.

"Well well, if it isn't our feisty little friend," the man declared, raking his eyes over her.

"Well well yourself," Amanda retorted, unable to help herself. The man really irked her; no wonder he was the only one of the party who wasn't married. He was so cocky!

Fabio rocked back against the counter and folded his arms against his chest, his eyes alight with interest.

The big man finally broke their locked gaze and looked over at the blonde woman, "I was wondering where you'd got to—why don't you come out and enjoy the sun?"

"I'm just making Michelle tea," Amanda heard herself say firmly.

"Well, Michelle can drink her tea outside," the man said, "can't you?"

"She's drinking it with us," Amanda said with finality, and thumped the mug down in front of Michelle emphatically.

"If that's the way it is then I'll join you."

Sighing heavily, Amanda asked, "What do you want to drink?"

"Nothing." He smiled smugly and looked across at Caleb and then at Fabio. "I don't believe we've met. I'm Allen Fairbelt."

"Fabio." Fabio took the man's hand but he did not smile. Amanda watched the visitor curl up in pain under Fabio's lingering handshake, his lips tightening into a white line. Clearly Fabio liked the man just about as much as she did.

Amanda glanced at Caleb, who was caught between playing host and feeling vindicated.

Allen Fairbelt clearly did not have a talent for making friends. Warmed by the support of Fabio and Caleb, Amanda settled down beside Michelle.

"So where you from, Michelle?"

Was it her imagination or did the woman glance nervously at Allen?

"Uh—we flew in from Sydney."

"But that wasn't your original starting point?" Amanda guessed.

"Prague," Fairbelt cut in, ignoring a question that Caleb had just asked him.

Amanda's brow rose. What was the man doing listening to their conversation while involved in his own?

"I see you are very protective of Michelle," Amanda challenged, holding his eyes which burned with sudden anger, or was it fear?

Once again he was the first to look away.

"What about yourself, Amanda, what are you doing in Zimbabwe?" Michelle encouraged, breaking the silence.

Amanda reluctantly met the worried gaze of the woman before her. Something was very wrong here.

"There's not much to tell," Amanda said, unwilling to open up. It was strange how easy she had found it to fit into the Jacobs family and how comfortable she had been to share about herself, but definitely not with this woman—or with Fairbelt.

"I'm from Scotland; I'm here spending time here with my friends," was all she said.

Michelle nodded, as though enlightened, but her eyes said that her mind was far away.

Just then Penny rushed into the kitchen, her cheeks flushed with excitement. "The meat is cooked, do you want to come out and say grace?"

Fabio thumped forward as he brought the stool back onto all four legs. "Now we're talking!"

He hustled them all out of the kitchen with his arms outstretched, and then strode past them rubbing his hands. "Jeff, you're getting slow in your old age. My stomach was rumbling hours ago."

"No doubt," Jeff answered dryly, looking pointedly at Fabio's extended stomach. "Where's Georgie and his family?"

"Should be on their way." Fabio, seemingly immune to the heat, poked at the meat that was still on the grid over the fire.

Amanda, standing near Caleb, couldn't believe how many people had come.

Mickey was dribbling a football through a shouting crowd of teenagers that must be his school friends, towards a slender girl who looked lost between the two shoes that marked the goal posts. Penny was hopping hopefully around Sophie, and behind her stood two girls with little shorts and grubby feet, both pleading for Sophie to say "yes" to whatever the question was.

Then there were the older people, gathered together on deck chairs under the shade of the pepper tree; the mothers hovering around the table that had been brought outdoors, checking that everything necessary was on it; and all the men standing around the fire, turning over the barbequing meat—no, what was it the family called it? A *braai*, not a barbeque. Amanda shrugged: *Same thing.*

Andy stood apart from everyone, watching with arms folded across his chest. Amanda's heart went out to him, but not enough for her to go and join him. She didn't have the strength to try and encourage him to open up. When his eyes met hers she turned away and pretended to be listening to Caleb and the man he was talking to.

"What a row!" Jeff said, coming up beside her.

Amanda shook her head. "I haven't the faintest clue how you're going to get everyone's attention."

"Watch this!" Lifting his fingers to his mouth he let off a piercing whistle, which had the effect of stopping everyone in their tracks—everyone except Mickey, who pulled the ball back around his body with his right leg and then slotted it behind the goalie with his left foot.

"Two-nil, and in the final minute of play!" he yelled, punching the air.

"Whatever!" a chorus of voices protested.

"Mickey!" Jeff called warningly, "Let's thank the Lord. Come over here, Son."

Putting his hand on Mickey's shoulder, Jeff prayed: "Lord Jesus, we thank You for this wonderful sunshine and for the first rains yesterday. Thank You for blessing us with Mickey these eighteen years, and for all the joy he brings to our lives. I just pray that You would continue to bless him, and guide him into the future that You have planned for him. Thank You for this delicious food, and may the rest of the day be filled with fun as we spend time together. In Your Name we pray. Amen."

"Amen!" came the combined response.

"Watch, it'll be Grandpa that leads the way," Caleb said, leaning in close. "He never follows protocol, it drives Mom crazy."

Amanda grinned to see Jack fulfil Caleb's prediction as he strode over to the table with his plate, the meat already on it, and proceeded to help himself to the thick white stuff that Mickey called *sadza*. No-one but Sophie seemed agitated with Jack's forwardness; Sophie buzzed around him, telling him off for his lack of manners, while at the same time apologising to the ladies that they were not being served first. Jack just dug into the food on the table and ladled it onto his plate, whistling to himself as he did so.

"I like your family," Amanda said, smiling. She glanced unconsciously towards the spot where Andy had been standing, reconsidering her statement, but he was gone.

The afternoon sped by. Amanda couldn't remember a time when she had enjoyed the company of so many people, but everyone she met was friendly and warm. Even the tourists sought her out to chat with her, despite their unfortunate initial encounter—all except Allen Fairbelt.

Just before they left Michelle touched her arm lightly and whispered, "Amanda, be careful. I don't know what the connection is but Allen Fairbelt knows you and I think he's got something bad planned. That's what I've been wanting to tell you – I just didn't know how to—"

"Michelle!"

The woman's hunted eyes flicked over in the direction of the waiting group. She impulsively touched Amanda's arm, "Watch yourself, Amanda."

Amanda nodded, searching the woman's face for any clues that might give away what was going on, but Michelle turned quickly away and hurried after her friends. Michelle's warning was a far cry from the one she had expected. Not only had Michelle not accused Fairbelt of poaching, but she thought Fairbelt knew her.

Allen Fairbelt knows me? Amanda stared across at the departing group, her eyes on the lanky figure of Allen Fairbelt with his cowboy hat jammed down on his head. The woman must be wrong. *Yet why be so determined to warn me? This just doesn't match up. If Fairbelt is not the one shooting the impala, then...?*

"Well, now you've met my friends." Mickey sauntered over and slung an arm over her shoulder in his usual style. "What did you think of them?"

"Noisy!" Amanda exclaimed. "But nice. The girl in the goal posts—was she Suzanne?" As she spoke she caught a glimpse of Andy driving the tourists out of the gate. What on earth could the woman have meant? She didn't know Allen Fairbelt, did she?

Shrugging the woman's words off, Amanda turned back to Mickey. "She was a decent goalie."

Mickey nodded. "That was her. Did you get to speak to her?"

Amanda shook her head regretfully. She would have loved to have met the girl who had won over the lively Mickey.

"Hey little brother, take your hands off the woman, she's coming with me." Caleb strolled up, hands in his pockets.

Mickey didn't move. He grinned cheekily at his brother, "Is that so?"

Caleb suddenly dove at Mickey's legs. Amanda squealed and ducked out from under Mickey's arm as Caleb connected with Mickey's legs toppling him over.

Penny shot by, her two friends at her heels, all yelling at once.

"Haven't they been left behind?" Amanda asked, pointing after the girls as Sophie came up to them and let out a big sigh, running her hands through her hair.

Amanda followed the girls thoughtfully with her eyes. Had Mickey or Penny spoken to their mother about Penny's night excursions?

"Nope, they're here for the night. We'll take them in to church with us tomorrow and they'll go home from there. Wow, I'm exhausted!"

"You must be! Here, let me help you with those dishes."

"Wait!" Caleb called, flipping Mickey over onto his back and pinning him down with an arm across his chest. "Mom, I just got a phone call from the South Mission. They want me to come and check on a possible outbreak of cholera. I was hoping Amanda could come with me and see the Mission—if you'd like to, Amanda?" he checked.

Amanda hovered between Sophie and Caleb, unsure what to say.

"Go on with him," Sophie encouraged. "Just bring her safely home, Caleb."

Amanda inwardly cringed at the subtle undercurrents in Sophie's warning. Why did Sophie always remind Caleb to take care of her? Did she think Caleb wouldn't?

"Hey Caleb..." Mickey propped onto one elbow and tried to appease Caleb as he rose forebodingly. "She didn't mean it like that."

"Of course she did," Caleb answered darkly. "She just can't forgive me, can she?"

Mickey's eyes met Amanda's knowingly but he said nothing more.

"So—you want to come, Amanda?" Caleb asked, still looking after his mother as she headed into the house.

"I'd love to." Amanda followed his gaze. "Let me just grab my hat." She flashed Mickey a small smile and dashed into the house. What a shame that such a pleasant day might be ruined by one thoughtless comment.

"Please God, show me what to do," Amanda whispered as she found her borrowed hat squashed under the sofa, which had been rolled back over it. "Mediating is a not a strong point for me."

Chapter 14

S tanding just behind Caleb's shoulder, Amanda had a good view of the village huts and the villagers while still feeling fairly sheltered from curious eyes. The crowd that was gathering around them felt quite overwhelming to her. Little children with threadbare clothes darted in and out amongst the adults' feet. One small girl staggered past carrying a baby almost as big as herself. Women paused and turned slowly to look at Caleb and Amanda, careful to keep the buckets of water balanced on their heads. Some of the women had babies tied to their backs in colourful towels, round little cheeks pressed against their mother's backs as they stared out at the world through big brown eyes.

A few of the people looked ghastly. Their eyes were wide and hollow and they seemed to stare right through Amanda. She examined them with sharp quick glances, noting their hopeless expressions and weary movements.

"Doctor Caleb! We are glad you're back." A man who could have been twenty or forty stepped forward. He didn't greet Caleb with the usual exuberance that Amanda had seen elsewhere; it was as though he was too tired. His shoulders slumped beneath a huge invisible, yet somehow tangible, weight.

"What's been going on, Tobias?" Caleb asked, concern in his eyes.

Amanda pressed right up against his back and unconsciously grabbed a bunch of his shirt in her fist as a group of little children crowded around her and tried to hold her hand, and patted her jeans to attract her attention. One little boy even bent down and stroked her toes, touching each red toe nail one at a time through the leather bush-sandals Sophie had lent her.

"Have people been using the river for drinking water again?" Caleb strode forward and Amanda trotted close behind him, smiling nervously at the children, Caleb's shirt still in her tight grasp.

The children looked so sad and beseeching, little eyes that had grown old before their time, and they were just as close on her tail as she was on Caleb's. Bare toes left soft footprints in the dust. One little girl reached up and slid a hand into Amanda's. The tiny palm was rough and calloused, and the wide eyes so entreating, that Amanda felt her discomfort drop away. Other children pressed around her, separating her from Caleb who moved on ahead, but Amanda barely noticed that she'd relinquished her grip on his shirt. She could not even begin to imagine what kind of life these children lived—but it was a far cry from her own relatively comfortable existence.

Amanda felt her heart flipping over in her chest. She was moved more than she had ever thought possible. It was as though all these little eyes looking up at her were asking something of her—yet what did she have to give?

She looked away from them, turning the question over in her mind as she made her way over towards Caleb and Tobias, her pack of adoring little followers sticking to her like glue.

"We have warned them not to use the river, but our water pump broke down and our well was dry." Tobias looked around at the people helplessly. "So many are sick, but there is not enough medicine."

"What the villagers need is proper education," Caleb said severely, "and then they need to apply that education to their lives. Where is *Mai* Shiri?"

They were approaching a whitewashed building with 'Hospital' painted over the doorway in big black scrawling letters. Tobias pushed open the door.

"Her husband went into the city to look for work last week, and she went with him. The children have not been taught since she left."

Amanda shook her head in disbelief, very aware of the little hand still cradled in her own.

Caleb grimaced, his mouth working angrily, though no words came out. He looked furious as he flipped open his case and then paused again: "And Pastor T?"

"Gone to the other Mission."

Jaw clenched, Caleb turned back to his medical bag.

Amanda watched him deftly arrange the supplies into an accessible order. He worked swiftly and silently, long hands moving fast with practise.

"Alright, line the sick up," Caleb ordered.

Tobias hurried to the door and shouted out something. People slowly bunched together in what resembled a queue—only it was at least three people wide. The elderly were brought to the front, and then the men. The women and children clustered together at the back of the line.

"This is ridiculous!" Caleb swung on Amanda. "These people need support and education. The government provides no funding whatsoever, yet it expects their devotion to the government's cause. The two Mission pastors are stretched between our three Missions, just like the other doctor and I are, and now the school teacher has run off into town, abandoning her post! And what's more, I don't blame her for going either, she just couldn't make ends meet here; no-one can," he hissed, and then slowly let out his breath and tried to regain control of his emotions.

Amanda nodded, helpless.

Caleb's dark eyes burned with frustration, but he nodded for Tobias to let the first patient in.

"*Mai* Mutsenga." He smiled in genuine affection as Tobias guided in an elderly woman and helped her to the designated chair. Caleb's muscular frame seemed so strong and healthy beside the toothless little woman, who was leaning heavily on her shaking cane as she teetered over the chair before collapsing onto it.

Amanda wasn't able to follow the conversation after that. It seemed Caleb could speak the native language fluently. He would ask something and after a moment of thinking the woman would touch a part of her body.

"Amanda, would you pass me that bottle there, please?" Caleb twisted around on his haunches: "The morphine."

Amanda shifted through the supplies and gently extracted a dark bottle. "This one?"

Amanda watched Caleb's hands as he gently prodded the woman's stomach—long lean hands.

175

"*Mai* Mutsenga has cancer, Amanda."

All thoughts of strong hands and tousled hair evaporated as Amanda gazed at the elderly woman through new eyes of compassion.

"Where—where is it?" she asked, smiling tentatively at the watery eyes of *Mai* Mutsenga.

"Everywhere," Caleb answered harshly.

"And she isn't able to get treatment?!" Amanda gazed compassionately at the woman, already knowing the answer to her question. "Surely there is more that you can do for her?"

Caleb rose, his frame straightening slowly, his eyes dark and piercing.

Amanda held her breath but forced her gaze to stay steady.

"So you think I don't know what I'm doing?" Caleb challenged, his eyes scrutinizing her face for answers.

Amanda closed her eyes and rubbed her forehead in confusion, "It's not that at all. It just doesn't make sense. I mean—I'm not questioning your judgement, but..." She trailed off and stared at *Mai* Mutsenga and then at Caleb's chin.

"I'm sorry Caleb," she said humbly. "I just wish there was something more that we could do other than masking the problem." Her little friend was still at her side. Amanda sighed softly, her eyes taking in the threadbare clothes of the child. "I wish there was more that *I* could do."

"Well—there isn't!" Caleb glared at her. Amanda searched his face; he was inexplicably upset by her comment. "Now either you can help me or you can leave, but I can't have a critic while I'm trying to the very best that I can with what I have. What will you do?"

"I'll stay and help," Amanda whispered meekly.

Amanda hovered around Caleb the rest of the afternoon, mutely obeying his barked orders. She kept an eye out for the little girl, who had been called away, but did not see her again. Amanda was sorry she had not been able to talk more with the child and dig up some information on what it was like to grow up in such poverty. Was the child happy? Was her family happy? It was more than just a research question to investigate and answers to keep Doug at bay;

she had met with individuals now—not just distant faces—and it had changed everything about the way she saw her work.

The sun had long since set when a man came up alongside Amanda and offered her some water.

Caleb swung around and glared at the man, demanding: "Is that water boiled?"

The man nodded mildly and backed away a step.

"Thank you." Amanda smiled at him and accepted the water, casually tucking it behind a chair leg. "I brought some water with me, but I will keep that there for now." She was touched by his thoughtfulness, but Caleb had thought to pack a couple of bottles of water from Shamwari, which she had been sipping throughout the afternoon. She wouldn't risk drinking potentially contaminated water.

The man smiled and stepped back a couple of paces, beckoning for Amanda to follow.

"I have been talking with the leaders of the village. Would you be willing to come and teach our children twice a week? We need a teacher, even if it's only part time."

Shocked, Amanda stammered: "Me? No, no—I'm not a teacher."

"But you are educated," the man persisted. "Our children need to be taught." He gestured towards the unseen children outside, their young voices heard above the lower rumbles of the adults. "They like you."

Amanda thought again of her research project. This was a wonderful opportunity to get right in there and be able to observe the children for symptoms of depression while she taught them. It would be true participative research. She couldn't see Doug having a problem with it. In fact, if the telephone lines weren't so bad she might have wondered if he had contacted someone and set this all up; it would be the kind of thing that Doug would do.

"Well?" the man pressed, sensing a weakening in her.

Amanda shook her head. "It wouldn't be right. I am a researcher. I want to research the people of Zimbabwe, the children of Zimbabwe. I am not a teacher."

She watched his shoulders slump slightly, and then just as quickly lift again as he said, "Well, you don't have to answer me now, think about it and then let me know."

"But—" Amanda began to protest but the man was already heading towards the door, waving goodbye as he went.

"Well *he* didn't want to take 'no' for an answer," Amanda muttered, wondering that she was not completely against the idea. If she had received such a proposition three weeks ago she would have shoved it forcefully back at the person who had even dared suggest such a ludicrous thing; yet here she was, daring to consider it.

"Oh no Amanda, you're letting yourself go," she breathed, glancing across at Caleb who was carefully setting a child's leg in a white plaster-of-Paris cast. "You have a Great Aunt to deliver, parents to greet, and a job and sick friend to get back to. Don't lose focus now!"

She strolled over to the window and stared out at the white moon against the navy blue sky, at the crowds of shadowy figures still lined up outside the hospital, and at a tired-looking woman with one baby on her back and two clinging to her skirt, standing slightly apart from everyone else. Here and there she could see little flares of camp fires and spirals of grey rising up against the dark sky. She could smell the wood smoke; she breathed in deeply, enjoying the pleasant feeling that it invoked inside of her. It reminded her of childhood camps that Kari and she had held in the back of Great Aunt Marie's garden.

She stared out at the night. It was strange how a place could grow on you so quickly.

A grinning face suddenly popped up on the other side of the window. Amanda squealed and jumped back, her heart racing as the child wobbled, clawed at the window sill for a hold and then abruptly disappeared.

"Amanda, stop playing about and come and help me." Caleb didn't turn around to look at her.

"I'm right there." Hand still on her chest trying to soothe her frantic fright, Amanda grabbed a clean pair of rubber gloves. She hadn't the heart to tell Caleb how many people were still queued up outside the hospital waiting to see him.

Chapter 15

A manda clambered sheepishly up onto the passenger seat and shot a quick glance at the tight jawline beside her. Caleb started the Jeep in silence, his hand idling on the gear stick. He didn't look her way as he finally shifted into gear.

They raced along the dirt track in silence. Caleb was grim.

It was very humid and the dust they churned up must be sticking to the sweat that had started trickling down Amanda's face within minutes of getting into the car.

"The wind is so hot!" Amanda said, and fanned her face.

Caleb said nothing.

"Maybe it will rain later."

Still nothing.

"Okay!" Amanda burst out, "so I commented that I wished there was more that I could do. You took it like I was challenging your professionalism. You got it all wrong. My conscience wouldn't let me stay silent; I always thought I had a tough childhood but when I look at..."

"Your conscience!" Caleb exclaimed, cutting her off. "For goodness sake Amanda, you practically accused me of having no heart; of being uncompassionate! And you didn't do this once, or twice, but you did it four times! Four times you got in between me and my patients and interfered. You'd think I was out to murder them through negligence!"

"That's not fair!" Amanda was incredulous. "You're exaggerating dramatically."

Both stared straight ahead, eyes burning, waiting for the other to weaken first and break the stormy silence. It was Amanda who spoke first, and only because she couldn't keep her thoughts in.

"All I said was the man needed a hospital."

179

"Well, what about the child?" Caleb shot back, knuckles white on the wheel.

"The child *did* need more care than she was getting and I assumed you knew who to contact that might be able to help."

Caleb growled but said nothing.

"And that other child..." She shrugged, unable to speak; fresh tears came to her eyes as Amanda remembered the peaked little face with tight skin moulded over a tiny rib cage and his bloated stomach. She shrugged again, trying to swallow back her tears, knowing she wouldn't be able to hold back the flood if she continued talking.

Caleb glanced at her, and after a minute or so he eased up on his maniacal driving, but his stony expression remained firmly in place.

"You've projected your own feelings of shortcomings and worries into this," Amanda choked out when the clog in her throat was almost gone. "It's all your memories about that boy, James Stewart. It affects everything you think about other peoples' attitudes to you."

The conversation with Mickey came back to mind.

"You're going to *have* to forgive yourself and let it go. If you claim Jesus took your sins away through His death, then you're going to have to start *believing* He really did do this for you, even in this horrible situation!"

Caleb snorted.

"Well, it's true," Amanda insisted, turning back to face the road just as a huge antelope leaped across the road. "Watch it!" she yelled, arms flying up to shield her head.

Braking hard, Caleb just avoided hitting the animal. "Suicidal kudu!"

Breathing hard, Amanda didn't wait to catch her breath. She was determined not to let this opportunity go, even if her blood was coursing through her body at twice the usual speed.

"Everyone in your family is blaming themselves, and its time someone took the first step to move on beyond this tragic accident—and I say that *you* are the one to do it, Caleb." She peered over her shoulder into the darkness, wondering what had happened to the animal.

"Whoa! And since when did Miss Scottish think she can

just rock up and start sorting me and my family out?"

Amanda gulped, tears stinging her eyes at the harsh words. Thoughts of her own family's messed-up situation flooded through her. Maybe Caleb was right, maybe she was the wrong one to challenge him. What had she ever done to try and mend the broken ties in her family?

But I'd never find the courage to confront my own motley crew, God. Amanda shook her head at the thought. *I just hoped that I could try and do something for this family that has welcomed me so warmly. I'm sorry for messing up, Jesus, and maybe interfering with Your plans for the Jacobs...*

"I'm sorry Amanda, I shouldn't have snapped at you." Caleb's voice sounded far away, but when she looked at him he wiggled his eyebrows at her and gave her a lopsided smile. "You must have hit home."

Amanda stared at him, taken aback, and then shrugged. "I guess you know I pretty much say what I think by now."

He pulled a face and Amanda reluctantly giggled; Caleb grinned fully then.

They drove in silence for the next twenty miles, Caleb whistling under his breath while Amanda mulled over their conversation. It was annoying that Caleb had apparently put their brief battle behind him. Amanda tried to study him covertly, hoping she didn't attract his attention. His straight nose and defined jaw, with that quirky smile and ruffled hair, made quite an attractive package, but it wasn't fun when he got mad—then everything about him froze over.

He's hurting, but that doesn't excuse him, Amanda told herself firmly. *And just because I find him attractive it doesn't mean he can get off the hook so easily. He can sit there as chirpy as anything, but it doesn't change anything—*

"What doesn't change anything?" Caleb asked, his eyes glinting.

Amanda frowned at him. She must have been talking aloud again! "Never mind, the main thing is that you need to think through this, Caleb. You're hanging onto something that you should have let go of a long time ago." She held her breath and crossed her fingers as she waited for a fresh spat of anger, but his expression remained open.

Letting out her breath cautiously, Amanda said: "I've been thinking about this. I realise that I'm not much of a

Christian, I don't depend on God like you or your family does..."

Thoughts of the family prayer times and Jeff reading exciting Bible stories came to mind. Young Penny would be squashed into the chair with Jeff, and everyone else scattered around the room as he brought a story to life, Penny sometimes reading the women's lines.

And then there were the informal times when Amanda had been so aware of God being present in this family, like Penny singing along with her favourite Christian band while making toast for breakfast, and Mickey strumming on his guitar as he turned Scripture verses into songs. And how many times had she seen Sophie's lips moving in silent prayer as she charged up and down in her hectic day?

"What I'm trying to get at is that all of you love God—like really *love* Him—He's not just a pleasant addition to your lives." Amanda flung a hand in Caleb's direction. "I mean even *I* can see that you are devoted to Him; me—a person who has had little time for God."

Caleb quirked a brow at her, but she could see he was listening.

"So what I don't get, Caleb, is how you can be so devoted to God but yet still not *believe* Him?"

"Whoa, hold up now," Caleb interjected. "Where are you getting that idea from?"

Flipping her dark pony tail off her shoulder, Amanda said, "Your dad read that story last night about the lame man who was lowered through the roof. Jesus forgave him and healed him. I understand that Jesus forgives all who ask Him to forgive them because of the cross, but if you're not letting go, then you either are saying you don't believe Jesus has forgiven you, or you think His death just isn't good enough for you to accept."

The Jeep seemed to jerk to the side of the road of its own accord. Amanda glanced nervously at Caleb. She sure chose bad times to debate such deep issues.

Caleb's silence was deafening. Amanda's ears roared as she watched the still profile, memorising his features. Caleb was quite a man, a man of deep emotions and thoughts.

She sighed softly. She had a gut feeling that she wasn't going to be here much longer. She just hoped that by the time she got her flight out the country they would at least part on a good note.

In an attempt to lighten the air she said, "I'll just add here that I don't fancy landing in a ditch for the night while there are all these critters running around the bush."

"What a nightmare—stuck out in the bush with you!"

Shocked, Amanda swung on Caleb, her mouth opened indignantly.

He grinned, "Just joking." He began to whistle again casting long glances at her to see her reaction.

"And what do you mean by that?" Amanda demanded, relieved the air had cleared, "I'll have you know I am excellent company, even when out in the bush!"

Caleb chuckled and nonchalantly leant back in his seat, "I don't know about that. Last time you were out in the bush with me you were stressed out about the lions and about us driving over trees."

The sound of crickets crowded the air, and that familiar high-pitched ringing. "I don't think I've heard the cicada at night before," Amanda remarked. "It doesn't annoy me now as much as when I first arrived." She let out a soft breath, her thoughts turning to Allen Fairbelt and the poaching. She was so confused. She had convinced herself that he was the poacher and that she would solve the Jacobs' poaching problems. But according to Michelle, Fairbelt was actually *her* problem—not the Jacobs'.

"Caleb, I've been thinking a lot about the poaching." Amanda moistened her lips, her brow furrowed as she asked cautiously, "Is it possible that someone, like Allen Fairbelt—that tourist, could be the one responsible?"

Caleb glanced at her curiously, "I know you don't like him but I didn't realise you would start accusing him of something as serious as poaching. You know the consequences for poaching are severe here."

"No—it's not because I don't like him," Amanda hastily denied, but her conscience twisted inside of her. Wasn't it? What had he really done to indicate he was the poacher? His only crime was to have arrived at the same time the poaching had started and to be a very unlikable man.

"But to answer your question—no, I don't think Fairbelt is our poacher. Dad thinks it could be one of our workers from the compound."

"Oh?" Amanda was surprised.

"Yeah," Caleb nodded. "Those wounded impala were shot in very awkward places. It was definitely an inexperienced hunter and they were not able to follow the impala to finish them off. Maybe they were frightened, maybe they wanted to save their bullets." He shrugged. "Maybe they just couldn't keep up."

Amanda's breath slowed, Caleb's words ringing through her head. "Maybe they wanted to save their bullets," she echoed, then shook her head. The idea forming was ludicrous. She had already wrongly accused Fairbelt, although he didn't know it, of a crime that was likely not his; she'd better not do it again. But then again, it made a lot of sense...

"Anyhow, now that we're talking about family, I noticed you don't speak much about yours. You have a sister, Kari, right?"

He had changed the subject so quickly!

Amanda blinked slowly, leaning back to look up at the stars. "No, Kari's my best friend." Amanda stared up at the night sky. She might have known that if she challenged him on his family he would want to know about hers. "So what do you want to know?"

"Just curious. You always seem cagey when your family is brought up. I take it that things aren't exactly pretty with *your* family, either."

"You got that right," Amanda nodded. She shrugged; what did it matter if she spoke about her family? "I don't communicate much with my parents anymore. They abandoned we four children when we were growing up, and went off to look after other people and *their* children. They're missionary doctors," Amanda said, answering Caleb's unspoken question.

"Ah."

"Yeah." Amanda watched the road light up ahead as they came around the bend. "Ruth was the oldest and I think she coped best. She bossed Polly and me around. I think Polly was glad to have someone telling her what to do, but I hated it. Every time Ruth got on my case I got mad because she was doing what our parents should have been there to do."

"And where was the fourth child while this was happening?" Caleb asked.

"Cobs? Cobs was put into a different boarding school, a boys' school. We saw him only on holidays. He was so much fun to be with, growing up. I got on with him best in my family. But something changed when he went into high school. He went off the rails. He pulled away, grew really bitter, and eventually we stopped seeing him. I haven't seen him for years. None of us knows how to get hold of him." Amanda laughed bitterly: "Perhaps he chose the best way—breaking off connection with the family completely. It must be much less complicated."

"And Kari, your friend?"

At the mention of her friend Amanda smiled, "Kari is the closest thing I have to a family. Her parents were killed in a car crash when she was about ten. She often came back with me for the holidays to Great Aunt Marie's house. If it wasn't for her I think I would have taken Cobs' route out."

"And this Great Aunt Marie?" Caleb asked, "Where does she fit in the picture?"

"Everywhere!" Amanda exclaimed, "Aunt Marie with her iron fist and tight words. She was my father's aunt. Those were long holidays when we landed up at her place."

"But if it wasn't for her you wouldn't have had a place to go?" Caleb confirmed.

Uncomfortable, Amanda nodded, pressing her finger tips together. "I guess so."

"And was she supportive? Did she check on how you were doing at school, and socially?" Caleb asked in a quiet voice.

Amanda nodded again. She didn't like what Caleb's questions were doing. They were giving a whole different twist on Great Aunt Marie that she had never thought of, and it wasn't fun.

"So she basically was the parental figure in your life."

"Okay, so you've made your point," Amanda snapped. "Don't rub it in so hard."

"And now you are going to South Africa because...?"

"Because Great Aunt Marie died and decided I was the one to carry her body around the world, that's why! I am her undertaker! I wish you wouldn't ask me all these questions. Now you see what an unhappy family life I have."

"It's almost as thrilling as mine, but apparently more blatantly disrupted than mine as well." Caleb flashed Amanda a smile. "Cheer up lass. If I recall right it was you that reminded me we're suppose to believe God is interested in our lives."

Only the light at the front door was on when they arrived back at the farm house. Using a remote to open the gate, they parked under the spreading acacia tree and Amanda waited while Caleb locked the Jeep.

She giggled. "It's open-topped; why lock it?"

He looked sheepishly at her. "Habit?"

"The stars are so bright here. It must be because there aren't so many city lights around," she said, leaning against the side of the 4x4.

"My favourite is Orion's Belt." Caleb pointed out the three stars in a row. "I used to imagine big Orion, the warrior, kitted up in it ready for battle."

The phone was ringing when they stepped into the house.

"Kinda late for a phone call," Amanda said, peeping around the lounge door to look at the clock. "It's twelve-fifteen."

"Hello?" Caleb listened. "Just hold on, I'll get her for you." He turned and held the receiver out for Amanda. "It's for you."

Surprised, Amanda took the phone, "Hello? Kari! Yayee!"

Caleb closed the front door and smiled at her as he went into the kitchen, signalling that he would make something to drink. Nodding, Amanda pressed the phone to her ear.

"Oh Amanda, when are you coming home? It's been weeks now and you're still there."

"Kari, is everything okay?" Amanda asked, concerned. It was wonderful to hear the sound of her friend's voice again, but why was Kari phoning so late? "What's happened?"

"Nothing! Everything!"

Amanda's fears were confirmed.

"I'm just so unhappy!" Kari wailed. "I don't know what

to do. I can't talk to Sally because she'll think I'm a nutter and then phone some shrink or something. I wish you were here."

Things were sounding bad, she had never heard Kari so distraught. Amanda was careful to keep her voice soothing and low. "Where are you now?"

"At the flat. Sally's in bed already, she has a big date tomorrow."

Mind racing, Amanda frantically tried to come up with a useful idea. Kari was clearly at the end of her tether. So the big crunch in Kari's pent up emotions had finally come and here she was miles away—too far to be of any real use. *Why God, why now?*

"Kari, I'm still waiting for a plane, but I'll take the first one out—wherever it goes—and get back home as quickly as possible."

"What about Great Aunt Marie?" Tears choked Kari's voice.

Frightened for her friend, Amanda clutched the receiver. This was not the tough, in-control Kari that she knew.

"God knows, Kari," she heard herself answering, and swallowed hard. Shrugging back her thoughts she pressed on. Now was not the time to worry about what Kari would think of her tentative new-found relationship with the God she had rejected for so long.

"I'm all alone, what do I do Amanda? What do I do?"

"Kari, listen to me." Amanda tried to speak calmly but firmly: "I don't know what's going on there but I'll be back as soon as I can." Her heart was thumping fearfully in her chest. She didn't know enough about anorexia to understand what Kari was going through. Were there stages in anorexia? Was Kari at risk of suicide? She was starving herself to death—perhaps she was bone-thin and about to disappear away into nothingness? There was nothing she could do!

Oh God, help me—what do I say?
—Church.

The idea just dropped into Amanda's mind.

Clutching at straws, Amanda said cautiously, "Kari, it's just an idea but rather than you spending the day alone tomorrow, why don't you go to church?"

The silence that followed was so long that Amanda almost thought Kari had hung up. She stared at the mouthpiece for a moment and then was just about to jiggle the phone when she heard a little sob.

"Kari?" She pressed the receiver back up to her ear.

Another little sob.

Eyes closed, Amanda couldn't even think straight to pray, all she knew was that God was going to have to do something to help Kari in the crisis she was in because she was out of her depth. Tomorrow she would phone Samuel Chiwedza and get on his case. It was time to go home.

Chapter 16

"Amanda, wake up."

Groaning, Amanda rolled over, shielding her eyes from the sunlight.

"Amanda, the airport has just phoned. A plane has come in and will leave within the next two hours."

Amanda was wide awake in an instant. "What time is it?"

"Five o'clock. Do you want to take this flight out?"

Kari! Sleep clearing from her eyes, Amanda looked into the gentle eyes of the woman she had come to admire deeply. Sophie was waiting for an answer as though she truly was suggesting that Amanda might stay longer.

"Yes Sophie," Amanda nodded. "I *must* take this flight out."

Sitting on the edge of her bed, Sophie caught her hand, "We'd honestly love you to stay longer. You've just become part of us so quickly."

"And you to me," Amanda answered sincerely, squeezing Sophie's hand, "but I need to go. It's the right time now." God must have heard her desperate prayers that had flowed from her until sleep had claimed her.

Sophie smiled sadly, but nodded. "Alright then. I'll get you a quick breakfast ready. See you just now."

The next hour was a mad rush. Amanda tried to sift through her clothes and separate borrowed stuff from her own. She hurriedly pulled up her sheet and puffed her pillow out. Sophie would probably strip it later, anyway.

Grabbing a piece of paper from her research file she scribbled a quick thank you note, wishing she had nicer writing paper.

This was all happening too quickly, too suddenly for her. "But not too soon," Amanda muttered, the sound of Kari's fearful tears still ringing in her ears.

Amanda pushed her window a little wider and gazed out.

A lone kudu stood beside the water hole, its beautiful curved horns glinting in the morning sunrise—a magnificent, fitting farewell.

"So this is it, God," Amanda breathed, her eyes burning with unshed tears. "Have You done what You wanted to do?"

Red and orange colour splashed across the sky on the horizon, and the early morning dove cooed from nearby. Caleb had called it an Emerald Spotted Wood Dove.

"Just like that, my last morning here," Amanda whispered, swabbing at the tears that landed on her thank-you note. She only succeeded in smudging the letters.

Tucking the note half under her pillow, she slowly zipped up her bag. As she squashed her research file into her kitbag an envelope dropped onto the floor. Picking it up, Amanda studied it. It smelled of lavender.

Mrs May's letter! Amanda rubbed the soft paper between her thumb and finger. It somehow did not seem as fearsome as when Mrs May had handed it to her in the church car park. *But still a little unsettling,* Amanda decided, pushing it back into the research folder.

The last thing she did was to find a spot for Aunt Marie's ashes in her kitbag. She had come too far to misplace her now.

Packed and ready to go, Amanda did not linger in her little room. If she stayed any longer she might have a fresh bout of tears.

She dragged her bag into the kitchen and tears instantly rushed to her eyes as she saw the entire family had turned out to say goodbye, even Andy.

"You have no idea how wonderful this time has been," Amanda whispered as Penny came and slid an arm around her waist. "I didn't want to come and now I'm not sure I want to go."

"We'll keep your bedroom ready for you," Sophie promised, slipping her hand through Amanda's other arm.

"Can we pray a blessing on you before you go?" Jeff asked, coming over and putting a hand on Amanda's head at her assent. "Lord Jesus, thank You for blessing us with Amanda for these weeks, and for how she just mucked in with all of us. Thank You also for the changes we've seen in Amanda while she's been here. Please be with her as she goes on to the next step of her journey. Protect her as she travels and as she completes her business. We ask this in Your Name Jesus—Amen."

"Thank you," Amanda smiled shyly as Jeff pulled her into a hug.

"Do you *have* to go?" Penny asked. "It'll be weird not having you around, and then Caleb will disappear again and—and nothing will be fun anymore!"

"Hey!" Caleb chucked Penny under the chin. "Things *will* be different if I can help it. Okay?"

Penny nodded miserably.

Caleb glanced up at Amanda, "I'll take your bag out to the car. See you there."

"Well, I'll miss our *blethers*," Mickey said as he sauntered up. Amanda was already reaching for his arm before he had quite got it over her shoulder.

"And I'll miss the *sadza*," she grinned up at him. "You'll have to tell me how everything goes," she said, emphasizing 'everything'. "Keep in touch with Kari when you can."

"You bet," he nodded, looking down at her affectionately. "Don't stay away too long."

Amanda's breath grew jerky as Mickey moved away. She glanced across at Andy who looked unsure of himself.

"Bye Andy..." Amanda hesitated, then held out her hand, "I hope things go well for you."

He nodded, shaking her hand stiffly. "And you."

"I wish you didn't have to go!" Penny slid an arm around Amanda. Amanda stroked the soft hair and gently guided the child out of the earshot of the rest of the family. She drew Penny away from her and crouched down so she was on the same eye level as the girl. "I do have to go, but I'm going to miss you so much!"

She really was. She couldn't believe how much her heart seemed to have grown and been filled with so much love.

"I do have a question and I'm hoping you answer me honestly." She met Penny's soft eyes and saw the small squirm. Penny already knew what she was going to ask.

"Penny, that food you were giving to your friend at the fence—was it really food?"

She wasn't surprised when Penny reluctantly shook her head.

"It was your dad's cartridges, wasn't it?"

Penny nodded slowly. "I only wanted to help. Everyone was so busy with their lives and I really wanted to do something to make a difference. I didn't know Jimmy couldn't shoot straight, and then he couldn't kill the wounded impala because he had run out of bullets. I told him he was wrong to have left them like that but there was nothing else he could do." Tears filled her eyes. "There was nothing else *I* could do. We didn't have enough food to give away. Mom would have missed it straight away."

"You dear *bairn!*" Amanda cupped Penny's jaw and smiled. She felt such love for this girl who had such a gentle spirit. "I only wish my heart was as big as yours."

Penny pulled her close. "I'll talk with Dad. He'll understand." She laughed shakily, "Although it's not going to be fun to explain. I'll miss you Mandy. Don't stay away too long."

Amanda closed her eyes, breathing in the scent of the shampooed hair.

"You ready?" Amanda rose and smiled unsteadily as Sophie scooped her into another hug. "Now, I've packed a little travelling lunch for you, and you must phone us when you reach your parents' place. Alright? Here, let me take their number just in case you can't phone us."

Amanda had to dig in her kitbag for her address book. There were so many crossed out numbers for her parents; she hoped she picked the right one. She tried to wipe the corner of her eye discreetly.

At the door she caught Sophie's hand. "Please tell your parents that I am truly sorry I never managed to come and visit them." She hesitated. "It just never seemed to be the right time, but if I come back they'll be a top priority."

"When you come back," Sophie corrected. "I mean that Amanda, I'll be expecting you back."

Warmed, Amanda climbed up onto the seat beside Caleb and watched as Mickey rolled the gate back by hand. The generator must be switched off.

"This is awful," Amanda sniffed, waving at the family until they were only specks in the dust behind them. "This wasn't the way it was meant to happen."

"Is that so?" Caleb didn't look too happy himself.

"No. If I hadn't been packed off to Africa then I would never be leaving here so sad to go. I should never have come."

"Do you really mean that?" Caleb asked, his eyes boring into her.

Amanda shifted, "No, but—but I am sad to go."

At the airport Amanda could barely meet Caleb's eyes. He made light conversation about this and that, joked with Samuel Chiwedza and the elderly man who was now manning the tea tables, and generally seemed as eager to avoid her imminent departure as she was.

"So, how do you like our beautiful country?" Samuel Chiwedza leant over the counter curiously. "My brother says he offered you a teaching post at the Mission school."

"He did?" Caleb looked at Amanda surprised.

Amanda shrugged, "I didn't realise he was your brother, Samuel—yes he did. But I said no. I am a researcher, not a teacher. My intentions would all be wrong if I accepted such a position."

"But you *can* teach," Samuel argued.

"Teach and research," Caleb agreed. "Why don't you consider it?"

"You can't be serious?" Amanda stared at him. "No, it just wouldn't work. I have to finish my undertaker job and then get back to a friend who is in a crisis. Besides, I'm sure my boss would never agree." As she said it Amanda knew she was lying. Doug would be there like a shot, helping pack her bag if necessary, as long as an excellent research opportunity was snatched up.

"Well, my brother said you might come," Samuel persisted.

"You don't look like your brother," Amanda said, diverting the conversation.

"He's my cousin."

"But you said he was your brother," Amanda argued.

Caleb clucked his tongue. "Come on Amanda, don't get

into a fight."

"But he's the one who said—"

Caleb shook his head in mock disappointment.

"Hey!" Amanda lightly punched his shoulder. "If anyone starts a fight it will be you."

"Anyway, here in Africa any member of the family—or outside it—can be called a brother or sister. See?"

Yes, she did see. She liked that.

They checked her luggage in, then mosied slowly over to one of the tables and sat down. The airport was much busier than when she had flown in. Obviously word had travelled about the flight going out. It was quite incredible how it had, because the phones could be so unreliable.

"So it's to Cape Town, and then back to Edinburgh?" Caleb said, studying her newly re-booked tickets. "I see you have fixed dates. You fly from Cape Town to Johannesburg and then directly on to Edinburgh."

"You got that right. I wasn't going to give my boss any opportunities to extend my stay here."

"Ah." Caleb slid the tickets back across the table. "What are your plans for Christmas?"

Amanda shrugged. "Kari and I usually eat Christmas lunch out together. Last year Polly and Sam invited us round, but this year they'll have a *wee bairn* to occupy them." She glanced up and smiled shyly: "I think this year I want to go to a Christmas service. It's been a long time since I've done that."

Caleb smiled but it did not quite reach his sombre eyes.

"What about you? Will you be—Oh no! What are *they* doing here?" Amanda broke off mid-sentence as the five tourists from Black Rhino lodge careered through the airport doors, the tall man leading them as usual. Michelle avoided her gaze; she looked peaky.

"Oh, they've also been waiting for a flight out. Andy brought them," Caleb said, turning to watch the group check their bags in.

"Well—I guess your family will be having some peace and quiet for a bit," Amanda said, waving at the blonde woman. Michelle didn't wave back.

"So are you ready to meet your family?" Caleb asked. He seemed to be fumbling for words.

"As ready as I'll ever be."

Amanda looked past Caleb to where people were starting to move beyond the barriers into the waiting room.

Caleb followed her gaze and pulled a face. "I guess that's you then."

Nodding, Amanda reluctantly pushed back from the table. Caleb followed suit, slinging her kitbag over his shoulder.

They paused awkwardly at the rope barrier before Caleb leant forward and gave her a quick hug. "Don't cause too much chaos on the flight if you can help it."

"Very funny." Amanda reached out for her kitbag, memorising the face that had once only been a picture to her and had now become a living, breathing person with great depth and personality.

Just as she turned to go Caleb caught her hand and gave it a squeeze, his mouth moved but no words came out. Amanda lightly returned his grip, waiting for him to speak.

When he did not, she reluctantly stepped away, her voice small. "Bye Caleb. Thanks for everything."

She didn't linger after that but ducked through the barrier, waving at the elderly sweeper-slash-everything-else-man as she went. He grinned and waved back. Samuel Chiwedza was, for once, nowhere in sight.

Amanda couldn't resist looking back just before she crossed into the waiting room. Caleb was just where she had left him, his arms folded across his broad chest and his hat jammed down over his brown curls. He didn't return her wave, even though he was staring right at her.

"Bye Caleb," Amanda whispered, before slipping through the doorway, vaguely aware that the lean Allen Fairbelt was close on her heels. The man really gave her the creeps.

"So we're on the same flight out."

Amanda gritted her teeth when the objectionable man settled down on the chair beside her. There were more than enough vacant seats he could have chosen.

"Where are you going?" Amanda asked, trying to be polite. This man really got to her with his slimy little moustache, dark beard and hard eyes.

"Cape Town, same as you."

Amanda's eyes narrowed, "And what makes you think I'm going to Cape Town? This flight is for Johannesburg."

Allen's answering smile sent fear shooting into Amanda's heart. He tipped his hat away from his eyes and proceeded to rake them over every occupant of the waiting room. Nothing missed that penetrating blue gaze, Amanda was sure of it. Perhaps there was something in Michelle's warning after all?

Shuddering inside, she turned her body slightly away from Allen and stared out of the full-length windows. About four hundred metres away a plane was parked, and beyond was the familiar long grass, now more yellow-green than the brown colour it had been when she had arrived.

We both were really dry when I arrived, Amanda mused, studying the grass. *I just hope the changes in me will be as evident as yours are...*

The Tannoy hissed and echoed: "Passengers travelling on Flight SA103 to Johannesburg, please get your passports ready."

At the call, Amanda looked up. She was disappointed to see that it was not Samuel Chiwedza at the exit gate. She would have liked to have thanked Samuel and said goodbye properly before she left.

"I hope you have your passport with you, it'd be most unfortunate if you don't." Allen leant into her.

Amanda scooted over and scowled suspiciously at him. Was that a threat of some kind?

She dug through her kitbag and pulled out her passport, hoping he had not seen exactly where she had pulled it from, in case he did decide to swipe it.

"So how long is your stopover in Jo'burg for?" Allen asked, following her to stand in the queue that had rapidly formed.

"How long are *you* staying over for?" Amanda asked, determined not to remain at the airport with him any longer than necessary. Perhaps she could get a different flight on to Cape Town.

"As long as I need to." The crocodile smile slid across his face again.

Eyes narrowed, Amanda scanned his lean face. What was this man's game? Perhaps she could get Doug to contact his connections in the law enforcement offices. Maybe they could run a detail of his profile and see if they come up with something. They would need to have his description...

Amanda turned back to Allen Fairbelt to carefully examine him. He had a lean face, a thin moustache, beard newly cropped since she had last seen him, thin wide mouth, piercing blue eyes and black eyebrows. He must be at least six foot two, and very lean. The hat covered his hair, as usual, but Amanda spotted a dark strand of hair near his ear.

Anything else?

Ha! She turned away smugly, satisfied that she had a substantial description of him now. The unusual heart-shaped birthmark on the left underside of his chin, just below his beard, would be a sure detail that the police would have if he was a convicted criminal.

Heart-shaped birthmark? Amanda swung sharply back to look at it but he had tucked his chin against his chest and was now watching her warily.

Amanda pretended to be fascinated by something behind him, and then tried fiddling with her shoelace, but he kept his chin down, his eyes never leaving her.

It's just a weird coincidence. Amanda breathed hard, heart racing as she pulled her laces tight and knotted them. *More than one person can have the same peculiar birthmark—surely!*

She held out her passport to the round man at the door. He studied it in detail and handed it back to her with a smile. "Have a good flight, ma'am."

"Thank you." Amanda flashed a brief smile, troubled about Allen Fairbelt.

A glance over her shoulder and she spotted the familiar maroon-coloured passport. Was it possible that Michelle was right and that he had been following her for longer than she had realised? But if so—why? *The birthmark was so similar...could it be...?*

Amanda shook her head at the idea. *Surely not.*

Thoughts of Allen Fairbelt melted away as Amanda stepped out of the cool airport and into the glaring sun. The cicada beetle was singing again, and to the far left she spotted two of the speckled ground birds she'd seen on her first day.

"The guinea-fowl are still here." Amanda paused and

adjusted her kitbag. The sky was so blue and the air so clean and fresh. The silence and stillness that had bothered her on her arrival was now only a vague memory.

"They're just birds." Allen strode past her, calling over his shoulder as he went.

Amanda ignored him, lingering a moment longer to watch the two guinea-fowl rummage around on the border of the grass. They were more than 'just birds'. Their speckled bodies and bald necks were a glimpse of God's detailed handiwork—they were beautiful.

Then, steeling her resolve, Amanda reluctantly trailed after the rest of the passengers who were climbing the stairs onto the plane.

Chapter 17

The temperature is a warm 28 degrees Celsius on the ground today in Cape Town, with only a scattering of cloud. We'll be landing within the next ten minutes, so please fasten your seat belts." The pilot spoke on: "If you look out your windows on the left you will see Table Mountain. It often has a tablecloth of cloud over it, but as you can see, today it is clear."

Amanda obediently clipped the belt across her body and pressed her forehead against the cool window. The flat-topped mountain towered above the city, and to the right was the glittering sea. From up above, everything looked very green.

Amanda murmured a thank you as the air hostess came and removed her untouched tea. She felt too nervous to drink anything. Her stomach was churning and her heart kept doing panicked flick-flacks.

It was highly unlikely that Dad and Mum would be there to fetch her, but even if she delayed seeing them until tomorrow, the inevitable meeting would not be put off forever.

It's just too bad I'm the one who has to come crawling across continents to find them! Teeth gritted angrily together, Amanda tried to swallow her resentment.

God, it's just not fair. They should never have been parents if they weren't going to parent us! How many times did I have to fight on Polly's behalf, listen to all her worries and be big for her when all I wanted to do was curl up and cry? They shirked their duties!

Dabbing at the tears threatening to spill over, Amanda pushed the fold-up tray back into the seat in front and straightened her seat.

I just don't know if I can do this Jesus, she confessed, leaning forward to tuck her kitbag under the seat in front.

Sticking out from the top of her bag was a white paper corner. Amanda tugged at it.

"Mrs May's letter," she whispered. She stared at her neatly printed name on the cover and got a waft of the familiar lavender smell.

Cautiously, Amanda slid her finger under the fold of the letter and slit open the top of the envelope. The letter she drew out was soft and delicate.

Heart slowing, Amanda gently unfolded it. She wasn't sure what she had expected but she knew it wasn't a lonely two lines on a stretch of lilac coloured paper.

Psalm 68:5, Amanda read. *A Father of the fatherless, a defender of widows, is God in His holy habitation. God sets the solitary in families.*

The tears trickled unchecked down Amanda's cheeks as she clutched the paper, the words she had read repeating through her mind. How had Mrs May known to write this? Amanda had never told anyone what she truly felt except for Kari—and now, Caleb.

—I am your Father, Amanda.

The single thought dropped into Amanda's mind and she couldn't shake it. It just kept echoing through her until she found herself mouthing, "God is my father."

"We are entering our final descent. Will the crew members please take your seats."

The aircraft lights dimmed but Amanda barely noticed. She sat, overwhelmed, clutching the letter in her hand.

God was her father. All along when she thought He had abandoned her and given her too heavy a load to bear He had been there, fathering her. Why had she not seen Him in her life? A memory of the drive with Caleb back from the Mission came to mind. Caleb had practically suggested that God had put Great Aunt Marie in her life as her parental figure. It seemed such an unlikely choice, but why not? Aunt Marie had been attentive, interested, very involved—too involved sometimes.

And then there had been Kari, the friend that had stuck with her through thick and thin when the rest of her family had faded away from the scene; Kari with her sense of humour and zest for living—a sister in every way except by blood. And then there had been the Jacobses, the closest she had ever come to being part of a whole family. Sure, they had their problems, but they had been genuine. They had included her, a stranger, and just somehow...loved her.

Awed, Amanda fumbled to get the letter back into its envelope and eventually gave up. She tucked it in her jeans pocket instead.

God surely hadn't abandoned her, even though there had been many lonely times.

The plane glided above the grey runway and then connected, bumping Amanda up in her seat. "Welcome to Cape Town, South Africa, ladies and gentlemen. Please stay seated until we have come to a complete stop."

Amanda was one of the last to get into the baggage area, and she took her time loading her case onto a trolley.

Help, God! she prayed as she nervously wheeled the trolley towards the exit. What if her parents were here? *You are My Father, You haven't abandoned me.*

Legs trembling, Amanda paused to one side of the exit and tried to calm her frantically racing heart. A movement to her right caused her to glance up.

She found Allen Fairbelt watching her with an odd expression on his face.

He must have been on the same flight as her.

Amanda slowly uncurled from the trolley handle and took a deep breath, "Here we go then." She pushed towards the exit and watched the automatic doors slide open. Faces loomed before her, all crowded against the rope barrier.

Amanda spotted them immediately. They were directly opposite the exit doors, watching it with wide eyes.

I'll just be calm and friendly, hand over Aunt Marie's ashes, stick out the two days, and then run home. I can do that.

She saw her mother's eyes rest on her before flitting past, still searching through the passengers. A bitter taste filled Amanda's mouth.

"You are my Father," Amanda whispered, turning as Allen Fairbelt stepped out beside her. Their eyes connected for a moment and then he glanced towards her parents before looking back at her. She almost imagined she saw some sympathy in his eyes before he slid into the masses of people and disappeared.

"Amanda."

It was Michelle, her eyes strained. "I won't get another chance to tell you this: watch out for Allen. I don't know what he's up to but I'm sure it involves you."

She vanished with the same fluidity that Allen had, leaving Amanda standing uneasily on her own.

Everything was happening at once and Amanda wasn't sure she could handle it. There was so much up in the air. At least she felt some comfort in the knowledge that Caleb would be facing a similar challenge with his family.

"Amanda?"

Her father was clutching the rope staring at her.

Amanda glanced towards the place where Allen had disappeared once more before turning back to her father. He was still eyeing her questioningly, leaning slightly over the rope. He had aged. His hair was as thick as ever but it was almost completely grey now, and there were many more lines in his face than she remembered.

"Amanda, is that you?" Her mother was now looking at her: "It *is* you!"

Roused into action, Amanda pushed the trolley over to the rope.

"Hi Dad. Hi Mum." Her awkwardness was swallowed in a tearful hug from her mother and a firm one from her father.

"Darling, I can't believe you're finally here, and so brown!"

Amanda laughed nervously, "Sun does that to you, I've discovered."

"Well, let's not chitter-chatter over here. Darling, help Amanda with her bag. We'll find a little place to talk—unless you'd rather go straight home, Amanda?"

"Uh…" She wasn't quite ready to go to her parents' home, not yet. "A cup of tea somewhere would be nice," she said, looking up at her mother's eager expression. She didn't know what to think when her mum slid a hand through her arm and bounced excitedly along beside her, at least an inch shorter than she was, grey streaks blending in with the fair hair.

"Oh, we have so much to catch up on. Your father and I have arranged to have a week's leave while you are here. As soon as we heard there were flights leaving from Bulawayo again, we were here like a shot."

Amanda glanced over at her father who smiled slightly at her before drawing ahead of them so that they could all fit on the pavement.

"We have your bed all ready for you, and tonight we'll have supper together, just the three of us. But of course tomorrow everyone will want to meet you. Your mind will be a boggled heap with names and faces by the end of the week. And we mustn't forget to phone Polly—she'll want to know you arrived here safely."

"Here we are." The smooth voice of her father interrupted the excited chatter of her mother.

"Nice car," Amanda said—the first thing that came to mind. She flushed slightly as she realised it had to be at least ten years old and had a couple of deep scratches on the rear end. They probably thought her caustic.

"We got her second hand but she pulls her weight." Her dad pulled open the boot and hauled her heavy bag up into it.

"Please, won't you get in?" Amanda's mother nodded at the car and gave a little smile.

The woman was nervous! Amanda slid into the car. She couldn't believe it. *Her mother* was nervous—nervous to meet *her?*

"How about we take you for a drive before we find a place to stop?" Amanda's father suggested.

"Sure, anything is fine with me." Amanda forced herself to lean back against the seat of the car. She clipped the seat belt across her hips.

"So how are Polly and Ruth?"

Sitting behind her father, Amanda absorbed every detail she could, from the sweat stained collar of her father's shirt to the tiny scratch on her mother's cheek. The rear view mirror also gave her angles of her dad which she used when he wasn't looking.

"I haven't seen Ruth recently, but I saw Polly just before I left. She was looking very—pregnant."

"So we gather. She had a little boy three days ago. Our little family is growing."

The news that Polly's baby had been born was lost under

the latter statement. Amanda's brow shot up dubiously. Whatever world her parents were living in, it had a vastly different perspective to hers. What family? There was no family.

"Do you ever hear from Cobs?" Amanda asked casually.

Her mother swivelled around and stared at her. She looked surprised Amanda was even asking the question. Amanda shrugged, but waited.

"Of course we hear from Cobs, darling. Not as often as we'd like, but then—your father and I long to have a better relationship with *each one* of our children."

"Ha!"

"Amanda?"

Amanda looked back at her mother innocently.

"Amanda darling, we were called to be full time workers for God. Sometimes such a calling requires a sacrifice. Our sacrifice was being away from our children. It's been a mighty painful one, too—but we know we have done the right thing."

"Mum!" Amanda couldn't believe what she hearing. "I have to disagree with you. You are pointing at God and blaming Him for the situation, when I don't think that was what He was really asking of you."

So much for keeping cool and friendly—there goes that plan.

"Amanda, you don't know that," her dad gently chided.

"No, I don't," Amanda admitted, "but I'm heck of a certain that you pawned us off plenty of times when you could have made much more effort than you did."

"Maybe now is not a good time to talk about this; you must be tired after all your travelling."

"Now is just fine with me, Dad," Amanda asserted. "I'd rather get this all off my chest now, at the beginning of my visit, than pretend everything is okay until the last day of my stay. This has been eating me for years and after these last few weeks I am finally ready to talk about it, and I mean to talk."

"If that's how you feel darling, go ahead."

"Fine, I will!" Amanda folded her arms and asked the question she had never thought she would get to ask, the question that was branded into every cell of her body:

"Where were you guys when we were growing up? Where were you when we needed a dad and a mum?"

They didn't answer the question straight away. In truth, Amanda had half suspected that they would not answer it at all.

After a long while her dad said, "Amanda, I always knew I wanted to be a doctor, there was never any doubt about that in my mind. I was going to be a big-city surgeon who raked in the bucks, owned a big mansion, and lived a life of luxury. In my final year of medicine I was out on a date with my fiancée. It was after a long day in the hospital and both of us were so glad to be let loose. We had eyes only for each other as we crossed the road.

"And then, just like that, she was gone. A guy on a motorbike didn't stop in time, and we never checked the road. He connected with her full on. She must have taken the main blow—she was killed instantly."

Pale, Amanda listened. She had never known there had been another woman before Mum.

"I was in hospital for weeks. The chaplain visited me regularly and I cursed him and his God every time he came. It was good to have someone to vent it all on. Anyhow, to a cut a long story short, God got through to me through this man's persistence and dedication.

"Over the next two years the desire in me grew stronger and stronger to become a doctor in countries that are economically poor. It can only have been God that planted this desire in me, because I know that it was not the dream I had always had. So I now had a choice between *my* dreams and *my* ways, and God and His plans. I chose His.

"I've never dared to look back, Amanda, just in case I falter. Maybe I have been too tense and fearful, and if that is so then may God forgive me, but it was just too much of a risk. A little less of God meant a little more room for me. More room for pride, idols of wealth, earthly treasures. The price of such a tipping in scales has just never been worth it."

He looked up in the mirror, eyes the same green colour as her own; something inside of her twisted wistfully.

"Amanda, I do want to ask your forgiveness for the years that we never got to spend with you. I can only hope that

God in His great mercy will let the years ahead be precious and sweet."

Her ears were burning. "Dad!" She shook her head incredulously. "So you're sad that I was standing between you and God? Then *why* did you and Mum have me? *Why* did God let you have me? Huh? Tell me! From the little I've discovered about God He is attentive and loving, He doesn't discard His own and I don't think He expects parents to, either!"

He didn't answer quickly. She had forgotten how he took his time to respond, choosing his words carefully, not letting himself get ruffled.

"Sweetheart, *you* were never the problem. It was *me*. I am just a man who is weak and frail and yet so eager to serve my God. Back in the hospital I had to make a choice: to serve God one hundred per cent, or not at all. To give any less than I can give would not be good enough. When your mother and I had you children, we were thrilled. We loved each one of you."

"But you were never with us!"

"No, you're right." He nodded slowly: "We sent you back to the UK because we thought it was the best thing for you. We wanted you to get the best schooling and grow up in your own culture. Some of the places we lived in were not places we wanted our children to have to grow up in. There were some really rough conditions. We did what we thought was best."

"Well you made the wrong decision!" Amanda snapped.

She leant back against the seat. Her head ached. Was she being unreasonable?

If her parents had lived in some of the conditions she had seen in Zimbabwe, like at Caleb's Mission, then she could understand why they had sent her to Scotland. She wouldn't have wanted her own children, if she had any, to grow up in such poor conditions. The memory of the calloused little hand of the child at the Mission came to mind. Could she blame her parents, with that in mind?

But wouldn't it have been so much better to be part of a family than not being part of one, even if it did mean she had grown up in primitive conditions?

—*I am your Father, Amanda.*

The words came back to her. Amanda dug in her pocket and pulled out the neatly folded paper from Mrs May. She unfolded it, the paper crinkling softly, and read it silently again.

A Father of the fatherless, a defender of widows, is God in His holy habitation. God sets the solitary in families.

"God sets the solitary in families," Amanda whispered. She shook her head wearily, gazing up at the scattering of clouds in the blue sky. God would have to reveal that part of the verse to her because it wasn't making any sense right now.

Sighing heavily, Amanda lifted a tired hand. "I need to think through what you've said to me." She flicked the letter gently. "I think I'm ready to go to your home."

Her mother nodded, her eyes watery as she touched her husband's arm. "Is that alright?"

"Of course." He looked up at Amanda in the rear view mirror. "I'm glad you've talked with us. Thank you Amanda."

"Not a great start," Amanda mumbled, feeling a little bad, "but I really needed to get it out. I just want to sort out the mess in our family. We're all over the place, all confused, all hiding in some way." As she said it she realised she really meant it. She was tired of being in a shattered family, tired of being lonely, tired of carrying the weight of the world on her own.

Her mother looked back at her, eyes glistening, "I'm sorry Amanda, sorry that we were not the parents we should have been." She leant back, an arm out-stretched, eyes pleading for Amanda's forgiveness and understanding.

Amanda stared at the hand for a long moment. She was not sure how ready she was to forgive...She met her mother's watering eyes for a long moment, and then gently touched her mother's fingertips before withdrawing her hand again. She turned to look out the window, relieved when her mother also looked away.

God still had to do a work in her, but at least her pain was out in the open now.

She fingered the verse, clinging silently to the promise from God that had been given to her. He had been her Father during all those fatherless, parentless years, even if she hadn't realised it until now. He would have to be the One who set her in a family, because she was solitary, and He had said He put the solitary in families.

Amanda noticed little of her surroundings as her father guided the car through the unfamiliar territory. All she could see was the back of the heads of her parents. She was filled with such a mixture of pain and pleasure. How many times had she longed to be with her parents? It wouldn't have mattered where they were going, just to have been with them was enough.

"Here we are."

Amanda sat up and peered between her parents' heads as they turned into the driveway of a beautiful red-brick house with a well-kept lawn. Two red-brown Rhodesian Ridgebacks barked excitedly from behind the green metal gate as her mother got out of the car, their tails beating the air furiously.

"Sshh! No, don't jump."

"Welcome to our home Amanda." Her father turned and smiled at her, his eyes at once searching and kind.

Amanda smiled timidly, "Thanks Dad." She choked back her emotions. "And thanks for hearing me out and—and really listening."

He leant back and caught her hand in his. Amanda stared down; his hand was strong and rough, hers slender and smooth. A dad's hand and a daughter's hand.

From her bedroom window in her parents' house Amanda could only just see the blue of the ocean, but the cool wind that blew in brought with it a strong sea smell. It reminded her of her flat in South Queensferry.

"Nothing like my room at Shamwari," Amanda whispered, the sea fading away as the memory of the arid land and the waterhole filled her mind's eye. The kudu with his head lifted gracefully, standing in the red light of the rising sun...was that only this morning? Had she really only been arguing with Caleb in the truck just yesterday?

She sighed softly. "I hope things are going better for you than they are for me, Caleb. I wish you were here."

She flung her kitbag down onto the pink bedspread. Wandering over to the polished wood dressing table she picked up the hand mirror and fingered it absently.

What was Caleb doing now? Had he gone straight back to the Mission? She doubted he had. Caleb was a man of his word. He had told Penny that things would change. Between him and God she hoped things would be different, for she knew he would surely try.

A knock at her door brought her sharply back into reality.

"Amanda, can I come in?"

"Sure."

Her mum was holding a hand phone. "It's for you. Kari."

"Kari!" Amanda's heart froze as she jerkily took the phone. She squinted at her departing mother. *Oh God, help!* she thought, taking the phone without a word. *This is harder than I thought it would be.*

"Hi, Kari?" Amanda closed the door gently behind her mother.

"Amanda, so you've made it to Cape Town at last." Kari's voice was strangely shrill; things were not right and it only made the tightness in Amanda's stomach grow tighter.

"Made it to Cape Town," Amanda echoed without emotion. "Uh-huh, I'm here." Putting aside her own worries, Amanda asked, "But how are you, Kari?"

She heard Kari's broken, almost nervous, laugh. "I thought you were mad yesterday when you suggested I went to church." There was a pregnant pause. "Well, today I was so miserable that I took your advice and went. I got there a bit late, but Mrs May was at my side like a hawk."

"So you sat with Mrs May?" Amanda pursed her lips thoughtfully.

"Uh-huh. She looked absolutely thrilled to see me. After church I went back with her for lunch. See how desperate I was?" Kari sounded sheepish.

Amanda smiled. All she could think was that God wasn't letting go of either Kari or her. From the little she had seen of Him in the last few weeks, this had "God" written all over it.

"And how was lunch?"

"Not bad," Kari admitted. She coughed slightly, "I've told Mrs May I'll see her next Sunday. Will you be home by then?"

"Yeah." Amanda rubbed a loose strand of hair between her fingers, studying the split ends with a frown. "With the whole delay I'll only get to be here until Tuesday. After all my worrying, I'll only be with my parents one whole day."

"And how do you feel about that?" Kari asked, sounding concerned.

Amanda smiled sadly, "I think a day will be enough for all of us for now. I might have already blown it when I caused an explosion in the car from the airport." She shrugged unhappily. "Hopefully by the time I go we will at least be able to part at peace with each other. That'd be something."

"I hope so," Kari whispered. "But I'm so glad you're coming home."

Amanda nodded. She said goodbye a few minutes later, her heart heavy.

Scotland was a long way from here—a long way from the Jacobs family—and Caleb, to be exact. Her weeks with them had turned out to be a time of nurturing and belonging—a time of cleansing and healing. She had barely touched her work during her whole stay there.

—*He sets the solitary in families.*

Amanda's heart leapt.

No, I'm just imagining it.

She shook her head, afraid to hope. *But what if—*

Shaking her head firmly, Amanda dug in her kitbag and pulled out the green alabaster jar.

"Well, here we are Aunt Marie. Our little journey together is over and you're still in one piece." She tapped the jar disrespectfully. "I call that pretty good."

Slipping out of her room, Amanda followed the voices to the kitchen and found her parents working there together. Her dad was stirring something at the stove, a butcher's apron on, and her mum was chopping up carrots like a pro.

"Mum, Dad—" Amanda held up the jar "—here's Great Aunt Marie. The tough cookie has finally reached her destination."

Her mother looked shocked, but her dad grinned. Wiping his hands on his apron, he took the jar. "She sure was a tough cookie. I don't know how many times she broke the wooden spoon on me."

"Dad!" It was Amanda's turn to be shocked.

"Just joking," he grinned, shaking the jar slightly to listen. "But I'm sure she would have liked to. She was actually pretty kinky. Every Saturday she would take us for a walk to the park at exactly eleven o'clock. She timed it perfectly so that we caught the ice-cream van just as he passed our corner. She'd make out like it was a huge problem that we kids wanted ice-creams—but she always had ice-cream money on her."

"Huh!" Amanda nodded in wonder. "Now that you mention it, I remember she did the same with us. We were always so scared to ask her for ice-creams though. We could hear the music of the ice-cream van getting louder and we'd fight over who was going to do the deed." Amanda laughed at the memory. "I was usually the one that got pushed forward."

"No, don't put that there." Amanda's mother fluttered over to the stove when she saw her husband balance the alabaster jar beside the meat. "Honey, what a place to put her!"

Amanda hid a smile as she watched her mum scold her dad with her eyes. Her father shrugged innocently and left the kitchen, holding the alabaster jar out before him.

Poor Aunt Marie.

"Honestly." Her mother rolled her eyes at Amanda, "You'd think he'd know better. Sweetheart, do you mind setting the table?"

"Sure. Where do I find the cutlery?"

"Just in the drawer by the stove." Amanda's mum turned back to her carrots and scooped them into the salad. "There you go, that's the salad done. How's that meat coming, darling?"

Her husband wiped his hands on his apron as he returned from depositing Aunt Marie somewhere. Amanda wondered where he had put her this time—hopefully he'd found a spot far less precarious than a stove.

"Just fine," he said, leaning over the pot. "I'd say it's just about done."

Their meal passed in relative peace. Amanda talked about her job, a little about Kari, as much as she could about Polly and Ruth—which wasn't overly much—and then about Caleb and his family.

"I couldn't believe how patient everyone is there. There was always some problem or other but everyone just got on and lived." She smiled at the memory of Caleb picking the cherries out of the biscuits and looking so guilty when she caught him.

"You liked it there?"

Amanda smiled dreamily, "Yes, very much. I hated it when I first arrived but the Jacobs were wonderful. It was just like being part of a family." She realised too late what she had said, but both her parents were smiling, looking genuinely glad for her.

"Well..." Amanda cleared her throat uncomfortably and added quickly, "anyway, I'm glad I'm here and that Aunt Marie made it to her destination."

"Well," her dad drawled, "actually, she really wanted to be buried in Botswana."

Horrified, Amanda only realised he was joking when both her parents beamed at her.

"Oh! You had me really worried there!" she exclaimed, laughing with them.

"Imagine how many more adventures you could have," Amanda's mum smiled, her brown eyes sparkling.

"I don't want to even try!" Amanda shook her head firmly. "Half of what has happened so far has gone way beyond my imagination."

After that the conversation drifted on to her parents' work in the Cape Flats townships. They also shared what God was doing in the church and what He was doing in their lives.

Amanda listened, soaking in every word they said, picturing what they were describing. She vaguely recalled her parents sharing about another of their Mission bases when she was younger, but she couldn't have listened properly back then because she couldn't remember a word of what they had said.

At some point her father got up to make tea. Amanda signalled for sugar and milk.

"My few weeks in Zimbabwe have given me a new passion for sugar," she said, laughing; wondering what other changes had happened in her that she wasn't aware of.

Eleven o'clock came quickly, and when Amanda left the

table she did so with more peace in her heart than she'd had in a long time. As she settled in for the night she replayed scenes of their conversation, picturing her father's easy smile and her mother's excited eyes. She was all talked out, but it had to be the first time in a long while that she had spent so much quality time with her parents.

"And spent it with them both at the same time," Amanda whispered, slipping into bed. She smiled up at the ceiling, "Thanks God."

She whispered a prayer into the darkness for Kari. "There's nothing I can do for her God, I'm trusting You to do something." A measure of peace stole over her heart as she surrendered her friend into the hands of her Father.

But the final prayer on her lips was reserved for the young man who had taught her the importance of prayer. She missed him already.

Chapter 18

The sand was white; white and wet. Amanda dug her heels into the coldness, turning back to look at the heavy imprint she left behind. Her trail wound along the edge of the waves, the prints filling up with water from beneath before the waves washed over them.

Amanda stepped into the water to avoid a grinning Labrador that raced towards her before abruptly veering off to her left and dashing up the slope into the grassy bank, its dripping body covered with sand.

"Lucky you," Amanda smiled at the dog's owner. The woman grinned and rolled her eyes, before bracing herself for the wet onslaught.

Amanda drifted past the pair. Table Mountain rose up in the distance. It was covered by a heavy blanket of cloud, the only cloud visible in the stunning blue sky. She stopped to watch a kite surfer, shielding her eyes as she saw him skim along the water further and further out to sea. Table Bay was seemingly a kite surfers' paradise, for at least twenty of them skimmed the water, some circling around the jutting rocks behind her, heading out into the bay beyond.

Her eyes were drawn back to the mountain. It held a magnetic pull for her. She was almost sorry she wasn't staying longer to experience this spectacular place. Now that the initial meeting with her parents was over she would have loved to have explored the area, perhaps climbed the mountain...

The shudder in her pocket drew her attention reluctantly away from her surroundings. She dug her cell phone out of her jeans. "Hello? Hi, Mum." A sea gull swooped down in front of her, legs stretched out for its landing. "I'm still on the beach." She scuffed some sand at the bird with her toe. The gull hopped a few steps back, head tilted to eyeball her with a severe look. Kari hated sea gulls. "Breakfast?...Okay, I'll head home now."

Pocketing the phone, Amanda sauntered up the slope towards the nearest gap in the wooden posts that separated beach from road.

She wandered slowly past the street sellers and their wares. Beautiful bead necklaces and bangles, wire cars, and little windmills with plastic fans that spun as the wind caught their blades: all were handmade. She shook her head and smiled regretfully at them as they held out their bounty to her. "I didn't bring any money with me." She patted her pockets to indicate: no cash.

Once she was beyond them she stopped to rub the sand off her legs and feet before rolling down her jeans and slipping on her sandals. The ice-cream shop on the corner beckoned to her as she passed it before turning to the left and following the pavement alongside the road. Her parents' house was about a ten minute walk away from Table Bay.

Ten minutes to pour out her heart to her Father before the day began in earnest.

"I've just got to go to the bank, where should I meet you?"

Amanda looked between her father and mother, waiting to see what her mother would decide.

"Well, I want to show Amanda a dress I spotted in Mac's shop. How about we meet at the benches by the smoothie bar?"

"Righto."

Amanda watched her dad weave his way through the crowds, before following her mother along the shop windows. She could barely believe she was actually here—with them.

Up ahead she could see her mother pointing out something in the shop window and talking to the empty space beside her. Giggling, Amanda hurried forward just as her mum looked around.

"Oh, there you are! I was just giving you the whole lowdown of my plans for this dress. Ah well, long story short is I fell in love with this dress the moment I saw it." She laughed and patted her waist. "Only catch is that it won't fit me. But you—it'd fit you like a glove."

Amanda laughed softly at her mother's enthusiasm. Her

cheeks were flushed with excitement and her eyes sparkled. It was hard for such zest not to be contagious. She glanced up at the mannequin in the window, and at the dress. Her breath caught.

"Do you like it?" Her mum caught her arm anxiously, brown eyes wide.

"Oh Mum, it's absolutely stunning!" Amanda breathed.

A beautiful wine coloured dress, chic and uncomplicated, with a full drop to the ankles, graced the unbecoming mannequin. A pair of high-heeled matching coloured shoes poked out from beneath the soft fabric, and just beside them was a petite matching handbag.

"It's yours."

"Mine?" Amanda gazed at the dress stunned before turning to meet her glowing mother. "Oh Mum, I don't think so."

Her mum leant forward and tapped the glass, pointing at a little tag that Amanda had not noticed. Amanda leant forward to read it.

SOLD, she read, her heart thumping as she understood what her mother was saying. "You've already bought it for me?"

Absolutely radiant, her mother caught her hand. "Your dad and I raced down and bought it the moment we knew you were coming. We just took a chance on your size, but looking at you I know it'll be just perfect! Oh Amanda, I'm so excited. You have no idea how impatient I have been to show you this. And with your shiny dark hair and height— you'll look exquisite!"

Amanda let her mother pull her into the little shop. She was almost floating on air under the motherly attention and delight that enfolded her.

"Mac, this is my daughter Amanda."

"Oh Mrs McCree, she is delightful!" the man behind the counter exclaimed, his big beard wobbling when he spoke.

"Of course she is," her mum answered smoothly, "and we are here to pick up our dress."

"Ah," he nodded wisely. "I am surprised you did not come sooner. I could have sold this dress twenty times at least since you bought it."

"Well, I notice you didn't take it out of your window," her

mum remarked dryly.

He laughed guiltily, "Ah well, it is eye-catching. The people come flocking into my shop when they see it. Perhaps I'll have a drop in my business now that you are taking it."

Hands flying into the air in pretended horror, Amanda's mother backed away from the counter. "If that's the case we'd better leave it—we wouldn't want to be accused of causing you to have bad business!"

"Of course," Mac countered, "but I can't give you your money back."

Both laughed. Amanda listened to the pleasant banter between them while she glanced around the store. It was a cluttered shop; or perhaps 'busy' was a better word. Necklaces and chains hung down the walls, with little jewellery display boxes dividing up the room into colour codes. The clothes appeared to all be fashionable dresses, but towards the back Amanda spotted one little section of smart ladies' suits.

It was quite a dingy shop. For some reason Mac had chosen a dim orange light for his globe, creating a mystical sort of atmosphere.

From the corner of her eye Amanda caught a movement at the door. She glanced up just in time to see a tall man with a black hat duck out of sight.

*Strange....*But she shrugged it off.

"That's us. Are you ready to go and meet your father?"

Amanda nodded, smiling as she thanked Mac and followed her mother out of the shop. "Mum, this dress is beautiful. You have no idea how thrilled I am that you and Dad thought of buying it for me. This dress is going to be hung in a very treasured place."

"Well, as long as you wear it darling," her mother admonished, but Amanda could see she was glowing with pleasure.

"Mac may be difficult at times but he is a really a great guy. We first met him at the waterfront when he used to have a shop there. Somehow, through his wheeling and dealing, he rented a store in this mall. I think he's actually done really well for himself."

"A shrewd business man?" Amanda guessed.

"For sure!" Amanda's mum wrinkled her nose at Amanda,

making Amanda laugh.

"Ah, there's your dad." She quickly walked ahead, waving furiously.

Amanda followed behind at a leisurely pace, wonderfully contented.

Suddenly a hand shot out and dragged her into a little passage.

"Let go of me!" Amanda gasped, jerking her arm free as she spun around. "Allen Fairbelt!" She stared up at the despised face which was twisted into a smirk.

"How dare you man-handle me like this!"

"How dare you man-handle me," he mimicked, his face contorting into a menacing scowl. "That's pitiful, Amanda."

Palms pressed against the wall, Amanda glanced to her right. At the far end of the passage was a door with a picture of a woman on it—the ladies' public toilets. And just to her left people were passing back and forth, but no one took any notice of them if they did happen to look down the passage.

Allen gripped her upper arm. "You're not going anywhere until I'm done with you."

"What is it you want?" Amanda snapped, hiding her fear behind an angry front. "You're becoming a pest."

"Bold words, little sister."

Amanda's brows rose, silently echoing his words. Her gaze flitted down to the heart shaped birth mark just under his chin.

He smiled slowly. "That's right. Your big brother Cobs, and you didn't even suspect it was me until I was in your face and you had nowhere to look but at me—or at my birth-mark, to be precise."

"Cobs?" Amanda stared up into the lean face with the hard blue eyes and slash of a mouth, the pitted skin dark with the sun, and something far less healthy …

This couldn't be Cobs! Nowhere in him could she see the brother she had once known and loved. Cobs had been well-built and strong, with kind eyes, smooth skin, a generous heart—this man was just the opposite! *Soulless!*

It must have been the drugs that had ravaged him so terribly—in body, mind and spirit—she realised with horror. Yes, he'd fought his way through hell to the other side and come out drug-free at last, but this man, this—haunted *shell*—was nothing like the Cobs she had known!

But he did have the birthmark.

Was this why he had stayed away from them all for so long?

Covering her eyes with her hands, Amanda tried to block out his painful grip on her arm. Surely this was not her brother! *Please, God …*

She lowered her hands, hoping to see him in a new light, but all she saw was the same cruel eyes and menacing smile.

"It's me, Amanda, and I mean to get what's mine."

"What's yours?" Amanda stared at him in confusion, her eyes flicking up to his eyes and then away again. "What do you mean?"

"My inheritance." He smiled again, his eyes cold.

"So why are you snatching me?" Amanda exclaimed indignantly, trying to jerk her arm free. His fierce hold only tightened.

"Because you, little sister, were always the favourite of Great Aunt Marie. All her wealth is going to you—or didn't you know, you cunning little wretch?"

Shocked at his callousness, Amanda managed to jerk free this time, her anger giving her extra strength. "You're speaking through your nose Cobs! What trash! Great Aunt Marie despised me. She was always punishing me and teasing me unmercifully. I spent more time digging the vegetable garden or running errands or having to tag along with her on some excruciating mission of mercy than any of you others!"

"Precisely." Cobs wasn't smiling now. "You were her favourite. She could barely spare the rest of us a glance."

"That's not true!" Amanda disputed.

"It's completely true. You were just too self-focussed and full of self-pity that you never realised how good you really had it. Well, it doesn't matter now. But what does matter is you're getting Aunt Marie's inheritance and I mean to have it. You can't have the love *and* the money."

"What nonsense Cobs!" Amanda was incredulous. "This is just your one-sided opinion; I never saw it that way. Don't you want to hear my viewpoint?"

"I never stopped hearing your viewpoint, Amanda. You were always moaning about being abandoned by Dad and Mum, never wondering how *they* felt being separated from their children, or how hard it must have been for them to decide what was best for us, or suppose that they might have felt lonely and culturally incompatible in the places they landed up in."

"You're siding with them? After all those years of being ditched in boarding school and then with Aunt Marie?"

"I'm siding with myself!" Cobs' eyes flashed. "But I have a bigger mind than yours. I am capable of seeing past my own little world and into others."

"But—"

"Enough!" Cobs yanked her forward. "Dad and Mum are going to take you to the lawyers at some point to sign for your inheritance. You'll sign it over to me."

"Well, if what you're saying is true why don't you just come with me and we'll sort it out one time, instead of you sneaking around worming your way in without ever having the guts to show your face!"

She never saw the backhanded slap until it was already too late. Gasping, Amanda held her stinging cheek, her eyes blazing with fury. "Coward!"

There was no inheritance, and even if there was it didn't matter if Cobs had it. She certainly wasn't going to fight with this beast of a man for it.

Gripping her in the same tender spot on her arm, Cobs marched her out of the passageway. "Where are they? Let's get this over with."

Almost lifted off her feet, Amanda scrambled along next to him. Her heart was racing when she saw her parents standing near the smoothie bar scanning the mall. Their faces lit up in relief when they spotted her.

"What are you going to do to them?" Amanda whispered fearfully. "Don't hurt them Cobs. This inheritance is between me and you."

"Don't be ridiculous, they *are* my parents."

Sagging in relief, Amanda didn't fight him any longer. Cobs jerked her to a halt in front of her parents and gave her a slight shake. His eyes were hooded and his lips pulled into an arrogant line.

"Umm, Dad and Mum, this is—"

"Cobs! Darling, you're back at last!"

To Amanda's horror her mum dived forward and planted a kiss on both of Cobs' cheeks. "My son!" Her eyes glistened with unshed tears as she caught onto her husband's arm, "God has been so good to us. We get to see two of our children within two days of each other!"

In disbelief, Amanda watched as her father stepped forward and drew Cobs into a gentle embrace.

Cobs was as stiff as a rod and his expression never changed but Amanda's mum was radiant.

"We've treasured that last letter you sent us! All your news, the photo..." Her eyes sparkled with unshed tears.

Amanda's gaze darted between her parents and Cobs, marvelling how they looked past this terrible man to their son beneath.

Her mother smiled joyfully at Cobs. Then, beaming at Amanda, she confided, "I've been telling Cobs all the family news, keeping him up to date on all of you. He was fascinated by Aunt Marie's request for you to come here with her ashes."

Cobs' lips twisted into a semblance of a smile as Amanda's stunned expression transformed into anger. *So this was how he had been able to track her movements!*

Abruptly, cutting right through their parents' pleasure, Cobs growled, "I've come for my money."

"Money?" Their mother looked confused.

"Oh Mum, Cobs has this ludicrous idea that Great Aunt Marie has left me some money."

She watched her parents exchange a knowing look.

"Tell Cobs he's got it wrong," Amanda said, feeling a little doubtful now. "Aunt Marie didn't like me—she'd never leave me any money!"

"Well..." Her father hesitated, and after a nod from his wife said, "actually, Cobs is right Amanda. Aunt Marie had a soft spot for you. She arranged through her lawyer for you to come and sign some papers when you brought her ashes across. That's really why she wanted *you* to bring her ashes here."

Unable to absorb what she was hearing, Amanda covered her ears. This was not fitting in with anything she had believed all these years—someone had it wrong! This was one big setup. Caleb had suggested Aunt Marie had cared for her, Cobs had accused her of being self-pitying and selfish, and now her parents were saying Aunt Marie *had* liked her best!

This was all wrong! She'd hated Aunt Marie because the woman had hated her! Had she really got it so distorted all these years?

"Amanda, darling..." Her mother gently drew Amanda's arm down, her eyes compassionate and concerned.

"Mum!" Amanda didn't care if they were drawing a whole lot of attention. She clung to her mother, silently pleading for her to hold her world intact. Her mother stroked her back in silence, holding her while tears poured down Amanda's cheeks.

Was it possible that things really had not been the way she had seen them? Well, there was only one way to know for certain.

Feeling shaky all over, Amanda drew back from her mother and glanced between the three faces before her. "Let's go to the lawyer then and straighten this all out. There must be some mistake."

She couldn't quite ignore the look that passed between her parents. Deep inside she knew they were right, that Cobs was right. Somehow along the way, in spite of all that bickering and fighting with Aunt Marie, the woman had developed a soft spot for her.

To the exclusion of her brother and sisters.

The lawyer's office was starchy white and extremely neat. The name plate on his door read *H.R. GREBE*, followed by a flurry of letters.

Amanda sat on the edge of her leather seat. Out of the side of her eye, she could see that Cobs was sitting up straight, his expression grim. To her right, her parents held hands and waited in silence.

The lawyer was the only one of them who appeared relaxed. He sat across the table from her, flipping through his file, pausing every now and then to check a page before turning over.

"Ah, here we are. Miss Amanda McCree. That is you,

correct?" He looked up at Amanda. "Have you brought any proof?"

"I have my passport?" Amanda whispered, digging in her kitbag. This was all like a bad dream. She handed the document over to him, glancing again at Cobs and catching his eye. He glared down at her dourly.

"Yes," the solicitor nodded, "that's fine." He looked up with a smile on his face: "I congratulate you on receiving a substantial inheritance Miss McCree; your Great Aunt was a wealthy woman."

Amanda gasped, clutching the edge of the table. "Are you *sure* you have this all right? You have the right Aunt Marie and the right Amanda McCree?"

Mr Grebe nodded, smiling.

Groaning, Amanda hid her face in her hands. *God, how did I grow up believing something so different to what was really there?*

She knew what she had to do. Letting her hands drop into her lap she said, "I'd like to sign it over to my brother." She gestured at the stiff figure beside her.

Frowning, the lawyer began sifting through his papers again. "Well, I'm not quite sure that is possible. You see, you can sign over whatever *money* your Great Aunt left you, but the bulk of the inheritance is actually a piece of land that has a clause attached which does not allow you to sell it for a certain period of time—or give it away," he added meaningfully.

Amanda glanced nervously at Cobs. "Is there no way around it? I mean, I don't need any more money and I don't want a piece of land."

"I'm afraid not," the lawyer shrugged, looking up at her. "If you wish we can draw up a form for you to sign over everything except the land?"

Letting out her breath slowly, Amanda glanced up at Cobs again. He nodded stiffly.

"Yes. Thank you."

Amanda was suddenly overwhelmed by it all; so much had happened in such a short space of time, and it was only just sinking in for her. To her right she could see her parents watching them both, their expressions unreadable; to her left Cobs—the brother she had once adored—sat, beyond her reach and equally indecipherable. She had inherited a fortune, and promptly given much of it away, all in the blink of an eye. It was all too much—and yet somehow not nearly enough.

She waited until the lawyer had left the room before she looked up at Cobs. Her voice was very small and humble when she spoke.

"Cobs," she gulped, almost unable to see him for the tears in her eyes, "I'm so sorry. I somehow must have got things very messed up along the way. I never imagined that this was how things really were. That Great Aunt Marie...liked me, and that you always thought I was so selfish and felt so sorry for myself. I just never thought—" Amanda broke off, unable to finish. She ducked her head down, hurriedly brushing away the tears.

Her mother slipped her soft hands over Amanda's.

"Let's just get the cash and get out of here," Cobs rumbled, suddenly sounding not quite as sure as he had been—or was that wishful thinking on her part?

Amanda looked up, her mouth quivering when she met Cobs' stony eyes. "I'm truly sorry Cobs," she whispered.

"Well, here we are." Mr Grebe strode back into the room, waving a piece of paper. "If you will just sign there Miss McCree, and then your brother can sign too, and the deed is done."

Amanda brushed at her teary cheeks and numbly signed the indicated spot, barely reading what was written. She watched as Cobs scanned through the form before signing with a satisfied flourish.

"You will note, Mr McCree, that this document you have signed states that you will never attempt to obtain your sister's land now that you have the rest of the inheritance?" the lawyer checked. Somehow, Amanda thought, the astute lawyer had seen fit to protect her. God again?

Cobs nodded, "That's fine with me. I've seen Zimbabwe and I have no desire to own land in it—and besides, it's worth peanuts on the international market."

"Zimbabwe?" Amanda whispered, reaching over to pluck the form from Cobs' hand.

She skimmed down the form until she reached the part about the land.

"Matabeleland?" she breathed. "But that's where—"

Cobs grinned darkly. "Where your precious Caleb lives," he finished for her. "What irony."

Heart fluttering, Amanda stared at the document in wonder. "But why did Aunt Marie have land there? I don't understand."

"Aunt Marie was a shrewd business woman." Her dad leant forward, his eyes dancing: "You'd be surprised what she put her hand to." He took the paper from her to have a look at it. "But I will admit that even I am surprised at this location." After studying the form he handed it back to her and shrugged.

"Well, that's us finished here, then," the lawyer said, standing up when Amanda had signed a couple more documents. "I'll finalise all the details and close this up."

Amanda stood, uncertain as to whether her legs would support her.

What was the likelihood that she would inherit a piece of land in the same province that she had been stranded for three or four weeks, in a remote African country? Not even Aunt Marie could have planned that.

She followed her family out into the street. They stood there, blinking in the bright sunlight as though everyone was quite overwhelmed by the whole situation. Amanda knew she was.

She glanced at Cobs. His lean face was still grim and tense.

"Well, that's that," Amanda said, uncertainly.

She half expected Cobs to bolt into the crowd and disappear, but he hovered beside them, looking unsure.

"Cobs, won't you come back with us for supper?"

Amanda's heart sank at her father's offer, yet at the same time she felt the stirrings of a yearning somewhere deep inside that took her by surprise. And it was impossible to criticise him now, because she was as much at fault as he was.

Staring across the table at Cobs that night, it dawned on Amanda that Cobs had known exactly where she was all along. He had known Aunt Marie had died, he had known her flight plans, he had known she was stranded in Zimbabwe, and he had known where to find their parents. He had cared enough about family to keep contact with their mother, and to know what everyone was doing.

Was this whole inheritance thing just a way he had found to connect with everyone again? Could it be possible that Cobs wasn't as self-assured and callous as he appeared to be?

Amanda patted her bottom lip thoughtfully as she studied the shifting eyes and stiff body of her brother. It was something to think on.

Another thing to think on was her inheritance from Great Aunt Marie. She didn't know what she'd do with the land, but there must be *something* good that could come of this?

Abstractedly she found herself wondering how close her land was to Shamwari ...

"Maybe tomorrow we can all meet at the beach?" her mum was suggesting, looking around the table. "What about a picnic, or a *braai*?"

Amanda swallowed, catching Cobs' curious look in her direction.

"Uh..." She cleared her throat. "I haven't managed to tell you yet but my flight home is tomorrow morning."

The disappointment in her parents' faces was heartbreaking.

"Can't you change it?"

Amanda shook her head, for the first time regretting her ticket choice. "It's a fixed flight."

"Oh, that is sad!"

Amanda caught her mother's hand, meeting her eyes, "I'm so sorry Mum—what with the flight delay and all, and Kari not being well," she added uncomfortably, "I was determined not to stay longer than I had to. But I'll come back again, I promise," she said eagerly. "There's so much more to work through between us, but I think I'm ready to, if you are?"

"Of course darling." Her mother squeezed her hand.

Amanda glanced at her brother and then down at her plate again.

"And you Cobs—are you going to be around for a while?" she heard her dad ask.

"Well..." Cobs sounded hesitant. "I might just hang around and get a wee bit of sun before heading back."

"Great! Our spare room is always open."

Feeling just a mite jealous, Amanda jabbed at a piece of chicken, then let out her breath. *Wasn't this what I wanted— my family beginning to mend broken connections? Hasn't God heard my prayer and graciously begun to answer it?—*

"You still talk to yourself Amanda."

Amanda looked up and shifted uncomfortably as she saw the moisture in her dad's eyes. She hadn't realised she'd been speaking her thoughts aloud, again!

"I don't know how many times I used to watch you chatting away as you busied yourself," he said lovingly. "My little honey-bee, never still...my little girl!"

"She's been talking to herself nonstop lately," Cobs observed dryly. "I was glad I didn't have to claim her as my sister." He suddenly flashed the briefest of smiles and his whole face lit up before settling back into the grim lines.

Too late, thought Amanda. *Caught you, big brother!* And a tiny curl of joy began in her heart.

She laughed softly, "A bad habit I guess. Kari says she hears what I think twice; once when I think through it myself, and the next time when I tell her about it."

A pleasant silence followed as they all ate, until her dad asked, "So what are your plans now?"

It took a moment for Amanda to answer, and when she did she wondered at herself.

"Well, a month ago I would have said it would be to finish my research on depression and then find a new research project to get my hands into, maybe one with a higher salary." She laughed self-consciously. "Now I don't know. The time in Zimbabwe changed my perspective a lot, and then coming here and seeing you all..." She shrugged. "Well, things aren't quite as clear as they were before."

She paused, moistening her lips nervously. "Actually, I have something to explain. Somewhere along the way on this trip God found me. I'm not sure what this is going to mean, but I know He's been the One Who has been orchestrating everything, and I think He's got something in mind for me, so I'm sort of waiting to see what that is."

She glanced up and smiled shyly at her family, nervously playing with her napkin as she measured their response. It didn't take a genius to see that her parents were absolutely thrilled, or that Cobs was looking out of his depth.

Cobs must have been feeling very awkward for he suddenly burst out, "Well of course, let's not forget Caleb, your 'honey'."

"Cobs!" Amanda blushed, her cheeks growing very warm.

"Caleb?" Her mother cocked her head curiously.

"You should have seen her!" Cobs leant back against his chair. "She practically attacked me and my friends while acting as our hostess, and we'd only just arrived. We were all gob-smacked and there she was, sizzling with anger!"

"Cobs," Amanda hissed, feeling the heat seep down into her neck.

"And during her rant this guy comes in through the door and is watching the whole scene, absolutely enthralled." Cobs leant forward, hand in the air. "Now, *I* know Amanda has never met him before, but the next thing I know she's calling him Sunshine or Honey or something like that, and he's doing the same thing. They were putting up a whole charade for us while negotiating some sort of peace treaty. I think he was pleading for Amanda to shut her mouth!"

"I know it sounds bad—but Cobs is really fluffing this one out!" Amanda protested, half-laughing.

"I'm telling you Mum, this guy was definitely Amanda's life-saver that day, because my friends were set to pack up and leave after she volunteered to drive us back to the airport. Amanda almost lost her hosts a lot of business."

"And this Caleb?" Their father leant forward seriously: "What's he like?"

Cobs flashed a sly look at Amanda, "I think you should ask Amanda that."

Hands clenched together under the table, Amanda shifted uncomfortably.. "He's nice, really nice." She shrugged and then confessed, "I like him a lot."

"Well, just know that I'll want to check out any man before you marry him, alright?"

"Yes, Dad," Amanda answered meekly, seeing that behind the smile he was dead serious.

"Well, that's dinner then!" Their mother clapped her hands together briskly. "Anyone for a cup of tea?"

Chapter 19

By the time Amanda had got her car out of the long-term parking it was almost eight o'clock. The street lights were on and the sun must have been set for a good three hours at least.

Home again. Amanda adjusted the heating in the car and pressed the radio on. A smooth jazz piece poured into the car, the leading saxophone hitting low melodic notes.

"Well here we are God, back in Edinburgh," Amanda murmured, guiding her car past the roundabout near the golf driving range. "And what a trip we've had."

A car flashed at her and Amanda hurriedly fumbled for her own headlights. *No wonder I couldn't see where I was going.* She lifted a hand in thanks to the other driver.

Only once she was off the airport road did she resume her prayer.

"I think I pretty much did everything I intended to do and more, the extra stuff obviously was what Your intentions were for me." Amanda tapped the steering wheel thoughtfully. "The only thing I didn't do was the research—and Doug sponsored everything but the flight. This is going to be a tricky one to explain, Lord. He'll want to know why I wasn't working while in Zimbabwe. I could pay him back, I guess, but I know he'll be bleak I didn't do the research."

Unable to let it go, Amanda pulled over onto the hard shoulder, dug around for her cell phone, and dialled Doug's number.

"Doug? This is Amanda. Yes, I'm back in Edinburgh, just landed in fact. I'm phoning because I have a confession to make. I assume Kari told you what had happened?" she checked. "Yes, I did have a lot on my mind...I did try and observe the children while I was there, but it was only a vague overview. No, I just didn't have opportunity." She paused, listening.

"Getting to see how the land lies? Well, I guess you could say that," she agreed, her heart quickening. "Well sure, I did meet some people there who said they would be glad to put me up if I ever came back...really? Well, yes..."

When Amanda hung up she shook her head in amazement. "Doug, you do beat all! Well God, You heard that. He wants me to go back and do the job properly this time."

She smiled as she pulled back onto the road: "But this time he's given me a choice. Now that is what I like." Her smiled broadened as she thought of Sally and Kari's frequent complaints about Doug. They couldn't stand it how much room he gave her as long as the job was done.

"You've definitely given me a hectically relaxed boss, God," Amanda said, flicking the left indicator on as she approached her street.

It was good to see Mrs Keene walking her dog up the road, just as usual. Amanda leant across the passenger seat to wave brightly at the woman who lived three flats down from her. Mrs Keene lifted a hand dubiously, as though uncertain if it was really Amanda or not. Her fat little terrier had its head down and didn't even turn to watch the car go by.

Which reminded Amanda of another duty she must carry out: she owed Mrs May an apology—though she somehow thought that the news of her accepting Christ into her life would more than make up for it all.

Ah, it's good to be home. Hopefully Kari will have a cup of tea and some yummy dinner ready.

Amanda pulled her car up beside her neighbour's before reversing into the parallel parking. She could see a light on in their flat, and a shadow moving around.

Beaming from ear to ear, Amanda almost fell out of the car in her eagerness. She slung her kitbag over her shoulder and yanked her bag out of the boot, pressing the remote button to lock the doors before dragging her case up to the door. She fumbled with her keys before finally finding the right one and sliding it into the lock. She took that moment to steel herself to meet Kari; she had no idea what to expect, but knew that Kari was going to need a lot of prayer and love.

"Kari, I'm home!" she called. She hadn't got the door fully

open when it was jerked backwards and a familiar figure launched itself at her.

"Amanda! Yayee!"

Amanda's heart wrenched at the bones she could feel in Kari's back. She stepped back and had a good look at her friend, her heart weeping when she saw how much weight Kari had lost since she had last seen her. Well, she was home now and with God's help she'd do all the praying and supporting that she could for Kari.

Hiding her thoughts, Amanda grinned at her friend, "Well I jolly well hope you have something for me to eat. I'm starving." She didn't miss the haunted look around Kari's eyes, or the depressed slump of her friend's shoulders.

"Yip, all done!" Kari took the kitbag from Amanda and waited while Amanda shut the door. "You're so brown!"

"*Ja,* she's browned off," a voice rang out from the sitting room.

"Kari, who—?" Amanda clutched at her friend's arm, heart racing and eyes wide as she saw the gleam in her friend's eye. Abandoning her bag she raced into the lounge and almost collided with a tall figure which caught her just before she connected with him.

"Well I know you missed me, but I never expected you to throw yourself at me," a familiar voice chided.

Tilting her head back, Amanda looked up into laughing blue eyes. "Caleb! What are you doing here?"

He shrugged, "A vacancy rose for a researcher-slash-teacher, and I thought I might know just where to find one."

"But how did you get here?" Amanda shook her head, dazed. "I mean, never mind that you managed to get a flight, how did you know where I lived?"

Caleb shook his head, "You'd be amazed at the things little brothers know. Mickey knew exactly where you lived. It beats me how!"

Eyes wide, Amanda glanced over her shoulder at Kari.

Kari nodded. "Mickey told me," she said simply.

"Mickey told you what?" Caleb asked, his hand still on Amanda's arm. "Wait, you've lost me now."

Amanda and Kari shared a look and both burst out laughing.

"Come on now, spill the beans."

Amanda shrugged, "I think this is something for your little brother to tell you. You'd be amazed at what little brothers *do*." She smiled up at Caleb, absolutely thrilled that he was actually here, that he had followed her.

"Let's just say I saw you before I actually met you."

Lips pursed, Caleb's brow furrowed in and then he shook his head, "I'll get to the bottom of this. But that's not what is important right now." He gently turned Amanda to face him.

"What I really want to know is, is there a chance that I have found a researcher to take home with me? She'd be doing pretty much what she was doing before, with some researching and teaching thrown in the mix. Word from the boss is that her room is still waiting and ready for her." He hesitated, his eyes searching hers.

"And maybe in time, for I wouldn't rush her, she could help to build herself a house? I know how to mix good cement..."

Eyes down, Amanda took her time. Then she threw her head up, eyes shining, "There is a strong possibility that she might agree to come."

She laughed when Caleb let off an exuberant whoop and pulled her into a hug.

"But it would be pretty cool if Kari would come out with me and check out where I've been hiding the last month." Amanda stepped back to look at Kari hopefully, keeping her tone light. "How about it Kari, I think you'd like it?"

Praying frantically that Kari would say yes, Amanda waited with bated breath. Her friend's answer would determine the direction her life would be taking, for she would not abandon Kari in her hour of need. Just looking at her made tears choke up her throat.

The beautiful brown eyes flashed between Caleb and Amanda, connecting with Amanda's for a long moment, and then at last Kari drawled, "Well I guess somebody has got to keep an eye on you. It appears that things do go wild when you're left on your own."

Laughing in delight, Amanda threw her arms jubilantly around her friend and then flung herself down onto a chair overwhelmed with the turn of events. She grinned up at

Caleb. It was so good just to look at him with his tousled brown hair and sparkling eyes.

"How about some tea?" he offered. "I know I could do with some."

"Sounds great Mr Jacobs," Amanda smiled, unable to contain her joy.

"I'll make it and let you two catch up," Kari offered, already heading for the kitchen.

"That's okay—" Caleb reluctantly moved away from Amanda "—I know just how she likes it. What about you? How do you like your tea?"

Amanda listened as the two of them moved into the kitchen and moments later had the kettle boiling. She heard Kari start a row when Caleb reached the sugar stage.

A piece of reddish paper sticking out from under the settee caught her attention. Snagging it, Amanda opened it up. Her heart stilled as she looked through it. It was a pamphlet advertising counselling for people suffering from anorexia. The email address had been circled and beside it a date and time was written.

"Oh, God!" Amanda whispered. Tears flooded so suddenly into her eyes that she couldn't see the words anymore. "Thank You so much." She brushed away the tears and stared at the paper again, confirming that Kari had set a time and date for her first counselling appointment.

Thank You.

Moments later Kari marched into the room indignantly, followed by a grinning Caleb. Amanda quickly tucked the paper out of sight, feeling it crackle beneath her, and tried not to look guilty. She would talk with Kari later—when the time was right.

"We're going to get this straight once and for all," Kari was saying, glaring at Caleb. "Amanda, he says you like two sugars in your tea and I say you don't have any. Which one of us is right?"

Amanda laughed softly and leant her head back against the chair to look at them.

"Two sugars will be just about right."

Glossary

Bairn	Child *(from the Scottish)*
Blether	Chatter, gossip *(from the Scottish)*
Braai	Barbeque (braai vleis: grilled meat) *(from the Afrikaans)*
Bru	Brother (also used to address friends) *(slang)*
Bundu	Bush (general term, orig. from an Indian town)
Bundu bash	Go off-road through the bush (usually in a vehicle, but can be on foot)
Frot	Dead; kaput *(from the Afrikaans)*
Hamba	Go, go away, move *(from Sindebele and other African lang.)*
Howzit	How are things? *(slang)*
Ken	Know *(from the Scottish)*
Lekker	Delicious *(from the Afrikaans)*
Nee	Not *(from the Scottish)*
Mai	Mother; respectful term for an older woman *(from Sindebele and other African lang.)*
Ndeipi	Informal "Hello"; "What's up?" *(from Sindebele and other African lang.)*
Sadza	Maize meal (staple diet in Zimbabwe) *(from Sindebele and other African lang.)*
Sekuru	Grandfather *(from Sindebele and other African lang.)*
Shamwari	Friend *(from Sindebele and other African lang.)*
Tsakupiti	Little Stout Girl *(from Sindebele and other African lang.)*
Wee	Little, small *(from the Scottish)*

The Author

KC Lemmer grew up in Zimbabwe amongst people who lived out the love of God and taught her what it means to be part of His church. She completed her university studies in South Africa, discovering God's faithfulness and compassion in greater measures, then trained as a Christian Counselor and English Teacher. KC now lives with her family in Scotland.

With a heart for Africa and for the hurting of this world, KC Lemmer writes with a desire to show the love of God and His compassion towards people. *A Flight Delayed* is KC's first novel, and she is currently working on a sequel. Watch her web site for more details:

www.kclemmer.com

PREVIEW SAMPLE CHAPTERS:

EMBRACING CHANGE

by

DEBBIE ROOME

Rose & Crown

Embracing
Change

DEBBIE
ROOME

Winner of the Rose & Crown Books New Novels Competition of 2009.

When Sarah Johnson's fiancé is killed by a hijacker in South Africa, Sarah carries out his wish to continue with their plan and moves to New Zealand, taking his ashes to scatter there. In her grief she hasn't counted on her gradual healing coming from two unexpected sources: Jesus Christ, and His new plan for her—Joel Baxter. But will Joel's old flame, Mandy, succeed in destroying Sarah's fragile progress in both her spiritual and earthly paths? And will she ever break free of the oppressive power still held over her by the hijacker who murdered her fiancé and attacked her? It takes a journey halfway back across the world for Sarah to face her demons, and finally forgive.

Embracing Change

by DEBBIE ROOME

Chapter One

I often wondered how it would feel to leave Africa. To leave the old and familiar; the heavy-blossomed bougainvilleas, and streets washed mauve with jacarandas. Would I miss the roosters crowing at 4am, and the jarring thump of mini-bus taxis as they cruise the streets? And what about the heat? Those searing days where the air hung thick and people gathered in dehydrated clusters. More than that, I wondered if I would find courage to leave my family and friends. To break away from all I had ever known.

From the journal of Sarah Johnson
Saturday, 1st March

They huddled together at the airport—Sarah, her parents, Luke's parents; a nucleus of pain in a swirling mass of humanity. This would have been a painful day anyway, but she'd never imagined it would be this hard. Small talk dwindled and they stood round her, guarding her, protecting her, but it was time to say goodbye. Time for her to fulfill her promise to Luke. His mother pulled her close and whispered final words in her ear: "Keep him safe, Sarah. Take him where he wanted to go."

It was almost a relief to leave their embrace, to walk towards security as their eyes followed her, tears streaming down all their faces. The staff had seen it before, this grief at parting. They appeared unmoved and disinterested as they processed her bags. Would they care, she wondered, if they knew what was in her carry-on bag? Would they care if they knew her story, the reason why her heart was breaking?

A short while later, she stared at herself in the restroom mirror. Splashing cold water on her face didn't help—her eyes were still swollen and blotchy, her cheeks pale and thin. Even her hair looked sad, hanging in dark flat sheets over her shoulders. "I'm doing it for you, Luke," she whispered to her reflection. "I must be strong."

She spent the next half hour wandering through the stores in International Departures. They were a concentration of Africa, a mass of carvings, feathers, colour and curios. She hadn't thought of this aspect of Africa. Would she miss the street vendors and their vibrant wares? Would life in New Zealand be bland by comparison?

I'll buy something to take with me, she decided. *A special memento.* It was a welcome distraction as she browsed through several stores, examining chess sets, holding up fabric paintings and admiring stone carvings. *What about a picture frame? An African one to put Luke's picture in,* she thought. *Maybe a carved one or perhaps a wire one with intricate beadwork.* She finally settled on a dark wood frame with inlaid giraffes in a lighter wood. *I'll put my favourite picture of Luke in it. The one of him leaning against a tree, smiling.*

The plane was massive compared to the small domestic aircraft she was accustomed to. *Like a hotel with wings*, she thought as she peered into its depths.

"Good evening, welcome aboard." A flight attendant glanced at her boarding pass. "You're in 43C, near the back on the right hand side."

She struggled down the narrow aisle, hugging her hand luggage in front of her. *Be careful,* she wanted to say. *Don't knock my bag.* She stowed it carefully in an overhead locker before huddling into her seat. People were still pouring onto the aircraft and yet she had never felt so alone, so vulnerable.

Concentrate. Think about what's happening around you. You knew this wasn't going to be easy.

After another ten minutes, most of the passengers were on board and the cabin crew made a few preliminary announcements. Their Australian accent was quite different to hers, but similar to Kiwis', so she'd been told. She liked the harshly melodic tones and wondered briefly how she sounded to them. Strange, stilted? What would it be like in New Zealand? How would it feel to live in a country of strangers who spoke differently? Would she be the odd one out? Would she be welcome there?

A flush of panic rushed through her body as doors were closed and crosschecked. There was no turning back now, no last minute escape. A few tears escaped, and she dabbed them away while listening to the announcements. "Welcome aboard Qantas Flight QF064 to Sydney. Our flying time tonight will be approximately twelve hours. Conditions over Johannesburg are calm and we anticipate a smooth take off."

She watched numbly as the crew demonstrated safety procedures. *Am I really doing this?* she thought. *Leaving behind everything I've ever known? Surrounded by all these strangers?* She pressed her head onto her chest, dizzy and afraid. Then she thought of Luke. Of the promise she'd made. She had to do this for him.

The pilot lined up behind several other planes, waiting his turn to thunder down the runway. It was dark now, with just a rim of fire where the sun had melted into the horizon. Sarah gazed at the terminal building in the far distance. She'd told her family to go home, but wondered if they were still there; if they were watching from the observation deck. She wished they were in the plane with her, surrounding her with love and comfort, as they had only hours earlier.

"Cabin crew, prepare for takeoff." The last crew members took their seats and the aircraft rolled into position, engines roaring, metal straining and vibrating until the plane surged into motion. She gripped the armrests as they hurtled down the tarmac, on and on until eventually the plane lumbered into the air, heavy and sluggish, as it banked to the right.

The lights of Johannesburg twinkled below them; gold and silver pinpricks, headlights on highways, people headed home to family, warmth, and comfort. Sarah felt like someone had ripped her heart out and left it down there. She tried to make out familiar streets but it was too dark, her mind too confused. Her gaze lingered long after the lights had disappeared. Each second, each minute, carrying her further from home, away from the place where she belonged.

Dinner was served soon after takeoff and she picked at chicken casserole and vegetables and toyed with blueberry cheesecake and cream. Her appetite was gone and she felt sick with anxiety. An empty seat separated her from a young Indian girl, about her age, seated by the window. She was striking to look at, with swirls of long black hair pinned up on her head. They smiled and acknowledged each other, exchanging names and nothing further.

"Hi, I'm Shiraz."

"Sarah."

She was grateful for the easy silence that sat between them. Any type of personal conversation would release fresh tears.

The crew dimmed the lights after dinner and she experimented with the entertainment system, scrolling through programs, movies and music until she came across ABBA. Luke adored their music, although it had been popular a couple of decades before either of them were born. After listening to his favourite tracks, she moved on to an episode of *House* and was engrossed in complicated medical procedures when the seat belt light came on.

"We're expecting some turbulence and request you fasten your seat belt as a precaution." All over the plane, bodies stretched out, rearranged themselves and clipped their belts into place. The plane lurched suddenly, dropping what felt like miles through the air. Then the bouncing and bumping started. A baby howled from the depths of economy class and Sarah huddled miserably in her seat. She had never liked turbulence and this was the worst she'd experienced. Would she even make it to New Zealand?

"We apologise for the rough ride." A confident voice reassured the passengers. "The pilot has requested permission to fly at a higher altitude which will lift us out of the bad weather." A sigh rippled round the cabin and she realised they had all been afraid.

She finally fell into a muddled doze, uncomfortable in

her seat and aware of the occasional bumps and bounces. She woke at 1am, then twice more before Shiraz woke her at 2:59.

"You're having a bad dream."

She struggled upright, tears soaking her shirt. The same nightmare had plagued her for months. Her mother would often come and hold her in the middle of the night; rock her until the terrible fear subsided and her trembling ceased. The dream always ended the same way if she didn't awaken first: Luke lying on the side of the road, life seeping from him in a dark stain.

"I love you, Sarah," he whispered. "I don't think I'll make it. Take me to New Zealand with you ... don't give up our plans ..."

Shiraz moved into the seat next to Sarah and handed her a tissue. "Are you alright? Is there anything I can do?"

A flight attendant paused at Sarah's side just then, her eyes sympathetic. "Can I bring you anything? A pain tablet, some juice, a snack?"

Their concern brought fresh tears to Sarah's eyes. "A tablet and some juice would be good. I'm sorry for disturbing you."

It didn't take long to organise and the attendant crouched down for a few minutes as Sarah swallowed the pill and thanked them both. "I feel so foolish. Sitting here, crying in front of two complete strangers. It's not the type of thing I normally do. It's just that I feel so overwhelmed. So afraid of the future and so alone." She couldn't tell them the whole truth but she shared this small part of it.

Shiraz placed a comforting hand on her arm. "Are you moving to Australia?"

"No, New Zealand."

The flight attendant smiled. "We get many immigrants travelling with us and I've seen the pain they go through. Most of them leave loved ones behind and find it really difficult. The great thing is that a year or so later, I see some of them again as they travel back to South Africa for a holiday. Most of them settle in really well and don't regret their decision."

Shiraz continued the conversation as a bell pinged softly, summoning the flight attendant to another part of the plane. "My uncle and his family moved to Sydney two years ago. It took them a few months to settle but they love it now." She smiled gently. "You'll be alright. I know you will."

To her surprise, Sarah managed to drift off to sleep again, the tablet having quieted the pounding in her head. This time she slept for two hours before the cabin crew roused them for breakfast.

Kingsford Smith Airport in Sydney was Sarah's first glimpse of a country outside of Africa. Although tired and emotionally drained, the terror of the night had subsided and she used the hour-long stopover to explore, absorbing the Australian accents and unfamiliar sights. The strangest thing was seeing white people doing menial jobs done by "blacks" in South Africa. *How different*, she thought as a middle-aged white woman walked past with a trolley of cleaning materials. *I see I'll have to adapt to a whole new way of life.*

By the time the boarding call came for her connecting flight, Sarah was eager to see the country she had studied so carefully and learned so much about. The anticipation took the edge off her tiredness and she settled into the soft embrace of leather. Outside, the Tasman Sea appeared to be a shiny blue cloth, interwoven with sequins and sparkles of silver. It looked so small on the map, but the reality was massive, a vast expanse that rolled endlessly from Australia to New Zealand, from one shore to another. It was a welcome distraction, this unexpected beauty. She knew the pain was still there, lurking deep within, but this was an adventure. She'd taken the first step to living their dream. "Oh, Luke," she murmured, "how you would have loved this."

An announcement from the pilot disturbed her thoughts. "If you're sitting on the left side of the plane, you'll see New Zealand in the far distance." She pressed her face up against the window and caught a glimpse of her new home, watching intently as the grey shadow started to take form. Greenery appeared, and then a fringe of yellow beaches. The sea lightened in colour and took on varying shades of turquoise, emerald and sapphire. This was a different world to the one she knew. A different kind of beauty, and she was captivated.

Her eyes moistened twenty minutes later as they crossed the Southern Alps; immense formations of grey rock, powdered in places with drifts of snow. This was where Luke had told her to bring him. She thought of the days ahead, the journey into the mountains. She thought of fulfilling his last wish; of taking his ashes and scattering them into mountain breezes. Of sprinkling them into raging waterfalls and majestic, braided rivers. Of making Luke a part of the land he yearned to come to. For the first time in months, a glimmer of hope shone into her heart.

Thank you, Luke. Thank you for making sure I would come here; that I would give New Zealand a chance.

Chapter Two

I have never felt so alone in all my life. There is no one here who knows me, no one who can give a smile of recognition. I never realised that moving means a total loss of identity and reputation.
From the journal of Sarah Johnson
Monday, 3rd March

She woke to a feeling of strangeness and disorientation; a bed that was too firm, shadows that were unfamiliar. A digital display told her it was noon. Uncomfortable and stiff, she turned and stretched, flexing her toes, calves and thighs, lifting her arms and splaying her hands into starfish. Eventually she pushed the bedcovers back and moved across to the window, separating the curtains to gaze out at Christchurch.

Her impressions of the day before jumbled in a mixture of neatness and beauty, strangeness and detachment. She knew the houses were wooden and wondered if the motel was too. Curious, she knocked on the wall with her knuckles, producing a hollow echo. She had only lived in brick homes and often wondered what wooden houses looked like on the inside. Could you tell they were made of wood? She thought of the homes she passed after leaving the airport. They were all situated on narrow pieces of land, and seemed to be an arm's length from their neighbour's.

What really caught her attention, though, was the openness. Many had knee high fences in white picket or natural wood. They were obviously there for the effect and not for security. Others had no barricades at all. Just smooth lawns that unfurled to stop neatly at the tarred foot path. All these impressions mingled together giving a sense of freedom that contrasted sharply with the barricaded suburbs of Johannesburg.

She pressed the power button on her laptop and the blue light flashed, signalling that life was flowing through its circuits. The motel had been booked over the internet, a full month with discounted rates and wireless internet access. She knew her family would be thinking of her, wondering how her trip had been.

She left the computer whirring and beeping and turned on the taps in the shower, twisting the silver knobs until warm water sprinkled the glass sides, running, sliding, making watery tracks. It felt good to rinse off the grime of the journey, and she inhaled the fragrance of herbal shampoo and soap as the bubbles swirled down the drain. After a long scrub, she wrapped a snowy towel around herself and sat down to connect to the internet. As she had hoped, there was a message from her parents.

Dear Sarah,
We are thinking of you, honey, and missing you terribly already. Hope the trip was uneventful and New Zealand turns out to be everything you hoped for and more besides. Let us know if you arrived safely and never forget—we love you very, very much.
All our love, Mom and Dad

She allowed a few tears to fall as she leaned back in the chair, wiping rivulets from her neck with a corner of the towel. It smelt faintly of washing powder and bleach and reminded her of laundry days at home. Their housekeeper,

Patience, would start the washing early in the morning and by midday, the scent of soap and clean fabric filled the house as she washed and ironed, folded and put away.

With a struggle, Sarah forced her mind back to the e-mail she wanted to write.

Dear Mom and Dad,

I'm here in Christchurch, in the motel we studied on the internet. It looks quite different to the pictures, but then, they always do. It's comfortable enough, however, and I'll be happy here while I look for something more permanent.

She wondered how much she should tell them. Did they need to know how difficult the journey had been and how much she was missing home?

The flight was mostly smooth and although I was tempted to turn round and come straight back, I didn't. I know I have an amazing opportunity in my hands and I'll give New Zealand a fair chance. It's coming up to 1pm here and I only got up an hour ago. I underestimated the effects of jet lag and the length of the flight, but feel better after having a shower. I'm going to go out after sending this and have a look around the city. I'm longing to see if it's as beautiful as the brochures made out. I'll write again soon and send some photos.

Much love, Sarah

The motel receptionist was barely out of her teens; a young blonde with braided hair and a short skirt. She pulled out a map and wrote down the information Sarah needed to get into town. "The bus stop is directly outside the motel. The buses run every half hour and any of these numbers will take you into the city. Get off at the bus exchange and you'll be in the centre of town." She drew a lopsided circle on the map. "This is the motel. If you follow the map on the trip back, you shouldn't have any problem finding us."

Sarah thanked her and went outside to sit in the shelter. The motel was situated on a main road and traffic was heavy, a blur of chrome and colour. Sarah was surprised at the variety of cars and recognised only a few models here and there. All the rest were foreign to her. She gripped her bag closely as she watched, wondering if it was safe to be sitting there on her own. The bus service in Johannesburg had folded years ago, giving way to the minibus taxi industry. These were used mostly by the black people and Sarah had never been on one. Many were poorly maintained and if accidents didn't pull them off the road, violence between taxi bosses often did. Patience told Sarah horror stories about the taxis she rode to get to work, and Sarah had felt sorry for her but thankful she didn't have to use them.

Her thoughts dissolved as a red bus pulled up, doors whooshing open as a group of teenagers disembarked, emerging like colourful butterflies bursting from their cocoons. They epitomised gaiety and freedom as they fluttered down the street, laughter drifting behind them.

Sarah climbed into the bus and smiled at the driver, handing over a $5 note. "I'd like to go to town please."

He punched out some change and handed her a ticket. "You visiting Christchurch?"

"It's my first day." Sarah guessed her accent marked her as a tourist.

"If you get back on the bus within two hours, you don't pay for the return journey. And look out for bus 19 if you want to come back to this stop."

She smiled thanking him for his kindness, and walked to the back of the bus. She sat in the second to last row, watching the suburbs unroll before her eyes. Everything looked the same, row after row of neat houses, stretches of lawn and an abundance of flowers.

After ten minutes, the driver turned left and entered a more commercialised area. Here the main road was dotted with businesses and motels, and the traffic much heavier. The driver stopped frequently and she noticed a large mall on the right. A little later they passed through a large park and she spotted Christchurch Hospital on the left before the bus entered the city centre.

The Bus Exchange turned out to be a cavernous building with glass waiting rooms, holding dozens of people. She followed the people out of the bus, stopping briefly by the driver. "Is this the town stop?"

"Yep. If you go up the stairs over there, you'll come to

the main office where you can get maps and directions. Remember to come back here to this platform for bus 19."

She thanked him and headed over to the stairs. Inwardly, she was feeling quite panicky. She wouldn't recognise the hotel stop. What if she missed it, or caught the wrong bus? "Stop it," she admonished herself. "You knew it wasn't going to be easy." She picked up a couple of maps and followed the signs leading out of the exchange.

Christchurch lay before her, a charming city with a mixture of old and new architecture. Tiny shops huddled next to big department stores, and brass and chrome mingled with the warmth of old-fashioned wood. She turned to her right and started walking towards Cathedral Square. From what she had read, this was the central point of town. It was only a couple of blocks away and she found it with no problem. The cathedral itself was impressive, a grey stone structure with a high tower and metal railed balconies. The square sprawled out from its base and was throbbing with activity.

A flea market spread across the far left and buskers entertained people as they wandered around. Near to Sarah, a group of young girls took turns performing Irish river dancing. A sign informed the public that they were raising funds for a trip to the championships in Ireland. Sarah watched for a long while, mesmerised by the soulful music and their shoes tapping on the wooden platform. A sudden surge of loneliness caught her by surprise. *Oh, Luke, if only you were here with me.*

# # #

To read the rest of this book, please
order it from your local bookstore,
or from all major online book retailers,
or from www.roseandcrownbooks.com

TITLE: Embracing Change
AUTHOR: Debbie Roome
PAGES: 256
ISBN: 978-0-9555283-7-8

MORE FROM ROSE & CROWN INSPIRATIONAL ROMANCE:

EMBRACING CHANGE: Sarah and Luke were about to move from South Africa to an exciting new life in New Zealand when Luke was brutally murdered. Sarah takes his ashes to NZ and starts afresh, but can her bitterness and hatred be overcome by the love of a new man? She finds she must return to her home country and face her demons, before facing her future. Brilliantly written by Debbie Roome, an emotional high-ride.

A FLIGHT DELAYED: *En route* to South Africa, Amanda finds herself stranded in present-day Zimbabwe and suddenly taken under the wing of an eccentric family on a safari game park. Finding out about the realities of life under Mugabe's regime, she is faced with challenges which change her heart and soul before she reaches her final destination. KC Lemmer has captured the essence of current-day Zimbabwe in this lovely bush setting.

BLUE FREEDOM: Bella thinks her life is taking a turn for the better when she lands a writing assignment that takes her on a journey across tropical islands, with two new men on her tail—if you don't count the contract killer, that is! A hair-raising thriller that chases our lovers across the South Pacific as rapidly as the professional assassin who is following them. Sandra Peut's love of exotic locations will light up your world, adding intrigue and drama too.

REDEMPTION ON THE RED RIVER: Cheryl Riley Cain offers an historical adventure romance set in 1800's America. Anna, a young teacher, takes a steamer downriver to Indian country, to teach pupils who barely understand schooling, with a war raging around them and an Indian vendetta that threatens her life. In the end she must choose between the man she almost married, and the man who has become her protector.

MORE FROM SUNPENNY PUBLISHING:

DANCE OF EAGLES: Explosive adventure set in 14th-century Africa, and in the 1970's bush war of Rhodesia-Zimbabwe. Tcana, daughter of a cattleherd, wife of a prince, high priestess of a new religion that rips apart her world; journalist Rebecca Rawlings, caught up centuries later in the remnants of Tcana's faith and a violent war of attrition; Peter Kennedy, commander of the famed Selous Scouts; his friend and right-hand man, Kuru—and Kuru's brother, trained as a top flight freedom fighter: the Mamba.

MY SEA IS WIDE: One man's journey, in his 70th year, to rediscover his purpose. In this beautifully lyrical work, with great depth of insight, internationally renowned missionary, trainer and speaker Rowland Evans takes us on a journey from Wales to the scatterlings of China and Tibet, and our lives are changed forever. Wondrously written, and lush with his love for the people and landscapes of all these lands. Thoughtful, thought-provoking, heart-searching, and definitely not to be missed!

THE MOUNTAINS BETWEEN: Blaenavon and Abergavenny surge to life in this vibrant, haunting, joyful masterpiece by Julie McGowan; a celebration of the Welsh people in the 1920s to '40s—a saga of two families and their communities, in a smorgasbord that keeps the pages in perpetual motion. It's a war story; a love story; a hate story; about the people of Wales, the people of the mountains and the valleys who formed the beating heart of that country in this chunk of Wales' lifetime.

GOING ASTRAY: At what precise moment does a church become a cult? Christine Moore writes a tense, gripping story of a family whose new community, meant to bring them into a life closer to that of the early church, becomes more and more of a jail. Their struggle to escape rips the family apart as the story builds to a terrifying climax. Told with empathy, insight, and great moments of humour, this book will get you thinking!

Lightning Source UK Ltd.
Milton Keynes UK
UKOW04f1128020315

247132UK00001B/60/P